Ruff Around the Edges

The Dogfather · Book Six

roxanne st. claire

Ruff Around the Edges
THE DOGFATHER BOOK SIX

978-0-9993621-1-2 – ebook
978-0-9993621-2-9 – print

COVER ART: Keri Knutson (designer)
and Dawn C. Whitty (photographer)
INTERIOR FORMATTING: Author EMS

Critical Reviews of Roxanne St. Claire Novels

"St. Claire, as always, brings a scorching tear-up-the-sheets romance combined with a great story: dealing with real issues starring memorable characters in vivid scenes."

— *Romantic Times Magazine*

"Non-stop action, sweet and sexy romance, lively characters, and a celebration of family and forgiveness."
— *Publishers Weekly*

"Plenty of heat, humor, and heart!"
— *USA Today's Happy Ever After blog*

"It's safe to say I will try any novel with St. Claire's name on it."

— *www.smartbitchestrashybooks.com*

"The writing was perfectly on point as always and the pace of the story was flawless. But be forewarned that you will laugh, cry, and sigh with happiness. I sure did."
— *www.harlequinjunkies.com*

"The Barefoot Bay series is an all-around knockout, soul-satisfying read. Roxanne St. Claire writes with warmth and heart and the community she's built at Barefoot Bay is one I want to visit again and again."
— *Mariah Stewart, New York Times bestselling author*

"This book stayed with me long after I put it down."
— *All About Romance*

Dear Reader:

Welcome back to the foothills of North Carolina where the Dogfather, Daniel Kilcannon, is once again pulling some strings to help one of his six grown children find forever love. On these pages, you'll discover my favorite things in life and fiction: big families, great dogs, and lasting love. And, I am delighted to inform you that a portion of the sales of all the books in this series is being donated to Alaqua Animal Refuge (www.alaqua.org) in my home state of Florida. That's where these covers were shot by photographer Dawn Whitty (www.dawncwhitty.com) using *real* men (not models, but they are gorgeous!) and *rescue* dogs (now in forever homes!). So you don't only buy a terrific book...you support a fantastic cause!

I couldn't publish a book without help. In this one, I had massive support from fellow author Silver James, beta reader Sandi Fitch Hutton, along with the team at Writers Camp who lived through every rewrite. As always, love and gratitude to my content editor, Kristi Yanta, who helps me see through the fog of a first draft; copyeditor Joyce Lamb, who might know this series better than I do; proofreaders Marlene Engel, Chris Kridler, and Maria Connor; cover designer Keri Knutson; and the formatting team at Author E.M.S. Of course, my deepest love goes to my husband who nourishes me body and soul, and the kids and dogs who call me Momma.

I hope you love the Kilcannon clan! Don't miss a single book in The Dogfather Series:

Available now
Sit…Stay…Beg (Book 1)
New Leash on Life (Book 2)
Leader of the Pack (Book 3)
Santa Paws is Coming to Town (Book 4 – a Holiday novella)
Bad to the Bone (Book 5)
Ruff Around the Edges (Book 6)

Coming soon
Double Dog Dare (Book 7)
Old Dog New Tricks (Book 8)

And yes, there will be more. For a complete list, buy links, and reading order of all my books, visit www.roxannestclaire.com. Be sure to sign up for my newsletter on my website to find out when the next book is released! And join the private Dogfather Facebook group for inside info on all the books and characters, sneak peeks, and a place to share the love of tails and tales!

www.facebook.com/groups/roxannestclairereaders/

xoxo
Rocki

Dedication

For Reggie, a basset hound with a heart as big as his ears and a howl that can be heard all over the neighborhood. Many thanks to his owner, my friend and one of my first readers, Faith Coulson, for teaching me how to be a "dogmother" and for never holding back opinions or love.

Chapter One

Bagram Air Base, Kabul, Afghanistan

"Major Kilcannon?"

The voice yanked Aidan out of the deep-state stare he'd been in for an hour, maybe two, making him blink at the sergeant behind the post-op desk. "Yeah?"

"Captain Spencer is in ICU recovery, sir."

Recovery? Then Charlie wasn't dead.

Aidan stood, the weight of a sweaty uniform and worry pressing on him as he looked down at the other man. "I need to see him."

"I'm sorry, Major. No visitors back there."

"Five minutes. Three. One." Aidan fisted his hands and leaned over the counter to get closer to the young sergeant's face. "I've known him since we were fifteen. We went through ROTC together. We've done three tours together. We survived Green Platoon together."

The other man flinched, maybe from the sheer force of Aidan's determination, or maybe the fact that

Aidan and the man he wanted to see were US Army Night Stalkers and they lived by one simple creed: *Night Stalkers don't quit.*

And Aidan wasn't about to quit until he saw Charlie Spencer again. He wasn't going to accept that a pickup of special ops troops down in Nangarhar got so ugly, so fast. Not after Charlie had *volunteered* to sit in the co-pilot's seat that night, since Aidan's usual co-pilot was throwing his guts up with the flu.

In a year and a half with the 160th SOAR Airborne, Aidan had transported special ops troops in his UH-60 Black Hawk through way worse conditions than what they'd expected tonight. This job, to pick up SEALs from a raid in an ISIS hellhole and get them back to Bagram, was *supposed to be routine.*

A flipping joyride, Charlie had called it. Stuck his head right in his crazy-ass dog's face and said, "I'm goin' for a joyride, Rufferoni. BRB, big boy."

But he hadn't been right back, because that night nothing had been joyous or routine. A brutal wind shear had forced Aidan to fly lower than he normally would over that region. Then a pack of Taliban bastards decided Aidan's chopper full of troops made for good target practice with their newly acquired ground-to-air weapons.

They started a bloody skirmish that the good guys won handily, but not without a price. That was paid by Captain Charles John Spencer, who jumped into the open door when the gunner was wounded. In true Charlie "There Ain't Nothing I Can't Do" Spencer fashion, the son of a bitch *co-pilot* managed to shoot three insurgents with master precision. But the fourth one landed a bullet right through Charlie's chest.

"Just tell me if he's on the CCATT list." Because if Charlie was being taken by the critical care air transport to the military hospital in Landstuhl, Germany, then the surgery had been successful. If he left Kabul alive, he had a chance.

Please, God, give him a chance.

But he knew that prayer might not be answered. They'd treated him in the chopper, and Aidan had managed to land at the airfield, where a team of medics had descended on the tarmac to whisk Charlie and the wounded door gunner to the base hospital. But Charlie's injury was serious. A clean shot, through the lungs and out the back.

"All I can tell you is Captain Spencer is out of surgery, and a CCATT team is loading up a C-17 for the trip."

"So he's going to Germany." As if saying it enough would make it true.

"I don't know," the man admitted. "There are two others in there, both wounded on patrol. Your door gunner is clear, but he'll be in overnight. Hang on until they bring them out. If Captain Spencer's on a gurney, I'll make sure you can follow him to the runway. If he's not…"

Then he wasn't going to survive. Or, he might already be dead.

Aidan closed his eyes and changed his prayer. *Don't let him die.*

Ten seconds later, the trauma unit doors smacked open, and the antiseptic stink and low-grade hum of horror rolled into the hall along with the first transportee. Three medics in brown coveralls marched out carrying a SMEED with a soldier so completely bandaged, Aidan couldn't see the color of his skin. But he could see that the special evac device that usually supported the patient's lower legs was being used instead of a gurney because...there were no lower legs.

Swallowing, he stepped way back and let them through, glancing into the trauma unit, which was packed with medical professionals and a few noncritical patients leaning against the walls, waiting to be seen.

The hall that led to the ICU was out of his sightline, so he waited until the next crew came through with a Marine on a gurney—Lance Corporal Rodriguez, according to his stripes and name tag, his hands completely bandaged, his eyes closed.

One of the CCATT medics passed by, her brown eyes holding Aidan's gaze long enough to give him the impetus to step forward. "Any more?" he asked her.

"Not on this flight, Major. These are the only two going to Germany. 'Scuze me."

That meant Charlie was staying. That meant Charlie was *dying*.

"Go on," the door guard said, his expression softening as he no doubt came to the same conclusion. "You'll need to stay out of the way, sir."

With a nod of thanks, Aidan walked into the trauma unit, turned left, and followed the signs to the ICU bay. His pulse thrummed with every step, his whole body itching for a different ending than the one he might be facing.

Finally, he reached the bay and found Charlie covered with a sheet up to his chin. He had IVs in both arms, oxygen pumped into his nose, and a visible chest tube. Shit, that wasn't good. Fluid in the lungs.

The room was eerily quiet, the only real noise the steady beeps of monitors and machines and the whispers of brief exchanges between nurses and doctors in and out of the ICU bays.

One of those doctors was a few feet from Charlie, looking at a clipboard, when Aidan approached.

"Can't be in here, Major."

Aidan peered over the man's shoulder at Charlie. "Please."

The doctor, with bloodshot eyes and two days' worth of beard, tipped his head toward the bed in consent. "One minute before he's moved."

"To Landstuhl?" He couldn't keep the hope out of his voice, the bone-deep belief that the transport medic had been wrong.

But the doctor gave a quick, nearly imperceptible shake of his head. "He wouldn't survive that trip, Major. I'm sorry."

Pain punched his gut, but he refused to flinch as he went to Charlie's bed. Instead, Aidan took a good look at the familiar face he'd known damn near twenty years. From the moment he found the new kid lost in the cafeteria and learned he could play center field, Aidan Kilcannon and Charlie Spencer had been inseparable.

But one close look at his bloodless complexion and the way-too-slow beeps of the monitor hooked up to him, and Aidan had a sickening feeling that *inseparable* might be coming to an end.

He leaned over Charlie's head to whisper, "Hey. Spence. It's me."

The faintest frown pulled at thick dark brows. He mumbled something, but Aidan didn't catch it.

"You're gonna be okay, man."

One lid opened enough to reveal a slit of brown. "Shut up, Kil."

Aidan understood *that*. "You shut up and get better."

Charlie managed to move his head from side to side. "Not happenin'."

"Oh yes, it is," Aidan insisted harshly, glancing around so the docs wouldn't make him leave. "You can do this. Don't give up, man."

"'S bad."

Yes, it was. As bad as it could get. But Charlie ran on optimism and an acute refusal to fail. It was what made him a great friend and an even greater soldier. "I've seen you worse, Spence."

He grunted.

"After Black Day? You barfed for two straight hours."

Charlie flinched a bit, either in pain or at the memory of the hardest day during their six-week training at Fort Campbell, where they fought to earn the badge and right to be called Army Night Stalkers. But they both knew the rigors of Green Platoon had nothing on the fight Charlie was in right now.

"No' as bad as spring break in Virginia," he ground out, making Aidan smile.

"Damn, we got some memories, bro." And he needed to live so they had more.

Charlie took a slow, deep, and agonizing as hell breath, the pain of it etched on every feature of his face and echoed in the black curse he muttered as he let it out.

"Lis'en to me," he said, forcing the words out. "Don't gimme shit."

"I'm not giving you shit, Charlie, I'm telling you—"

"Ruff."

At first, he wasn't sure what Charlie had said. "Ruff? Your dog?"

He gave a slight nod. "You...get...Ruff."

Aidan closed his eyes as he let the words sink in. Charlie knew he was dying, or he wouldn't start making final requests about the stray he'd found four months ago when they'd dropped into a bombed-out hospital to airlift troops and injured locals. Somehow, Charlie managed to snag the doggo and break every frickin' rule in the Army to keep him at their base. But Aidan wasn't about to accept this as Charlie's last will and testament. No way.

"I'll take care of him while you're laid up."

"Get him home."

He wasn't sure what that meant, but Aidan leaned closer. "I'll take care of him."

"Start now." Charlie got both eyes open and gave Aidan a harsh look. "Takes a long time. Lotta money."

Getting a dog out of Afghanistan and back to the States? And not an official military K-9, but a stray found after a bombing? It took time, money, connections, and a few miracles, but every soldier who got attached to one over here knew that from the get-go. Still, Ruff was irresistible and had given both Charlie and Aidan hours of desperately needed destressing.

"Your dad can do it."

Aidan inched back. His father? Come to think of it, if anyone on earth could transport a dog back to the

States, it'd be Daniel Kilcannon. "Get better, and you can both go home. You weren't going to re-up next spring. You and Ruff can go back to Bitter Bark and have the life you want, Charlie. You take over your uncle's business, make pizza night and day, and Ruff'll be right there with you."

Maybe that old fantasy would make him fight for his life. Because Aidan could swear that the will to live was slipping away with each labored breath.

"You do it," Charlie rasped.

Aidan snorted. "You know I'm a lifer, dude." Although, without Charlie, what kind of life would the Army be? Boring as hell. Broken.

"You take Ruff," Charlie repeated, his eyes fiery enough to be golden brown now. "He can live at Waterford," he added, referring to the homestead where Aidan had grown up, surrounded by siblings and dogs.

"Only if you're there, too, Spence."

Somehow, Charlie managed a *get real* look and another agonizing breath. "I'm goin' somewhere else, man. An' it ain't Germany."

So Charlie knew the CCATT had left without him. He had to know what that meant.

Aidan squeezed his lids against an unwanted burn. "Come on, man. *Fight.*"

"Listen," Charlie hissed, adding force and digging up some of that grit he had in spades. "You and Ruff...belong together. He's me in dog form."

Aidan smiled at their running joke, which was so damn true. Charlie and Ruff were both big, wild, loyal, funny, stubborn, and fearless as hell. And Aidan didn't want a world without either one of them.

He put his hand on Charlie's thick shoulder and leaned closer. "Night Stalkers don't quit," he ground out.

Charlie barely flinched at the motto that had been hammered into their brains and bodies during the grueling weeks of training and every day on this, their first tour of duty as Night Stalkers.

"This one is checking out."

The words sliced Aidan in two. "Charlie."

He looked up, a vacancy in his brown eyes that were always so light with humor or warmth. "Promise me."

"Just get—"

"Promise me, Kil. You get Ruff home. Work on it now. Get him to Waterford. He belongs wi' you. You. No one else."

"No, man, he belongs with you. So I'll get him wherever you are, I promise. He's your dog."

"Now...he's yours. Ruff is your dog. Do it...for me."

"Charlie, look—"

"Aidan. Your word, man. Gimme your word." Charlie leveled his gaze, pain and hope and humor gone from his eyes. Maybe life, too. But they never went back on their word to each other. It had been their code, their deal, the lifeblood of an enduring friendship. "Give it to me," Charlie insisted, battling for the breath to make the demand.

"You have my word," Aidan whispered.

The machine attached to one of the ten different cords pressed to his body started beeping, loud and fast, as Charlie closed his eyes.

A medic called an alert. A nurse shoved Aidan

away. The doctor hustled over and started firing off orders.

And someone grabbed Aidan by the arm and yanked him out of the way. "You need to go outside, sir," a nurse said. "Now."

He moved blindly through the doors, back to the cold fluorescent lights of the hallway, into the waiting room. There, vaguely aware of the sharp-eyed gaze of the sergeant still at his post, Aidan leaned against the wall and felt his whole body start to crumble, sliding toward the floor. As he sank lower, something snapped in his head. In his heart, maybe.

The smells and sounds of the base hospital swirled around him, like he was on psychedelic drugs and a bad trip. Grief rose up and strangled him, the way it had after his mother died. Regret. Remorse. Misery. Loss. Loneliness.

Every dark thing that he could feel closed in around his head, smothering him.

Just before he hit the ground, he launched up, so hard and fast his boots slid on the linoleum.

Without a word, he took off, running through the hospital hall and out into the dusty, filthy air of Afghanistan. He looked left and right, got his bearings, and headed straight to the yellowed adobe walls of base housing, breaking into a run so fast the air sang in his head.

When he got to the entrance, he powered through the common area, ignoring the sound of someone calling his name. He shot up the stairwell and threw open the door to Club 25, as they called the four-man suite. Immediately, a big brown head rose from Charlie's bed, followed by a deep, baritone bark of greeting. Aidan threw himself at the boxer, arms around his neck, and put his face in fur that sometimes seemed like God made it to absorb silent, secret tears.

But Aidan didn't hide these tears. They flowed hard, until Ruff put a massive paw on Aidan's shoulder in the closest thing to a hug a dog could give. They both fell on Aidan's bunk eventually, spent. Aidan didn't even take off his boots but let sleep be his escape.

It was barely sunup when two officers came in and quietly opened Charlie's locker, took a bag of his belongings, and stripped his bed without a word.

After a few minutes, Aidan got up, put a leash on Ruff, and took him out. Then he called his father, woke him up, and asked a special favor.

If anyone could pull strings and get a dog from Afghanistan to the US, it was the man they called the Dogfather. Yes, it would take money, which he'd happily pay. And it would take time. A long time. The only question was who would get out of this hellhole first, Aidan or Ruff?

Didn't matter. They both would, and they'd have each other's back just like Aidan and Charlie. Now it would be Aidan and Ruff, a couple of Night Stalkers who never quit.

Chapter Two

"He's on his way."

Aidan froze in the act of hosing out a dog kennel stall, letting his father's words sink in. As he flipped off the water, his heart slammed in his chest like the thumping blades of a Sikorsky taking off.

"How long?" Aidan asked.

"Cilla said they'd be here in ten minutes." Dad stepped closer, a note of pride in his voice that his good friend and skilled travel agent had the credentials needed to travel to Europe and bring home a very special delivery. "She said he's awake from the travel sedation and…rambunctious."

He laughed. "That's Ruff." On a heavy sigh, he put his hand on his father's arm. "I don't know how to thank you, Dad. This took a long time, longer than I thought it would, but you did it."

"We had a lot of help here and overseas," his father said with classic Daniel Kilcannon-style humility.

Aidan had been home from Afghanistan for about a month, but his own Army discharge when he hit ten years had been a breeze compared to the hell they'd gone through to get Ruff cleared to leave the country. Aidan had started the process—well, Dad had started it—the morning after Charlie died in November. And now, more than six months later, Ruff was ten minutes away.

"How do you feel?" Dad asked.

Aidan shook his head and tucked his fingers into the pockets of his jeans. "Overwhelmed, I guess. Like I'm coming full circle." And that there might be hope for him here at Waterford Farm, once Ruff arrived. But he didn't need to say that to his father. Didn't need to start another conversation about how much he'd struggled since he got back. Dad knew, so he also knew how important this was to Aidan.

"Because Charlie wanted you to have Ruff." There was something in his father's strange statement of the obvious that caught Aidan off guard. Was that a subtle warning? Doubt? Something didn't sound quite right.

Maybe his father wanted to have that conversation anyway. He'd never miss a chance to advise one of his kids, no doubt readying a low-key lecture on how Aidan should face his issues, unpack his baggage, and settle into life at Waterford Farm the way all the other kids had.

But his siblings hadn't been at war. They'd been bonding over dogs, building the largest canine rescue and training facility in the state, and moving on from the grief of their mother's unexpected death three and a half years ago.

All the while, Aidan had been fighting and training and flying and losing his best friend. But did Dad really want to talk about it now?

From the question in his father's piercing blue gaze, so much like his own, the answer might be yes. But Aidan didn't want to screw up his reunion with Ruff by getting into deep shit with Dad right now.

"I'm going to go wash up and greet him in the driveway." He tried to step past his father, but Dad didn't move out of the way, his six-foot-and-change frame blocking the opening of the empty kennel. He didn't say anything, either, but Daniel Kilcannon didn't always speak when he had something to say to one of his six kids. A good long look usually did the trick. Fact was, Aidan had faced hard-ass COs who couldn't deliver that look like Dad.

"What?" Aidan asked, not bothering to pretend he didn't feel the glare.

"You're absolutely certain?"

Aidan made a face, confused. "Of what?"

"That you should keep this dog."

His father could have hauled back and sucker-punched him, and it wouldn't have shocked him as much. "What? Is that a joke?" They'd moved heaven and earth to get Ruff here, and Dad had been integral every step of the way. "You know how much he means to me. You know Charlie gave him to me on his deathbed."

Dad stood stone-still and finally dragged his thick, silver hair back as if trying to pull something out of his head. The right words, maybe. But for what?

"There's no chance you misunderstood him, is there?"

Where the hell was he going with this? "No. I didn't misunderstand anything."

"He was on heavy medication, I assume, after surgery. In pain. Maybe delirious, even."

Aidan frowned, angling his head as if he wasn't hearing right. Delirious? "He was in pain and medicated, yeah. He was dying, not to put too fine a point on it. But he was lucid. And insistent. Why would you even ask me that right now?"

Dad crossed his arms and let out a noisy breath. "Have you, by any chance, been over to visit Charlie's aunt and uncle?"

Another curve ball he hadn't expected, but Aidan answered honestly. "Once. I went to pay my respects about a week after I got home." He lifted a brow. "I'm not sure Sarah Leone was that happy to see me alive when her nephew isn't."

"Grief can change people." Of course, who knew that better than his father, who'd lost the woman he loved more than anything or anyone on earth. "Charlie was like a son to her."

Aidan conceded that with a tip of his head. Sarah and her husband, Mike Leone, had been legal guardians to the two Spencer kids after their parents died in a car crash when Charlie was fifteen.

"What about Charlie's sister, Rebecca?" Dad asked. "Have you seen her?"

"Sarah didn't let me in the house. She said her husband was sick and Beck..." Aidan frowned, trying to pull up a visual of the girl he hadn't seen much since he and Charlie had gone to college. Rebecca Spencer, who was almost always called Beck, had been a kid back then, maybe fourteen. When they'd come home, she hadn't been around much, and then she went to the Midwest for art school, if he recalled correctly.

"Charlie told me she moved to Chicago, lives in a high-rise, and has some business that has to do with babies. I don't know any more than that about her."

"You have some of your facts straight," Dad said. "She's here now. Mike Leone had a mild stroke in the end of February, and Beck came back from Chicago, where she apparently has a baby-photography business. She's helping her aunt keep Slice of Heaven running."

Aidan felt a kick of guilt, knowing he should have done more to offer sympathies to the whole family. Maybe gone into their pizza parlor in town once or twice. But Sarah Leone had been frosty when he'd knocked on the door of their home north of Bitter Bark, saying little more than hello and goodbye to Aidan. They might not blame him for Charlie's death, but they sure as hell resented Aidan for being alive.

"Why are you telling me this?" Aidan asked, his wheels spinning as he psyched out the conversation and its timing. "You want me to take Ruff to see them or something?"

Two brows lifted. "Or something."

"Dad." Aidan let out a soft laugh of bewilderment. "Can the cryptic code. What's up?"

"Beck Spencer came to see me a few weeks after Charlie died."

"Okay." That didn't completely surprise him. Beck had lived in Bitter Bark a long time, and everyone in town knew his father, a highly respected local veterinarian and pillar of the community. People sought him out for advice, or favors, or to tour Waterford Farm. "What did she want?"

"Ruff."

"'Scuze me?"

"She wanted my help in bringing Ruff home from Afghanistan. For her."

He drew back. "Did you tell her you'd already started the process? For *me*?"

"I did tell her you'd asked me to initiate his return already, but I didn't know what your plans were with the dog. I knew you wanted him back here, so I assumed you knew that Charlie...Charlie..." He took a pause and searched Aidan's face while he looked for a way to say whatever he had to say. "Charlie left Ruff to his sister."

Aidan almost laughed at how crazy that was, but there was something serious in his father's eyes that stopped him. "Dad. He gave me the dog. He begged me to bring him back here and told me he wanted me to have the dog."

"But she's—"

"She's his sister, I get that."

"And next of kin."

He huffed out a breath. Yes, next of kin got everything unless a soldier requested otherwise, but not Ruff. "But he left Ruff to me, and anything else would be going against his request, and I can't do that."

"She wants Ruff."

"She can't have Ruff." This was not debatable. "We're bonded. We're one. We survived those last months without Charlie because we had each other." He heard his voice strain to make his point, but pushed on. "That dog is a part of my soul, Dad. And more than that, I gave Charlie my word I'd do what he wanted with Ruff. Hell, that's half the reason I didn't re-up, so I could honor that promise. That's all that matters."

Dad looked...unconvinced.

"No way," Aidan continued. "I'm not giving him to a stranger, even if she is Charlie's sister. I'll help her find another dog and disavow her of the notion that she automatically gets him because she's next of kin. Because she doesn't. She *can't.*"

Dad's expression barely registered the impassioned speech. "She has a letter from him, signed, dated, and unequivocal, instructing her to transport and keep the dog. It could easily be taken to court as a legal addendum to his official will."

"*Court?*" A white light popped in Aidan's head as he shook it vehemently. "That's wrong. That's... *Court?*"

"His letter is specific, with instructions that, should anything happen to Charlie, Beck was to contact me and do whatever was necessary to get Ruff and to keep him as her own."

This wasn't possible. Aidan felt the tiny bit of joy he'd been clinging to for days dissolve in a pool of pain. "Ruff is mine, Dad. I don't want to be an asshole about it to Charlie's sister, but this matters to me. More than *anything.*"

He hated that he had to add that, because it would open a can-of-worms conversation about why Aidan was so restless and unhappy now that he was back in the States and out of the Army, but Dad—*of all people*—should understand this. "Would you have given Rusty to someone else when Mom died? Wasn't that dog the only way you got through the worst times?"

"My family got me through it. My kids and this place." He let his shoulders drop. "But I wouldn't have been happy about letting go of Rusty."

"Thank you." He made one more attempt to step past Dad. "Can we drop this now?"

"You have to talk to her, Aidan. You have to work this out."

He choked softly, refusing to even dignify that with a response. He powered past his father, his boots pounding on the kennel tiles as he headed for the door. What kind of fresh hell was this? Talk to her about what? Shared custody? Dad was out of his flipping mind if he thought that was happening.

Just as he reached the open door that led to the sunshine outside, a loud staccato bark stopped his thoughts and maybe his heart. "Ruff!"

Aidan whipped around, blinking into the light as a large brown blur came tearing at him. Before he took his next breath, Ruff leaped into the air, slapped both paws on Aidan's chest, and pushed so hard they both slammed into Dad, who was right behind him.

"Whoa, whoa, boy!" Aidan half laughed as he managed to get his arms around the sturdy boxer and roll down to the ground. Immediately, the barking stopped and the tongue came out.

And everything and everyone else disappeared. The kennels, the sunshine, the grief and guilt he'd been carrying for months, even Dad and his crappy news.

There was nothing but Ruff, a wild, crazy, loving brute of a dog who was as much a part of Aidan as his soul. And the love was mutual, as anyone could see by the stubby tail knocking back and forth and that relentless tongue swiping over Aidan's face.

Paws beat against his chest until Ruff ran out of steam and collapsed in drooly satisfaction on Aidan's chest. All Aidan could do was laugh at the pressure of the seventy-five-pound beast who'd transferred all his love from Charlie to Aidan the day his real master was carried out of Afghanistan in a box.

Still chuckling, nuzzling, and rubbing the big head, Aidan pushed the dog up to look into his big, sad eyes. He never looked happy, even when he was. "That's my boy."

Except...was he?

Both of them still panting, Aidan managed to sit up and get Ruff to settle down. A little. But the dog barked and pawed and kissed a few more times, barely glancing up at Dad as one hundred percent of Ruff's doggie focus was on Aidan.

"You're a good boy, Ruffie," Aidan murmured into his fur, letting the full joy of having this dog in his arms again roll over both of them.

"That's a bit of a stretch," Dad joked, reaching down to give Ruff a scratch, which only sent the dog into another barking tizzy, spinning twice and pounding on Aidan again. "Looks like Ruff could use some Kilcannon training magic."

Which Aidan did not have. "He's untrainable," Aidan said.

"There's no such thing."

Aidan buried his face in Ruff's neck again. "You haven't met this one."

"But he's a military dog," Dad said. "I can't believe he didn't get trained overseas."

"He's an Afghani stray," Aidan corrected. "Not a working dog."

"Looks like a purebred boxer to me."

Aidan shrugged. "I don't know what he is, but he's not trainable, not like you guys do it."

He waited for his dad to correct the *you guys* into a *we*, as he had several times since Aidan came home. But Dad was silent, and when Aidan glanced toward the driveway, he saw Darcy, Garrett, and Liam all talking to Cilla Forsythe. His siblings were giving Aidan space for his reunion before they descended on Ruff and pronounced him yet another family dog and tried to turn him into some kind of rule-following specialist. *Good luck with that, guys.*

All this dog could do was play hard and give comfort. And Aidan needed both more than he needed food and water.

"As far as Beck Spencer," Dad said, pulling Aidan's attention back to him. "I'm not going to insist you do anything."

Aidan almost rolled his eyes. As if the man who breathed *Do the right thing* before he got out of bed every morning wasn't going to put his hands on Aidan's shoulders and push him toward Slice of Heaven.

"But I saw the letter to Beck, and I know that, at least when he wrote it, Charlie's request was that Ruff be adopted by his sister. There is no ambiguity about it, and the letter is proof in writing, something you don't have."

Irritation slammed him. "Dad, he was *clear* that night. He was determined. He made me give my word."

When that didn't sway his father, Aidan gripped

Ruff's big brown head, angling his slobbery face toward Dad. "Look at him. He's a guy's dog. A drooling, snoring, out-of-control jumper, licker, and eater of shoes and toilet paper."

Dad gave in to a smile, crouching down to get close to the dog and eye-to-eye with Aidan. "He's definitely a handful, but if your mother had heard you call any canine 'a guy's dog,' she'd have thrown you down for a good old-fashioned Annie Kilcannon talking-to. Then your sisters would pounce on you, too."

"You know what I mean. He's been at war. He's an honorary member of the 160th SOAR Airborne. He can't live in a city high-rise surrounded by babies and cameras. He belongs with me."

"That might not be for you to decide, Son. You have to talk to Beck Spencer."

"Does she know he's here?" Maybe he could put that conversation off for a while, until Ruff was too settled for another life change. Dad was known to fight for a dog's rights in a situation like that, and hard.

"She checks in with me periodically, and I've told her that we were getting closer, but there were no guarantees. You know we weren't certain we'd have him until Cilla got on that plane yesterday in Germany. I didn't see any reason to bring it up until we knew we had him. And, honestly, I didn't want to plant any seeds of discontent in you."

Because life had sowed enough of those under Aidan. "Does Beck know I'm home?"

"Yes, she does. But she has no idea you're thinking about keeping Ruff."

"*Thinking* about it?" He dug his fingers into the fur

22

he'd been stroking, the truth bubbling up. "I can't stay here without him, Dad. I know you don't want to hear that, but I can't."

"Aidan, you've been back less than six weeks. You have to give yourself time and space. We all are doing that."

They were, but he sensed his brothers' impatience that he wasn't all over the dog training business and his sisters' frustration that the Golden Boy they'd sent off to the Army was tarnished now. They all knew he wasn't enthused about this...this *institution* they'd built, though they were doing their best to include him.

But his family had done this all without him. They'd turned Waterford Farm from a peaceful family homestead into a thriving business. Yes, they'd done it as a way to mourn their mother and honor their father, and, of course, they'd done a damn good job.

But he didn't have any part of it. And he didn't belong here. Unless...

He stroked the big brown head, feeling Ruff's heated pants. Unless Ruff could change all that.

"Look, Dad. I know you want me to blend in and fall into the family business like I was born for it, but I don't know how to advise dog trainers or run rescues or train guard dogs how to sniff bombs. I'm no vet or groomer or whatever it is you've picked out for your kids to do here. At least with Ruff, I can have a piece of my life with me. He's going to help me fit in so I don't feel so lost here."

Dad flinched. "Lost? This is your home."

"Is it?" He gestured toward the massive kennel, the sprawling training pen, the outbuildings for admin and trainee housing, the on-site vet office. All of it in the shadow of a yellow farmhouse that used to be the only thing on these hundred acres, all full of a happy, whole family.

"You were conceived, born, and raised in that house, Aidan."

"But I wasn't here when this business was built."

"You're here now."

But could he stay? He had no idea where he'd go or what he'd do, only that he felt restless and itchy and out of place. But if he told his dad that he might leave, it would crush him after all these years of being apart. "I need this dog, Dad. Can you tell Beck that and see if she has a heart?"

"That would be your job, Son. Not mine."

He closed his eyes and let his head drop against the furry forehead of the sole piece of Charlie Spencer he had left. And the only thing that felt anything like that elusive, impossible concept of *home*.

No doubt, Charlie had known that when he made his final wishes crystal clear. All he had to do was somehow convince Beck of that, and this problem would be solved.

"I'll do it," he whispered. "Tomorrow."

Until then, he'd live on the hope that Beck Spencer would change her mind when she saw that Ruff wasn't some little furball she could stuff in a designer bag when she went shopping. She could be his "aunt" and visit him once in a while. And if she wanted a dog, Aidan would gladly find her one.

But not *this* one. Giving up Ruff would break his word. And his heart.

Chapter Three

"Thin, Rebecca! Thin like a windowpane!"

Beck closed her eyes and tried to shut out her aunt's instructions so she could concentrate on the dough. "Aunt Sarah, please. I'm trying." She stretched the gooey mass...and a hole popped open in the middle, making her grunt. "And failing."

"Well, so's this business," Sarah said on a sigh, hugging an old-school ledger to her chest as out of date as the fridge and decades-old oven.

"Maybe you need to actually install a computer and do those numbers on a spreadsheet, Aunt Sarah. I can help you with that."

Sarah dropped her head to look down at her books, the roots of her frosted hair looking more gray than brown. When she looked up, Beck could have sworn the crease between her brows had deepened in the three months since Uncle Mike's stroke. Her complexion was drawn, and her mouth was set in a perpetual pucker from the stress.

"You're doing enough," Sarah said. "I can't make pizza."

Beck snorted and slapped the doughball on the counter, making a yellow semolina cloud puff, probably because she'd used too much of the sandy base. "That's funny, neither can I."

Sarah didn't even smile, but let her narrow shoulders fall. "I'd hire someone if I could afford it, Rebecca. I'm already worried about paying Carly next week," she said, referring to the only part-time help they had left.

"I know," Beck said sympathetically. "But we'll get through this, Aunt Sarah. We'll get Uncle Mike better and back in here."

Sarah rolled her eyes. "He has to want to get better, honey. Right now, he doesn't want to get out of bed."

And without him making the best pizza in town, business was as thin as the last batch of sauce Beck made.

Well, they'd fix it, Beck told herself, shifting her attention to the doughball, which seemed even gummier than usual.

"I need to ask Uncle Mike about the water and weather thing again." *More water if it's warm, less if it's cold.* Or was it the other way around? She looked around for the tattered cheat sheet she'd memorized. Didn't matter if she followed his instructions to a T. She knew every aspect of making pizza, from yeast to oven. She knew the timing, the temperatures, the thickness of each topping. But she didn't have...the touch. That simply couldn't be learned, no matter how hard she tried.

"You can ask him," Sarah said. "But you know what he'll say."

Nothing, Beck thought glumly. Her uncle could

still talk after his stroke, and he was even mobile, but he'd sunk into a silence that was as scary as it was maddening.

When Beck didn't answer, Sarah turned and placed the book on the top shelf over a work desk. "You'll get the hang of it, honey."

Yeah? She'd been here almost two months and the *hang* still eluded her. If only she liked pizza, could stand the smell of red sauce, or wanted her hands covered in flour and dough. If only she were as good as Charlie, who'd be twirling a couple of perfect dough pies in the air like a circus juggler right now and cracking jokes as he performed.

Still, she appreciated her aunt's uncharacteristic optimism. That trait had resided firmly in Beck's mother, Sarah's sister, and Charlie had inherited it in spades. Beck had merely learned optimism, as a coping mechanism, she supposed. But to Sarah Leone, the glass was usually not only half empty, it was cracked, leaking, dirty, and sitting right in the spot where the sky happened to be falling.

That was only one of the many ways Aunt Sarah differed from her younger sister, Karen. Sarah Fitzgerald had married later in life, was childless by choice, and was not a natural nurturer. Karen, on the other hand, had made mothering an art form, was rarely bothered by life's ups and downs, and firmly believed that life happened and you made the best of it.

But there was no making the best of a car crash on the Pennsylvania Turnpike that took the lives of Karen and John Spencer. However, Aunt Sarah had tried hard to make a horrible situation tolerable, and Beck loved her for the effort.

As the legal guardian of her sister's children, Sarah hadn't hesitated to take in her niece and nephew after the accident, even though kids—and certainly not a teenager and a preteen—had not been in the plan with Uncle Mike. Sarah had stressed a lot then, too, thrown by grief and worry and the fact that the four of them didn't fit in the little apartment she and Mike lived in above this restaurant.

Once they'd moved, though, and settled into a new normal, Sarah had done her best to be a mother, especially to eleven-year-old Beck, who'd suffered mightily after her parents died. No, Sarah would never be the vibrant, joyous, witty, and tender nurturer that Beck's mama had been, but she'd tried. And Uncle Mike was gruff and opinionated, but he was funny and loved his unexpected little family, taking care of them like they were his own. They were not the ideal version of family that Beck once had, but they *were* family and all Beck had left. Of course, she'd do anything to help them in this difficult time.

If Mama were here, she'd say, *Turn your face to the sun and you won't see the shadows*, or something that sounded like it belonged on a coffee cup. And that was why Beck was standing in a kitchen she'd never enjoyed, stretching pizza dough she wouldn't eat, and living in a town she'd spent a good deal of her life wanting to leave.

She brushed the thoughts away with the stroke of her hand over a counter-top covered with semolina, clearing her workspace to start again. "Okay, Aunt Sarah, the pizza isn't going to make itself, even though it might taste better if it did."

Sarah smiled at that. "I tried your pepperoni

yesterday, and it…wasn't the worst pizza ever."

Beck laughed and pointed to the dining room. "On that whopping compliment, you go and be sure we're ready for the lunch rush."

"I think I can handle the three people that will storm the doors of Slice of Heaven."

"You never know," Beck said in a singsong voice as Sarah walked out. "Yesterday, we had four. Today could be five!"

Once Sarah left, Beck returned to her dough, squeezing it with all her strength to get the ever-elusive texture that would mean she had a snowball's chance—a doughball's chance?—of making this pie round. Hers were never round. Oblong, misshapen, and too fat on one side, Beck Spencer's pizza was not worthy of being served at the institution that had earned a Best of Bitter Bark medallion twenty-four consecutive times.

She rolled and folded and flipped the doughball. Or should she fold, then roll? Why did it matter so much?

At the slight smell of something burning in the oven, she dropped the ball and headed toward the stainless-steel beast that lined one wall. She eyed the red line, drawn with Sharpie on the dial, carefully setting it at 647 degrees, because ol' Bessie stopped working if you accidentally went over 650.

Shaking her head, she tamped down the money worry again. They couldn't afford part-time help, so they certainly couldn't get new kitchen equipment. What they needed was customers who lined up like they used to. That wasn't happening now, though many of the townsfolk had come after Mike's stroke to support the business.

But, over time, the customers had dwindled, choosing the far superior product at Ricardo's or one of the newer delivery places that had popped up with Bitter Bark's recent growth.

Truth was, Beck could coax a smile out of a gassy seven-month-old sitting inside a fur-lined basket to take the perfect picture, but she couldn't turn flour, water, and yeast into a decent pizza crust. And forget the sauce. She could mix Elmer's Glue and ketchup and it would taste better.

Not that she would actually *taste* it. The response from the customers, or lack of them, told her all she needed to know. And there was that one-star review on Yelp. Ouch.

She forced herself to hum a happy tune, but stopped when she heard a dog bark at the back door, slowing the kneading process to listen.

Funny place to walk a dog. There was nothing in that alley but parking spaces for the retailers on this street, shared dumpsters, and locked doors.

And if that was a lost tourist looking for a way into Slice of Heaven, they'd find the door locked to them in the front, too, metaphorically speaking. Because dogs were not welcome in this pizza parlor.

It sure didn't help their dwindling profits that Aunt Sarah's bone-deep fear of dogs meant she was one of the few storeowners in Bitter Bark who refused service to guests who wanted to come in with leashed dogs. Sarah had bucked the local tourism-building campaign that officially changed the town name for one year to Better Bark to position it as the most dog-friendly town in America. That decision cost as many pizza sales as Beck's not-thin-enough crust.

The barking dog reminded Beck that she still hadn't heard back from Dr. Kilcannon about the status on Ruff. Until she did, she wouldn't break that news to Sarah, though. She had enough to worry about, and a dog in the mix might put the poor woman over the edge.

Sighing, Beck lifted the dough and stretched it out, narrowing her eyes to gauge the thickness. A windowpane? More like a window shutter with that hole in the middle, but this was the best it was going to get unless she started all over.

So she did, throwing the dough down for another pass.

"Roll, sucker," she commanded of the dough. "Roll like you've never rolled before."

The dog barked again, loud enough to be right outside the back door. She thought she heard a man's voice, but that didn't quiet the noisy, persistent barking. Sarah came marching back into the kitchen, wild-eyed at the sound.

"Who's barking back there?" she demanded.

"My guess is a dog."

Sarah grunted. "This whole town is overrun by them."

"You know what's overrun, Aunt Sarah? Ricardo's is overrun," Beck said with a pointed look. "With customers who have dogs. Lots of customers. Paying customers."

Sarah shrugged. "We were fine before this whole Better Bark thing happened."

"Because Uncle Mike was making the pizza. Now the competition is beating the pants off us."

The dog barked again, followed by three hard

knocks at the back door. Beck lifted dough-covered hands. "I'll get—"

"No," Sarah said. "I'll send them away."

"You hate dogs."

"I'm afraid of them," she corrected, heading back there. "I don't hate anyone. I've got this."

Beck kept kneading, listening to the sound of the thick drapes sliding back as Sarah looked out the bank of windows to the alley.

"Well, I'll be damned," she muttered.

Beck glanced over her shoulder, but the walk-in fridge blocked her view of the door. Still, she heard the heavy lock unlatch. Almost immediately, the barking became deafening.

"Quiet." The man's voice was louder than the dog's, deep and certain, but still didn't drown out Sarah's loud gasp.

"Down, boy!" he ordered.

Finally, there was a second of quiet, long enough for Beck to hear Aunt Sarah ask, "What are you doing here?" The question was cool, making Beck huff out a breath of frustration. Okay, he had a dog, but was that any way to treat a potential customer? He might only want some takeout.

"Hello, Mrs. Leone. How are you?"

Beck abandoned the dough altogether, inching back from the counter as she tried to place the somewhat familiar voice. Who *was* that?

The dog barked again, making her aunt give a quick cry of fear. "Get it back! Please."

"He's harmless, I promise. Easy, Ruff. Sit."

Wait. Did he say...*Ruff?*

"Mrs. Leone, I need to—"

"I'm sorry, Aidan. We're getting ready for our lunch rush. Another time."

Aidan? And *Ruff*?

Beck whipped around, wiping her hands as she started toward the back, but the door slammed closed. As Sarah came around the refrigerator and into view, there was agony in her green eyes, and pain turned her thin lips downward.

"Was that Aidan Kilcannon?" Beck asked, knowing full well the answer was yes. "With a dog named Ruff?"

"I'm sorry, Rebecca. I'm not ready to make small talk with him." Her voice trembled, the way it did when life was too much for her.

"But I am." So, so ready. She launched toward the back door, but Sarah snagged her sleeve.

"Where are you going?"

She gave a grin. "To get my dog."

"*What*?"

Beck strode to the back door, yanked it open, and bolted outside to peer from one side of the alley to the other. Daylight spilled between the buildings, highlighting parked cars, dumpsters, and a full bike rack, but no people.

She started to jog toward Ambrose Avenue, her feet on the pavement thudding to the same tempo as the pulse in her head.

Then she saw a man with a dog, a big, dark boxer she immediately recognized from Charlie's pictures. They rounded the corner, heading toward Bushrod Square. She continued a slow jog toward him, her gaze moving between the muscular dog and the equally muscular man.

Aidan Kilcannon was older, broader, bigger than she remembered, but it was the same boy who'd busted into her brother's life in the dark times and made life brighter for Charlie. An old resentment bubbled up, but she tamped it down because nothing was as important as Ruff.

Her dog named Ruff! How she loved Charlie for this sweet parting gift.

When she was about twenty feet away, the dog turned and barked over and over, warning Aidan of her arrival. He looked, but she didn't see his expression, because all her attention was on the mahogany tones of the dog's face, those big dark eyes, the thick shoulders, and the enormous paws that pounded the pavement and fought the leash that held him.

This dog looked *exactly* like the original Ruff, even more so in person than in Charlie's pictures and descriptions.

"Ruff!" she called out, breathless as she ran. Just as she reached them, she dropped down to the dog, who reared up and threw both paws on her chest, knocking her on her backside.

"Whoa, Ruff! Stop!" Aidan yanked the leash, then dove forward to snag the dog's collar and pull him back. "God, I'm sorry. Ruff! Bad boy! Are you okay?"

Beck looked up at him—way up—and blinked at the way the sunlight poured over Aidan Kilcannon, making his tawny-colored locks gleam and his blue eyes match the sky behind him. "Do you remember me, Aidan?"

He didn't answer, but stared at her for a second, maybe two, long enough for Beck's beating heart to skip when a whole bunch of female hormones decided they liked the view. Whoa. Young Aidan Kilcannon had turned into one very fine grown man.

Then the dog made another playful lunge at her, barking and demanding all her attention.

"Oh my, you're a wild one." She dodged the giant head, laughing, trying to reach for a hug or at least a pet, but he was having none of it.

"Careful," Aidan said, who seemed to be using all his strength to hold him back. "He plays hard."

"Of course he does," she said. "That's why he's named Ruff." She looked up at Aidan in time to catch well-defined muscles bunch under an olive-green Army-issued T-shirt as he battled the excited dog.

"I'm Beck, if you hadn't figured that out yet," she said, wiping her hands as she pushed up to one knee. "And I can't believe he's finally here!" She punctuated that with another attempt at a hug, but the big dog jerked in the other direction. "That's okay, Ruffie. You'll get used to me."

Glancing up, she saw Aidan react with a slight flinch. "He's essentially untrainable, you know. You won't believe how bad he is."

That made her laugh, a cascade of pure joy rolling through her. "Thank you so much for bringing him, Aidan. I really thought your father would call, but I guess he wanted to surprise me. I love that."

"Yeah, yeah, it's a surprise for all of us." Aidan managed to get his hand on Ruff's head, and he must have added just enough pressure to calm the dog down. With his other hand, he reached to help her up, his gaze locked on her with more emotions than she could begin to read swirling in his crystal-blue eyes. "It's been a while, Beck."

She sighed and gave him an easy smile. "Yeah, it has. It's good to see you, Aidan."

He nodded, and she tried not to take it personally that he couldn't return the compliment. She looked enough like Charlie, at least in coloring, that he was probably being swamped by a wave of grief.

And if it weren't for this big, beautiful dog, she would be, too.

"I like that you brought him to me," she said, sensing he needed some reassurance. "I thought your dad would, but it's very thoughtful and sweet of you."

Ruff pulled on his leash, hard enough to jerk Aidan away from her. "Whoa, boy. Like I mentioned, tough to handle," he said. "Really a very strong and willful dog."

So was the first Ruff. "Boxers can be."

"But he's like really, *really* stubborn. And your aunt hates dogs—"

"She's afraid of them, no hate."

"—and even our best trainers struggled with him, so I'm happy to keep him. It'll be so much easier for you."

She looked up at him, feeling her face form a *you can't be serious* expression. "*Keep* him?"

"I mean, if you're dying for a dog, then I can get you one so easi—"

"Charlie was the one who died, Aidan," she reminded him. "And he left me his dog, as you know. So, if *you're* dying for a dog, get one. Ruff is mine." She slid her arms around the dog's neck and tried to nuzzle him. "Ooh, I've waited so long for you, boy." Seventeen years, to be precise.

But he jerked away, gave a deafening bark, and looked up at Aidan as if begging for an escape from her.

She didn't care. Charlie had found "the reincarnation of Ruff," as he'd written in his letter to her. It had been a long time since she'd had to say goodbye to the first Ruff and get in a car with Aunt Sarah and Uncle Mike to be taken away to a new, empty, pizza-heavy life with no Mama and Daddy and no Ruff. Her brother had kept his promise to replace Ruff. He'd gone across the world, given his life, but managed to keep that promise.

No one could ever take her Ruff away again.

She stroked his head and tried again to nuzzle him. "You're mine now," she said softly.

But his only response was a noisy bark and a sudden lunge. He almost knocked her over as he took off with the leash flying behind him, running at full speed down the sidewalk like he couldn't get away from Beck fast enough.

And just as he took off after the dog, Aidan's eyes flashed like he was a little bit happy about that.

Chapter Four

"Ruff! Ruff, stop!" Aidan didn't hesitate, taking off after Ruff and leaving Beck Spencer and her bad news behind.

He managed not to run into a single pedestrian as he tore down the sidewalk along Ambrose Avenue, zooming into the square twenty feet behind Ruff. As they passed the brick-columned entrance, Ruff took a two-second break to get his bearings and pant. Aidan launched at him, snagging the end of the leash.

"Nice work, dude," he whispered. "Good thinking in the face of enemy fire."

Ruff dropped down to his haunches and stared up at Aidan like he was shocked that his bad behavior had gotten such a loving response. Assuming he was in trouble, he let out his high-pitched Ruff whine of remorse, which Aidan knew would last thirty seconds, tops.

He really was a poorly trained dog, and the sooner Beck Spencer knew that, the better his chances of getting her to change her mind. So, yeah, maybe he'd held the leash a tad too loosely.

Now, he wrapped the strap around his wrist a few times and seized the looped end with a solid grip.

Turning toward the entrance to the square, he wasn't surprised to see Beck striding toward them, her gaze locked on Ruff with intention and, yeah, something that he supposed was happiness. He noticed only now that over jeans and a T-shirt, she wore a red apron tied around a narrow frame. Narrow, but a hell of a lot more filled out than when she was fourteen, he couldn't help noticing.

"Does he do that often?" she asked as she reached him.

"Yes," he said vehemently. "All the time. You really may want to reconsider your—"

"I'm not going to reconsider anything." She bent over to get closer to Ruff. "Neither are you, my friend."

Ruff barked in her face, which only made her laugh. It was a sound he might have found incredibly endearing under any other circumstances.

Damn it all. She *wanted* Ruff.

As she looked up at him, Aidan stared into milk-chocolate-colored eyes, opened wide under messy bangs that brushed the tops of her brows. The rest of her long brown hair flopped over a shoulder in a sloppy ponytail that looked like it might fall apart at any moment.

And he almost fell over again.

Holy hell, she looked like Charlie. A pretty, delicate, finer version, with a wider mouth and a dusting of freckles on a feminine nose and a...was that flour on her sculpted cheekbone?

Well, that *really* looked like Charlie. If he hadn't been sitting in the cockpit of a UH-60 or cracking up his comrades-in-arms with endless bad jokes, he'd been proofing dough in the DFAC kitchen so he could treat the entire team to world-class pizza.

His gaze dropped to the apron and the Slice of Heaven logo on her chest, reminding him that he and his dog—*his* dog—couldn't have been less welcome at that pizza parlor.

"Are you sure?" Something told him he was grasping at straws, but right now, he'd grasp at air to keep this dog. "'Cause your aunt—"

"My aunt isn't making this decision. I am." She crouched down in front of the dog. "I still can't believe he found a boxer who looks like this and named him Ruff."

"Yeah, well, he took a whole lot of grief for the total lack of creativity, but he insisted."

"He didn't tell you why?"

"He said it sounded like his bark and because he plays rough."

Her eyes twinkled, making them spark with a secret. "Exactly the reasons I named our dog Ruff, too."

"You and Charlie had a dog named Ruff?" How could he not have known that? "He never mentioned that."

She shrugged, her fingers finding the flop of his ears, which made Ruff bark and give a hard full-body shake to get rid of this new offense. "Charlie was so excited when he called me from Kabul. Said it was a miracle. Like my Ruff was reincarnated." She tried to pet him again. "And he was."

"Wow." Why the hell wouldn't Charlie tell him that? They had been side by side going through that shell of a bombed-out hospital the day Charlie found this dog curled up in a closet. "He never mentioned any of that to me."

She straightened and eyed him closely, as if this were the first time she'd really noticed him. "It was between us," she said. "Brother and sister memories. And thanks for bringing him." She looked at Ruff, and he could have sworn her eyes misted over. "I know it couldn't have been easy."

"No, it wasn't. A huge pain. Multiple international parties involved, volunteers, money, airfare, and a few twisted arms, all to get Ruff home..." *To me.*

"Thank you." She gave a brief smile and shifted her attention to the dog, who was sniffing some grass with clear intent to pee on it, and when he did, she smiled as if it was the cutest thing she'd ever seen.

Not good. Not good at all.

But Night Stalkers don't quit. Aidan took a breath and mentally regrouped.

"Maybe when Charlie suggested the possibility of you taking him, it was before we realized just what a, you know, *difficult* dog he is."

She flicked her hand as if that idea was a flea on Ruff's fur. Then her eyes tapered to slits as she looked harder at him, her gaze moving over his unshaven face and unkempt hair. "You mustn't be home on leave, unless they're letting you guys grow your hair longer than military regulations."

"I'm out," he said simply. And he'd started growing his hair after Christmas, when he decided not to re-up when he hit ten years a few months later.

"Oh." She did a terrible job of hiding how much that surprised her. "I thought you were career Army."

He'd thought so, too. He wasn't sure how to answer that, except with the truth. "The job wasn't much fun without Charlie."

Her shoulders dropped, and they both stood still for an awkward beat, but then Ruff pulled the leash, attracted to the bushes and grass of a place where dozens of dogs visited each day. Aidan went along with him and glanced at Beck in invitation.

He didn't need to issue one, though. Her gaze was locked on Ruff as she followed, a mix of wonder and joy and disbelief on her pretty features.

After a moment, she reached for the leash. "May I?"

"You really need to be strong to walk him." He glanced at her arms, exposed in a short-sleeved T-shirt, noticing they were toned but slender, like the rest of her. "I don't know if you can manage him easily."

She tilted her head to one side. "Are you serious? If I could handle a full-grown boxer at eleven, I can do it at twenty-eight."

He lifted his brows to show his doubt, but untwirled the strap and handed the looped end to her, his fingers brushing soft, feminine skin as she took it.

Everything about her was feminine, to be honest. Although the family resemblance to her brother was strong, she was smaller, sweeter, and a helluva lot prettier. And she wanted his dog, which took away some of that pretty and put her on the wrong side of this battle.

"Oh!" She startled as Ruff yanked and tried to go forward, grabbing the arm Aidan offered as she nearly stumbled.

"Told you."

"I got it." Although she didn't sound so sure. "I can manage him."

He waited a beat, then his curiosity got the best of him, still unable to believe Charlie wouldn't share a piece of history after he'd found and kept Ruff. "So you and Charlie had a boxer named Ruff when you were little?"

"Technically, Ruff was mine. My parents got him as a rescue for my tenth birthday."

"What happened to that Ruff?"

"My aunt…" She shook her head. "We couldn't bring him here when we moved, and our next-door neighbors adopted him."

"Oh, got it." Sarah might have just become his best and strongest ally. "She was not happy to see Ruff."

"She was bitten as a kid," she said. "I can't fault her for that fear, but I don't need to have them in the same room together."

But she would be at the pizza parlor all day, right? He sneaked another peek at the flour on her face and the apron, remembering Dad said she was working to help them out. Full time, he hoped. "Don't you have to work?"

"I do." She made a face and glanced over her shoulder in the general direction of Slice of Heaven. "I should go back soon."

"Okay. Then I'll keep Ruff for as long as you need to think about it. Longer."

"There's no thinking involved." She brushed some hair off her face and shot him a sideways glance. "But I'm getting the impression you're not keen on my having him."

Maybe it was time to change tactics and tug the

heartstrings. "We got real close in Afghanistan, Ruff and me. Especially in the last few months...after Charlie died." He pulled back, not wanting to tug so hard he hurt her. "I'm really sorry for your loss, Beck."

She nodded. "We both lost."

He appreciated her acknowledging that. "Ruff has been a real solace to me, honestly."

This time when she looked up at him, he could see the anguish in her sweet features. "I know you were close to Charlie, Aidan. I know you two were inseparable, and I resented you for that. I shouldn't have, since he loved being around you."

"So why did you resent that?"

"I guess because you swooped in ten minutes after we landed in Bitter Bark and stole Charlie from me when I needed a brother more than I needed anything in the world."

He tried to remember when Beck and Charlie had shown up in town as orphans whose parents had died in a car crash. He and Charlie had rarely discussed that, frankly. But then, they were guys. Guys who faced death every single day, so they didn't spend their spare time talking about it when they didn't have to. Maybe that was why he'd never mentioned having a boxer named Ruff.

"I didn't exactly kidnap him," he said, remembering the early days of his friendship with Charlie when the new kid arrived at school after Christmas break his sophomore year. The minute Aidan found out he'd played baseball at his old school, he'd taken Charlie straight to Coach Bergh and gotten him signed up for tryouts for the spring season.

From that moment on, Charlie and Aidan had been close friends on and off the field.

"You had him playing baseball or at your house or riding around chasing girls or whatever you two did, anywhere but home."

And they were all good times. Where had Beck been during those years? A child, to him. He couldn't remember anything more than a casual, *Hey, Beck, is Charlie here?* when he stood at the front door of that two-story house in a cookie-cutter development called Pine Woods Grove.

"Then you dragged him off to the ROTC," she added, yanking him from the past.

Dragged him? "He wanted to enlist and skip college," Aidan reminded her. "I'm the one who convinced him to go to Wake Forest and get a degree. He never wanted to do anything but the military."

She didn't answer as they walked Ruff from one tree to the next. Occasionally, Aidan stole another glance at Rebecca Spencer. It was impossible not to notice she was not a child anymore. She moved with grace, like a dancer, her skin luminescent in the sunlight, her messy hair silky, her body feminine with the right amount of curves under that apron.

And then he remembered why he was there. Not to be tempted.

Time to find a new front in this battle and quit looking at hers. "So where are you living in Bitter Bark?"

"With my aunt and uncle now."

Perfect. "Your aunt is not going to like this dog in her house."

"Oh, she won't let him in."

"Then I can—"

"I've already figured this out." She cut him off. "I'll move to the apartment above the pizza parlor. Then I can visit him when I have a break and take him out when he needs to go. Easy-peasy."

For her, not him. And not Ruff.

"Won't that disappoint your aunt? Doesn't she like having you live with her?"

She smiled as if to say, *Nice try*, and let him know she was totally on to him. Didn't care. *Night Stalkers don't quit, they find a new way to win.*

"I think she'd be fine if I moved up there," she replied. "I never really expected to stay this long, but things are worse than I thought."

Ruff finally found a spot of sun-washed grass, and they headed to a bench near it.

"I heard your uncle had a stroke. I'm sorry," Aidan said as they sat down.

"Yeah, he did." She held up a finger in warning. "And don't you dare use that as an excuse to keep my dog, too."

Actually, for once, he wasn't. "I like Mike. He's a good man, and I'm sorry he's struggling."

She nodded in full agreement. "And that's why I came to help."

"How bad was the stroke?"

"Not awful, but bad enough." Easing back on the park bench, she twirled the leash off her wrist and rubbed it where the strap had chafed a bit. "But it hit him hard mentally. He's sullen and doesn't talk much. He certainly doesn't work. He's in bed like he's ninety, not sixty. He's got some mild paralysis, but it could be treated and overcome with good physical therapy. He won't do that, so he can't make pizza." She choked softly and looked skyward. "And neither can I, but I'm trying to help them hold Slice together."

"Wow, that place is like an extension of him," Aidan mused. "I don't think I ever walked in the door that Uncle Mike wasn't in the back pounding dough and stirring sauce."

"He's owned it for thirty years," she said on a sigh. "And he'd always expected Charlie to take over when he got out of the Army."

"Charlie couldn't wait for that," Aidan said. "He was going to get out this spring...right now."

They were both quiet for a moment, then she said, "Uncle Mike knew that, of course, and now..." She shook her head. "He seems to not want to go on."

Aidan turned away, leaning his elbows on his knees, rubbing his hands together to brace for the expected wave of grief and guilt. They always came in a pair, those two. Sadness that Charlie was gone, shame that he was still very much alive.

"So are you taking over Slice of Heaven, then?" he finally asked.

She laughed without a drop of humor. "No, that isn't what I want to do. I have a great business and a full life in Chicago, but I can't leave my aunt and uncle high and dry. She has her hands full with him, and someone needs to make pizza and run the restaurant, or they'll lose everything. Money's tight, and hiring is impossible right now."

And all that left no room for a dog. He rooted for a way to remind her of that without beating the possibility to death, but before he thought of anything, she turned around and looked back toward the street.

"Speaking of which, I better get back to work. It's almost lunchtime, and we might actually get a customer, although I wouldn't hold my breath."

"That place used to be wall to wall. Best pizza in the state."

"Used to be." She closed her eyes with a slight groan. "And Uncle Mike has the Best of Bitter Bark awards on the wall to prove it. He won twenty-four consecutive years, since the contest and festival started."

Aidan laughed. "I think Charlie reminded me every single time we made pizza together, which was about a thousand."

Interest glinted in her eyes. "If you picked up any secret techniques during those thousand times, I sure could use some pointers."

He frowned, sensing she was serious, even though she'd made it sound like a joke. "Charlie always said the trick is in the hands."

"And the water. And the temperature. And the humidity. And the whims of the pizza gods."

"But mostly the hands."

She held out her hands, showing very fine-boned hands with long, slender fingers. "These haven't figured out the trick yet."

"I can see your problem." He took one of her hands, practically engulfing it in his much-larger, much-rougher grip. "You're not strong enough to make pizza."

She tugged her hand free of his. "How many times are you going to accuse me in one conversation of being weak? Can't hold the leash, can't roll the dough. Please."

He cringed, realizing the mistake. "Sorry, Beck. I'm sure you're strong in many other ways—the fact that you're here proves that. But Charlie always said that you have to knead full strength, rolling and folding with power. It's the only way to get the windowpane."

She dropped her head into those slender hands. "That freaking windowpane is the bane of my existence."

"You're really struggling, aren't you?"

"You have no idea. I can't even make the damn crust in a round shape, and it always seems not to have the right..." She held her hand out and let it fall at the wrist.

"Flop," he supplied. "Charlie taught me how to get that. Really has to do with the water ratio and how long you leave it in the oven. And the weather. Use more water in the dough mix during the hotter months."

She eased back, stunned. "You *know* that?"

"I told you, he taught me everything. Now that I'm home, I swear my family is bugging me to make pizza every week."

"Huh. Well, lucky you. I wish I knew the tricks of the trade. I mean, I *know* them, I just can't seem to apply them." She pushed up. "But I do have to get back." She tugged the leash gently. "So, let's go, Ruff. We'll get you settled in your new apartment and break the news to Auntie Sarah. I'm sure she'll be overjoyed with this turn of events."

Damn it, he'd completely forgotten the war he was supposed to be fighting, lost in an easy conversation with a pretty girl.

"You're taking him? Just like that?" Aidan stood, a

fresh punch of heartache at the realization that Ruff was leaving *now*. "You can't do that."

"Why not?"

"He needs a bed, bowls, toys, food." *And me. He needs me.*

"You didn't bring any of that for me?"

No, because he'd lived on the false hope that this would be a fool's errand. "I have emergency supplies in the Jeep I brought from Waterford Farm," he said. "Only enough for a day or two at the most. And by then…" He raised his brows in warning. And hope. "You might be ready to change your mind."

"No minds are being changed, Aidan. Sorry."

"Okay." He exhaled softly as they got up and started walking through the park, with Ruff content enough to lead but not pull, or do anything overtly bad, like he should be doing to help Aidan out.

Aidan dug through his artillery knowing he had to take one more shot. He knew he had the perfect weapon, but didn't want to use it. Deathbed promises would make her eyes well up again, and he had zero desire to hurt her in this process. There had to be a better way.

"What about when you go home?" he asked. "You can't take him to Chicago. You work and live in a high-rise, right? He'd go stir crazy. He needs a lot of exercise. Like, major amounts. All day."

A quick laugh bubbled up, which was stinkin' adorable and made him want to howl in the face of his obvious defeat. "Hate to break it to you, but dogs are legal in Illinois and welcome in my building. We actually have a dog run on the roof and a park that faces the lake across the street."

Great. "But, your work? You're a baby photographer?"

"Yes, I am," she replied.

He grunted. "Oh man, I wouldn't trust him with a thousand-dollar camera, and he'll probably make your babies cry."

"You *really* don't want me to take him, do you?"

He turned to her and looked directly into her eyes, out of excuses but not too proud to beg. And maybe pull out the deathbed promise after all, since Ruff was less than five minutes from *gone*.

How did he tell her what Charlie said on that stretcher without breaking her heart?

"Beck, your brother made it clear in the...end...that he wanted me to have Ruff. He was still quite lucid, but he..." He swallowed, aware that those brown eyes, so much like the ones he was seeing in his memory, were locked on him, riveted to his words—hanging on each one, as a matter of fact. "He told me quite clearly that he wanted me to have Ruff. He asked if my dad would start the process of bringing him here so he could live at Waterford Farm, our family's canine facility. I think he felt that Ruff belongs there, with me, someone who knows him well and can take care of him."

Her eyes didn't well up, and her gaze didn't flicker. For all her femininity and apparent "weakness" that he shouldn't have pointed out, there was a strength in her expression that nearly made him take a step backward.

"You think Charlie changed his mind sometime between writing a letter to make it official if something happened to him and when something did happen to him?"

He thought about that, and no real answer emerged. "Since he never told me that he promised you the dog, I don't know. All I know is what he said that night, Beck. And all I want to do is honor his request."

"As I do. Ruff is his legacy and his gift to me." She looked down at the dog. "I only want to do exactly what Charlie wanted, and I'm sorry that he told you that when he...then." She closed her eyes for a second, but when she opened them, they were clear and direct. "But I have a letter from him. It's signed, dated, and when you read it, you'll see that he not only wanted me to have Ruff, but the reason he took him from the rubble of that building in the first place was so that I could have the boxer I lost when my parents died."

He stared at her, remembering Charlie's determination, even though more than a few other soldiers had tried to tell him that taking the dog back to base was a bad idea. He'd been hell-bent on it, and Aidan had chalked it up to Charlie being Charlie.

But he'd been hell-bent about Aidan taking Ruff, too. "If what you're saying is true, then—"

"No *if* about it," she said as she started walking with purpose toward Slice of Heaven, letting Ruff lead the way.

There was an *if* to him, though. A big one.

Silent, as if she sensed she'd won this round, Beck concentrated on the leash, trying like hell not to get pulled by Ruff. Then her steps slowed and stopped completely when they reached the front door of Slice of Heaven, her jaw suddenly dropping as she peered through the glass window that faced the street. "What the heck?"

Aidan followed her gaze, seeing about eight customers at tables, with two more at the counter, ordering from a frazzled-looking Sarah Leone.

"Customers!" Beck exclaimed.

"That's good, right?"

"Not unless I make some pizza." She yanked the front door open, and Ruff went lunging into the restaurant, barking at DEFCON 1, only a little louder than her aunt's sudden shriek. Fighting to hold Ruff back, Beck whipped around and gave him a look of sheer desperation. "Help!"

"Give me the dog." He managed to get the leash from her.

"Don't you dare take him," she warned.

So this was it? This was goodbye? With the same deft control he'd use on a Black Hawk under fire, he dipped and rolled and hovered for another approach at his target. And then he got one.

"I'll help you," he said, giving Ruff a harsh tug and an order to calm down. "Let's get him upstairs and take me into the kitchen," he said.

"In the kitchen?"

"So I can make your pizza."

She gave that a millisecond of thought and then broke into a blinding smile. "I owe you one."

He raised a hopeful brow.

"Not *that* one, but I like your tenacity, Kil." With a sly wink and the use of a nickname only one man had used, she reminded him so much of Charlie, it took his breath away.

But he'd gained some ground, living long enough to get more time with Ruff and another chance to fly back into this skirmish with a winning strategy.

Because Night Stalkers don't quit. And pretty Beck Spencer would have to accept that, sooner or later.

Chapter Five

Beck waved off Aunt Sarah's howl of discontent as the dog made his way deeper into the dining room, and then she gave Aidan a solid shove into the kitchen. Inside the door, she snagged the master key ring and jingled it in the direction of the back stairs up to the apartment.

"Follow me."

Ruff bounded up the steps ahead of her, pulling Aidan along, and as the leash got between them, Beck nearly faceplanted on the second step.

"Careful," Aidan said, grabbing her under the arm, saving her from the fall.

"Doesn't he ever follow directions?"

"Never. Not ever."

She had to laugh at his continued attempts to talk her out of something she would never be talked out of. But he was cute. Wasting his time, but easy on the eyes.

In a half run, she stayed a step behind Ruff, who led the way like this was all his idea. Behind her, she heard Aidan chuckle, too, before giving another demand for Ruff to settle down, which was totally ignored.

For a second, she couldn't remember the last time she'd laughed, but couldn't take time to think of it, because Aunt Sarah's complaints and calls for assistance in the kitchen reverberated through the narrow wooden stairwell.

"I can lock him up here if you want to get started on the pizza," she suggested.

"Not until I check it out." Aidan looked around the small space at the top of the stairs while she flipped through the keys to find the one that opened the apartment.

"Will he be safe up here?" he asked. "Nothing he could ingest or that could hurt him in there?"

She managed to get the door open to the tiny one-bedroom, a power wave of bad memories hitting her as she did. Always the same moment flashed in her mind when she walked into this room. The week before Thanksgiving, when Aunt Sarah and Uncle Mike had climbed the steps with Charlie and Beck, carrying their suitcases, trying to stay chipper, telling them about the pizza parlor down below...

This is your life now.

She shook off the ancient ache and looked around at the apartment they'd moved out of not long after that. Over time, the living area had become a bit of a storage unit, but mostly for furniture, old restaurant equipment, and a pallet of paint cans from when Uncle Mike wanted to paint the pizza parlor dining room seafoam-green, but gave up after seeing how putrid it looked on one wall. So now they covered the lone seafoam-green wall with the Best of Bitter Bark awards and hoped customers looked at those and not the hideous color.

In one corner, a stack of sealed, unused pizza boxes towered nearly to the ceiling, and the rest of the place had a few boxes of files and papers.

"We never keep food up here," she said. "He should be fine."

Aidan glanced around, frowning. "Define fine."

"Unless he eats sofas or paint or..." She looked down. "Hardwood floor. I think he's safe."

Ruff started sniffing and exploring, pulling his leash taut, and Aidan still didn't look satisfied. "It's dark in here."

She rushed to a bank of windows along the front room, dragging the heavy drapes all the way open, immediately bathing the room in light. "And he has a view of Bushrod Square," she said with the flourish of a real estate agent working every trick she had. "It's really a lovely apartment."

"Water. He has to have water."

"Of course! The kitchen functions." She breezed to the galley kitchen and searched wildly for a dish, pulling cabinets open and snagging a plastic bowl like it was the Holy Grail.

"Here we go!" She flipped on the faucet, filled up the bowl, splashed a little in her haste, but planted it square in the middle of the living room. "Thirsty from all that barking, Ruff? Here you go, baby."

"And that means he'll have to pee."

She resisted the urge to glare at the man who never gave up when it came to this dog. Maybe to anything. "He peed sixty times in the square, and we'll take him out after we get a few pies served. Can we go now?"

"Let's see." He unhooked the leash and backed

away from Ruff as if he half expected the dog to bolt, jump, or leap out the window.

He did none of that, but loped toward the water bowl and slurped noisily.

"See? He's fine."

Aidan didn't answer, but watched him, then looked again at Aunt Sarah's old paisley-print sofa. "Sleep there, Ruff," he said. "Take a long afternoon snooze."

At the word *snooze*, he perked up his head, barked once, and ambled to the sofa with the speed of a hundred-year-old man thinking about his nap. *Come on, Ruff.*

"Snooze, boy," Aidan ordered.

Ruff climbed up, stretched out, knocked a throw pillow out of his way with his head, and let out the mother of all belches.

"Did I mention he's disgusting?" Aidan asked.

"Nope, but you will." She gave Aidan a good nudge toward the door. "Come on. A rush is rare. Like, unheard of. I don't want to lose these customers."

Aidan took one more look at Ruff, but she ushered him out the door. "He has to get used to this place. I'll clean it out tonight, and we'll both move in, all comfy and safe. Let's go."

Down the stairs, she pushed the door into the kitchen and nearly got mowed down by Aunt Sarah as she bounded in from the dining room.

"What is he—"

Beck cut her off by stepping between them, using one hand to point Aidan toward the pizza counter and the other flat in front of Sarah's face in the kindest, clearest way she could say *stop*.

"He's here to help. Isn't that awesome?" Beck said, dialing up the brightness with a wide smile. "He can make actual pizza that people will eat."

"But where's the—"

"Upstairs, out of your way. How many people, what pies, and do you need any salads?"

Sarah's jaw unhinged, and she pushed back a lock of hair, the lines even deeper now on her sixty-year-old face. "Four," she finally said. "All large. Two cheese. One pepperoni. One half mushrooms, half veggie. Six salads."

Beck gave a quick nod, calculating whether she'd made enough dough for four large pizzas. Well, she'd made it. How it tasted was anyone's guess. "We can do that. Get them drinks."

The second Sarah's gaze slipped over her shoulder toward Aidan, Beck got right in her face, blocking her view. "Drinks at the fountain. Behind the pickup counter. In the dining room." She tapped Sarah's shoulder. "Don't be paralyzed by the big rush of business, Aunt Sarah. It's an answered prayer."

With a flash of her green eyes, Sarah pivoted and got to work. On a sigh of relief, Beck turned and took that breath right back in again.

Aidan already had a Slice of Heaven apron on, his head down as he kneaded a doughball like the stuff was whipped cream made to conform to his hands. He pushed, rolled, folded, scooped some flour into his hand, and slapped that unresponsive ball of hell onto the countertop and started pushing it out to a perfect twelve-inch circle.

Wow. "How did you do that?"

He stole a glance at her, a lock of his hair brushing

his eyebrow, crystal-blue eyes glinting with a whisper of arrogance. "Told you. It's all in the hands." Then he sniffed. "Something in the oven, Beck?"

Was there? "No, it's been on too long. The smell goes away when we put something in it."

"Something like this?" He lifted his hands off the dough, spread his fingers wide, and flipped the pie back and forth for full examination.

Forget the dough. Look at those hands. They were…good. Damn near as big as that pie, tanned and strong with clean, clipped nails, and enough nicks and scars to make her want to know the story behind each one. "Oh yes."

He glanced up and gave a half smile that was almost as jolting as his hands. "Like it, do you?"

Yes. *No.* Damn, she wasn't going there.

Because if he got one whiff that she had so much as a single cell firing up over the sight of his big hands and blue eyes and shoulders that looked like they were made for a woman to claw with her nails, his next approach would be a charm offensive. And if a man as insistent and relentless as Aidan Kilcannon turned that charm on her, she might actually weaken for his claims that Ruff belonged to him.

And that wasn't happening, come hell, high water, or sexy hands.

Instantly, she spun on her heel, rounded the counter, and headed for the fridge to gather the ingredients for salads. She slipped into work mode, lining up bowls, adding cherry tomatoes, sending the uninspired concoctions to the pass. Uncle Mike would have cut the cucumbers with cool edges, sliced the olives, and made sure every salad was topped with a jaunty sprig of something fresh. But she wasn't Uncle Mike and couldn't have made edged cucumbers if her life depended on it.

Who'd care?

"That was a sorry-looking salad," Aidan mused as he passed.

She closed her eyes and grunted. "They don't come for the salad."

"From the way you're acting over a lunch rush, I'm starting to think they don't come at all."

She gave a careless shrug. "Well, this group did, for whatever reason. All the pizzas in the oven?"

"Yep. Where's the rest of the dough?"

"I have some proofing in the refrigerator, but I honestly thought it would be for dinner, not lunch."

He bent down to peer through the glass into the dining area. "I saw three more people come in."

She blinked in shock. "What is going on?"

"Um, lunch?"

"Haven't had a lunch like this in a long time."

He grinned. "I must be your lucky charm."

Just then, the kitchen door flew open, and Aunt Sarah came in with her face flushed. "They're travel agents!" she announced. "Apparently, a busload of them are on a tour through North Carolina small towns."

"That's great," Aidan said. "They'll tell their clients to come if the pizza's good."

"Big if," Aunt Sarah muttered, but Beck wasn't going to stand here and discuss it when there were actual paying customers pouring into Slice of Heaven.

"Did you get the order for those three new customers?" she asked her aunt.

"I sent them away," she said.

"*What?*" Aidan and Beck asked the question in perfect, shocked unison.

"They had a dog." She held out her hands as if that was all that needed to be said. And, of course, it was.

"Didn't read the sign, huh?" Beck said as she wiped down the salad-making counter.

"Oh, they saw the sign, but they were in line outside of Ricardo's and saw you come in here with…" She pointed toward the ceiling and, Beck assumed, the apartment above them.

"My new dog, Ruff?"

Sarah actually smiled, either at the name or the idea.

"He is," Beck insisted. "Aidan kindly brought him all the way from Afghanistan. He was Charlie's dog."

Sarah blinked as if Beck had spoken in Greek and not a word made sense.

"And he'll live upstairs, with me, as long as I'm here, then I'll take him back to Chicago," Beck finished. "You don't have to have anything to do with him."

Her aunt opened her mouth to argue, but the front bell rang, indicating even more guests had walked in. Sarah and Beck shared a shocked look, too slammed to argue over the dog.

"You better make more salads and start the next pie," Sarah said, turning toward the dining room. "I'll get their order."

"Unless they have a dog," Aidan muttered, opening the oven door.

Beck sighed. "Yeah. She's really got her heels dug in on that topic."

"Maybe you could tell her what's what." He opened the oven and slid a rickety old metal peel under a pie. "You're awfully good at it." He turned and caught her gaze, a glimmer in his blue eyes.

"Was I mean?"

"You were...strong," he said, shimmying the peel to get the pie in the middle. "Reminded me of Charlie."

That made her smile as she walked to the shelves to get more salad bowls.

"And it's pretty hot," he added.

She closed her eyes. Yep, he went there. Already. "You mean the pizza? It's supposed to be hot."

He just laughed, and Beck could feel the ground shift under her feet. *Oh no you don't, Aidan Kilcannon.*

But then she saw a pie coming out of the oven, as golden and perfect and bubbling as if Uncle Mike himself had made it.

"Oh...wow." She didn't even eat pizza, and she could tell he'd nailed it.

He lifted his brows, and his lips curled in a smile. "I could teach you for—"

She glared at him. "The answer is no. Ruff is mine."

But something in his smile scared her. Like he didn't plan on taking *no* for an answer where Ruff was concerned.

Well, too bad. She had the letter. He had...a story. And the bluest eyes she'd ever seen.

Chapter Six

"That's the last of them." Sarah Leone practically collapsed in a heap as she came in from the dining room after the short, but intense, lunch rush. She eyed Aidan as he wiped down a counter, mouthing the words, *Thank you.* Like she couldn't actually *say* it, but had to.

He responded with a simple nod, understanding how hard it must be to have him here. Every time she looked at him, she had to think of Charlie.

"I'll go up and check on Ruff," he said, having been waiting for the all clear from a steady stream of pizza-and dough-making to do that.

"I can check on him," Beck called from the back. "I was on my way."

"I should go with you." Aidan headed her off before she got all the way out of the fridge. "Ruff might not react well to a total stranger."

Beck sailed by him with an armful of clean salad bowls, turning to her aunt. "Ignore that, Aunt Sarah. Ruff is fine. Harmless. Big and clumsy, is all." She shot a look over her shoulder as if to say, *Like someone else around here.*

Of course. He'd totally forgotten about her aunt's fear, so he really shouldn't be talking like Ruff was a troubled dog that should scare her. "And we haven't heard any barking," he added quickly. "I bet he's been sound asleep for the last two hours."

"I'll get him." Beck dumped her bowls and stripped off her apron.

"He knows me." He blocked her from the door.

"He's my dog."

"But he might...lick you. He's persistent like that, and the drool?" He shook his hands like they were dripping. "You'll *hate* it."

"I'll love it." She inched closer. "Move, Kilcannon, or I'll hate *you*."

For a long moment, they faced each other in a standoff. What if she went up there and Ruff greeted her with his usual *you've been gone for two hours and look how miserable I am* face? All bets were off. Misery face was irresistible.

The stare-down ended when Sarah cleared her throat. "Well, I for one am not going up there. I'm off to check on my husband. I suggest you use the door at the bottom of the stairs to take him out on Ambrose Avenue." Aidan got the impression that was as close to *permission to keep the dog* as Sarah was going to give.

"Bye, Aunt Sarah," Beck said without taking her gaze off of Aidan.

Finally, he gave in, moving to the side so she could go through the side door that led to the stairs. She was in such a hurry, she didn't even close it behind her.

At least Ruff wasn't unwanted.

Wait, was he giving up? Not a chance. He took a

step toward the door, just as he heard a moan of pure disbelief.

"Oh my God..." The soft exclamation came floating down, followed by a whiny, moaning sigh of...remorse. Ruff's remorse. Only slightly more endearing than misery face, but it always followed something very, very bad.

"That's my boy," Aidan whispered to himself. No doubt, he'd left a chewed sofa. An unrolled trail of toilet paper. Maybe a nice big pile of—

"What did you do?" Beck's voice rose with the question, cracking on the last word.

Exactly what Ruff the Wonder Dog would be expected to do. Trouble with a capital T. Aidan bit back a triumphant laugh as he headed up the steps two at a time, coming to a sudden stop at the open doorway where Beck stood in utter shock.

Oh *man*. This was bad. Even for Ruff, this was...serious.

"Is paint toxic?" she asked softly. Considering that the sofa, floor, most of the boxes, and pretty much every visible surface was covered in a light turquoise paint, the last thing he'd expected her to be concerned about was Ruff's safety.

"Dude. What did you do?" Aidan inched by the shell-shocked woman to see Ruff flat out in the middle of the floor, his paws covered in paint, the open, empty can next to him, his face spotted with the color.

He stood, barked, and lifted both paint-covered paws in greeting. Aidan snagged his feet, holding the big dog steady on his back legs while he examined the state of his mouth. "He didn't eat any," he said. "He was too busy playing in it."

"Oh my." She came in as Aidan lifted the dog and got him off the ground.

He didn't even have to say, *I told you so*, since the paint kind of spoke for itself. He did have to keep himself from laughing, rewarding Ruff with affection, or asking her when he could take the dog home.

Of course Ruff would have his back. He was Charlie reincarnated. "Is there a bathtub?" he asked.

"Right through that door on the right."

"I'll clean him up, then get the rest of this."

"I've got it," she said, totally unfazed. "There are rags and cleaning supplies downstairs." And off she went, with no tirade, no tears, no foot-stomping or fury.

But she had to be seething inside, right? Seething and ready to give up this crazy idea.

"Ruff 'N' Ready, you are such a hero," he muttered into the dog's ear as he hoisted him up to avoid even more paint on the floor. "I mean, *bad boy!*" He turned his head toward the door so she'd hear the reprimand.

The dog barked once, sharply, as if to say, *It was nothing*. And then a few more times, which Aidan took as Ruff's reminder that he didn't like to be alone in a strange place, and oh, by the way, isn't paint fun?

Fighting a smile, he managed to get the beast into the bathtub and turn the water on, which pleased Ruff to no end. He let out a few happy barks, because this dog loved nothing more than a good bath and probably thought he was being richly rewarded for his horrific behavior.

Which he was.

The paint must have been water-soluble, as it

washed off easily, leaving a greenish-blue tint on the white tub that Aidan was sure would remind her every time she took a shower what a bad idea this dog was.

He closed his eyes as the image of her doing just that slipped into his brain, as unexpected and unwelcome as her laid-back reaction to this crisis. Okay, she was cool under pressure and pretty as a picture and not the pushover he'd kind of hoped she'd be. And she worried about the toxic paints. *And don't even* think *about her in the shower.*

She had plenty of points in her pro column, but no reason to retreat. He'd vanquished more formidable enemies, and he would again.

As he ran each monster paw under the faucet, Aidan listened for any noise from the apartment, but didn't hear Beck.

"I think we may have won this one, big boy." He scrubbed hard, getting between the dog's giant toenails, which might take on a permanent shade of turquoise.

Ruff answered by swatting the water like an elephant at play, panting at the pure fun of it. So Aidan took his time, but not too much so Ruff didn't start associating this apartment with bath-time fun.

Aidan finished the job by turning on the shower and closing the curtain, hoping that helped clean the tub and knowing Ruff was in dog heaven now. Not seeing a towel, he bent over to open a cabinet under the sink, and as he did, the curtain behind him came crashing down. Ruff was instantly over the pile of plastic, lunging for the door before Aidan took another breath.

Dude was *killing* it today.

Aidan shot up, ran after him, and barely caught him by the collar as Ruff went careening across the living room floor. The two of them stopped right next to a stunned Beck, who was on her hands and knees trying to get paint off the hardwood floor.

Next to her, Ruff gave a world-class shake, raining water over Beck and turning the paint into a blue-green puddle.

"Told you he's a really, really bad dog."

"He's a good dog, right, Ruff?" She put her hand on his head, spreading her slender fingers, and trying to press like he had. Which only made Ruff shake again and start to bark furiously.

She closed her eyes for a quick second in frustration, but then brightened. "Can you show me how you do that thing on his head?"

Aidan had opened his mouth to tell her that her hands weren't big enough when she held one up to stop him.

"Don't tell me I'm not strong enough. Or big enough. Or man enough. Or worthy enough. Just tell me what to do."

Chastised, he leaned back and let his backside hit the floor, keeping his mouth firmly shut, because she was all those things, and more. Well, maybe not *man enough*, but she was woman enough, all right. And that only made her more formidable.

Then he opened his hand wide and reached for Ruff's head. "If you put gentle pressure in the heel of your hand and flutter your thumb and baby finger under his ears, he usually calms right down."

He demonstrated, and instantly, the barking stopped and Ruff sat on his haunches, tongue out in a noisy pant as he looked from one to the other, waiting for praise.

"Good boy, Ruff," she said, trying and failing to make eye contact. "You're a good boy."

"Beck."

She gave Aidan a questioning look.

"Aren't you mad? Disgusted? Ready to scream at the beast for wrecking the place and getting on your last nerve?"

Still on her knees, she locked gazes with Aidan, her dark brown eyes so mesmerizing he wondered how Ruff managed to not get snared by them. "I'm not changing my mind, if that's where you're going." Then she turned to the dog. "You get that, Ruff? We'll figure this out. We'll dog-proof, paint-proof, goof-proof this place. We'll go on walks and watch sunsets and take Sunday drives with the windows down, and we'll sleep in front of the TV, and when you're really good and Aunt Sarah isn't around, we'll take you over to see Uncle Mike, because he secretly loves dogs. You got that, kiddo?"

Aidan could feel victory slipping away. How could he compete with sunsets and Sunday drives and long nights with a beautiful woman? Lucky dog.

"Well, you are being remarkably chill about this mess," he noted.

"Messes get cleaned up, Aidan." She turned back to the floor, her hair half out of the ponytail now and covering most of her face. She took a swipe with a wet rag that took the paint right off the floor.

As she reached for the next spot, Ruff walked in front of her and slapped a paw in the paint puddle, splashing it everywhere.

"Geez, Ruff, give the girl a break." Aidan reached for his collar and pulled the dog back, noticing then that Beck's narrow shoulders were shaking. "Oh man, are you crying?"

She looked up, but those weren't tears in her eyes. "Oh my God, no." They sparked with humor, and her straight, white teeth were on full display as she let out a belly laugh, then gasped for air and laughed again.

"You think this is funny?"

"I think it's hilarious," she managed, shaking her head and using the back of her wrist to wipe her eye. "Wonderfully funny. Don't you?"

It would be if she weren't so damn understanding. That's not what should happen. She should freak out and make the dog leave, and this whole thing would be over. But she was laughing and pretty. Why hadn't Charlie told him how pretty his sister was? Or that he had a dog named Ruff when they were kids? Or that he'd written to her and given her *his* dog?

"I'm a little ashamed of his behavior," he finally said. And maybe a little ashamed of himself. Maybe it was time to admit defeat.

"Don't be. He's not yours."

That wiped his smile away. "Beck, Charlie told me to keep him. He insisted. I know I don't have a paper trail, but you can see how connected we are. And you..." He swallowed while she let him dig himself deeper, but he didn't know how to make the same argument again when it was obvious she was intractable. "You..."

"I have a letter from my brother. Do you want to see it? I don't have it with me, but my friend and partner at work can send it to me. I can tell her where to find it in my apartment. She can text a picture of it to me in an hour, if that will get you to back off."

He held up a hand to stop her. There *had* to be another way. "What would you say to shared custody?"

"That he'll only be harder to handle when I get him back. Sorry, no."

"How about I find you another boxer? Exactly like him. My family can find any dog anywhere. We'll rescue a boxer, name him Ruff, and hand-deliver him to your door. Trained, even."

For a long time, the only sound in the room was Ruff's steady, noisy panting.

"I want this dog, not *a* dog," she said softly. "Because he *is* Charlie."

He frowned at that. "They were inseparable, that's true."

"That explains so much." She reached out to scratch Ruff's head, but he inched away. "This dog is exactly like him. Kind of klutzy, very endearing, all boy, and all heart. If my brother came back as a dog, he'd be Ruff." She stretched her arm again, but Ruff wanted no part of her touch. "Only, he'd like me."

"If your brother came back in any form, the world would be a better place." Aidan easily managed to pet Ruff's head, using the gesture to cover the pain that engulfed him. "Guess you already know that."

"I do." Beck sat back on her heels, sighing. "And it's so important to me to do what he wanted and keep this dog."

"That's exactly what's important to me. More than anything, I want to honor Charlie's wishes. Yes, I love Ruff. And need him, but at the bottom of this is respecting what Charlie wanted."

"If I didn't have that letter, I'd give him to you."

If she didn't have that letter, Ruff wouldn't be hers to give.

One more time, they locked gazes, both of them immovable in their position. Both, in a way, right. And both motivated by love for the same person.

"He's been through a lot," she finally said. "Shipped overseas, and everything is new. He needs some time."

He couldn't argue that. Ruff would settle down. He'd never be an easy dog, but she'd get the hang of it. Damn it.

She held her hand out to Ruff as a peace offering, but he trotted a few steps away.

She narrowed her eyes with a gleam of determination that Aidan already knew to respect. "You might not want me, big boy, but I want you."

"Ah, Ruff," Aidan said, shaking his head. "When a beautiful woman says something like that, you know what you have to do."

Ruff slowly lifted one leg in front of the sofa.

"Oh no you don't!" Aidan lunged at him, averting the disaster. "Outside, dumb-ass." Standing, he tugged on the collar, forgoing the leash in case Ruff was serious about peeing right then and there. "Where did your aunt want me to take him?"

"Me," she corrected. "She wanted *me* to take *my dog* out the back door at the bottom of the stairs. It leads to the street, not the alley." Pushing up, she wiped a wet, paint-splattered hand on her jeans. "Come on, I'll show you."

She headed down the stairs ahead of them, with enough bounce in her step to make him wonder if anything threw this woman. Also, enough bounce for him to appreciate that the back of her was every bit as attractive and feminine as the front. Ruff gave a good bark in her direction, as if he didn't know what to make of this startling, strong, stunning new creature, either.

All Aidan knew was that he had to back off and regroup. Retreat, not defeat.

Chapter Seven

"I need dog help."

"Um, Beck? I have two cats." On the other end of her phone, Jackie Saunders gave a low, throaty laugh that instantly sent a warm feeling of familiarity and comfort through Beck. From the day they'd met as first-year art students, Jackie had been Beck's sounding board and the closest thing to a sister she'd ever had. "But I know a little about dogs, since my mom never met a rescue she wouldn't keep. So it's not going well with the new puppy?"

Beck put her coffee cup on the table, her gaze on Ruff, who was flat on his belly, facing forward, staring straight ahead, as he had been since she'd brought him in from a morning stroll through the square. The walk had lasted exactly nine minutes, when Ruff did his business and slowly trudged home like an inmate who didn't have the spirit to make the most of his time in the prison yard.

"He's not a puppy," Beck said. "Don't think this is a cute little squirmy ball of adorable we're talking about here. He's almost eighty pounds of solid muscle and used to be wild, joyous, and noisy."

"Maybe he's finally settling down," Jackie suggested. "Animals need time to get used to new surroundings. You said he was completely out of control, so this should be a good thing."

Beck stood and crossed the small living room, crouching down to pet Ruff's head. He turned away from her instantly. "He doesn't like me," she admitted softly.

"He'll like anyone who'll feed him, walk him, and love him. It takes time."

Beck shook her head. "He's not eating at all. The first few days here, he'd tromp back and forth between the door and window and stare outside and bark at dogs in the square and eat bowls of food, but now he just...slumps."

"He's depressed," Jackie said. "That happened to my mom's last rescue for a few weeks, but he came out of it."

"I guess," she agreed, sitting back down. "His whole personality has changed. What should I do?"

"Well, if he's not eating, you have to take him to a vet, Beck. Is anyone open on a Sunday?"

"I can check, but..." She dropped back on the couch. "Small complication. The vet in town is a Kilcannon. Aidan's sister."

"So? She's part of the dog family. She's probably a great vet."

"I don't want him to know I'm failing with Ruff."

"Beck." She could hear the chiding in Jackie's voice of reason. For an edgy glass artist who could disappear for a solid weekend when working on a piece, Jackie had an uncanny logic about her that Beck loved and needed.

That trait worked in every aspect of their friendship, from sharing problems to running Beck's business schedule, which Jackie did with flair. If her glass artistry ever took off and Jackie didn't need her job at Baby Face, Beck would be hard-pressed to find an assistant so organized and efficient. And she'd never find a more honest, loyal friend.

"Where's my Little Miss Sunshine?" Jackie asked.

Beck smiled at the nickname that Jackie had given her when they first became friends. They'd met on student housing move-in day at the Illinois School of Art, drank their first bottle of wine together that night, and stayed up in Jackie's room until almost dawn. That night, they made pacts for change, as college students did.

Jackie was going to stop seeing herself as a misfit and embrace her artistry, and Beck vowed to adopt her mother's mantra and find the positive in every situation. Jackie dubbed her Little Miss Sunshine, but Beck, after too much wine, couldn't do better than Artsie Fartsie in return, which became the first of a million inside jokes they shared.

"Little Miss Sunshine is back in Bitter Bark, Fartsie, and you know what that means."

"It means you're meandering down memory lane, bumping into ghosts of the past, and wallowing in your darkest, pizza-filled days of your youth."

She didn't know whether to laugh or cry. "You know me so well. Most of the time, I'm able to stay directed and positive. But too much time in Bitter Bark, and I might revert."

"You can't change who you've become in the last ten years, Beck. And Ruff isn't the only one suffering from the blues. You miss your life, your job, and Wine Wednesdays with me."

She smiled at their after-work tradition when they finished hump day and celebrated with their favorite Pinot Noir. "I do miss you."

"And your life and job?"

"Of course I miss work." But life? A few dinners with friends, volunteering at a local high school once a month to teach kids photography, and the occasional yoga class or bike ride on perfect summer afternoons. Life *was* work, in Chicago. "How many new clients have you had to turn away?"

Jackie was silent a few seconds too long.

"Damn," Beck muttered. "Baby Face was having the best year ever."

"I know, kiddo. I do the books. No fears, though. You'll recover if you get back soon. Things slow down in the summer so it's not the worst time to be out of pocket."

"How many clients?" she asked again.

Jackie sighed. "You don't want to know. The ad in *Chicago Today* did, uh, really well."

"Oh." Beck grunted. "I totally forgot I booked that six months ago to boost our summer business. With a coupon, too."

"Well, it boosted."

"What did you tell potential new clients?"

"That our master baby photographer is away indefinitely on a family matter. And everyone understands, Beck. These are brand-new moms who'd kill for their babies, so they understand family issues."

"They also pay a fortune for their photo and won't

wait until their li'l darling is three months older and looks different. Ours is a time-sensitive business."

"Hey. *Sunshine*."

"I'm sure they'll want toddler shots," she added quickly. "And have siblings. And come back in the fall for that 'baby in a pumpkin suit' every mother has to have. We'll be wall to wall with chubby little models and their families."

"That's my girl," Jackie teased. "Speaking of family, any change in Mike?"

"He's exactly like Ruff. Despondent with a capital D."

"He needs his own vet."

"Physical therapy," Beck agreed, turning on her tablet to click through to the Kilcannon Veterinarian Hospital in town. "We can't seem to get him to go. Oh, they have Sunday hours at the vet."

"Take him in today. What's the worst that could happen?"

"I don't know. Aidan could come back and claim I'm an unfit mother."

"But you have the letter," Jackie reminded her. "You have the law on your side, if we're going to get, you know, custodial about it."

"Neither one of us wants that. We only want to honor Charlie's wishes. That's our number one priority. But, yes, I do have the letter and he has…his story. Which isn't strong enough to take Ruff from me."

"Would he? I mean, is he that much of a jerk?"

"God, no. He's…" She closed her eyes and pictured Aidan, with his too-long honey hair and blue eyes and tall, masculine build. "He's…imagine Matthew

McConaughey at thirty-two with bluer eyes. That's what I'm dealing with."

"Oh, that sucks. And I'm totally being sarcastic. Are there sparks?"

Beck snorted. "Only from the friction of a dog fight. Anyway, I'm done with him, now. No more Aidan."

At the mention of Aidan's name, Ruff lifted his head for the first time in hours, looking from one side to the other and pushing up.

"Oh God, Jackie. Ruff popped up the minute I said Aidan's name."

"Coincidence."

Really? "Aidan," she said again, louder this time.

Ruff turned, barked, and trotted to the door.

"Oh, Jackie. That's what's wrong with him. He needs to see Aidan."

"Take him to the vet first," she said. "Today. This morning. See what the vet says and then decide what to do."

There was no arguing with that logic. Or the fact that Ruff showed the first sign of life at the mention of a name she hadn't said in days. They finished talking while Beck made an appointment online with the vet, then she dressed and got both of them out the door in the next hour.

With Ruff on the leash and moving at a snail's pace, Beck walked slowly down Ambrose Avenue, taking in the quiet Sunday morning in Bitter Bark. The town sure had changed in the last ten years, though she'd been back enough times to see the changes as they happened.

The many small retailers, cafés, and businesses were flourishing, many of them enjoying lovely facelifts or a complete change of name. Boutiques like La Parisienne had popped up, appealing to tourists, and almost all of them had the dog paw on the front door, welcoming four-legged furry friends like Ruff.

She cruised by Ricardo's, the Italian restaurant in town and the only place that ever gave Uncle Mike a run for his money in the pizza department. The restaurant had been around as long as she could remember, but from the look of the brick exterior and shiny new sign, Ricardo Mancini was not suffering for business like Slice of Heaven was. He paid well, that much she knew from feeble attempts to hire help. Of course, it was a higher-end restaurant, but Slice appealed to the locals and college students at Vestal Valley. Or it used to.

She passed a few more buildings, then paused at a storefront to read the Coming Soon sign hanging on the door. Under that was yet another dog paw, this one accompanied with a logo that said, *Bone Appetit—The Place to Paws for a Bite!*

"What do you think of that, Ruff?" She tugged him closer and slowed her step to check out the list of doggie treats and supplies they'd be selling soon.

Ruff kept on pace, slowly making his way down the street until they turned on a road off the square, where Kilcannon Veterinarian Hospital sat in the shadow of the town hall. It also had a brick front and a picture window, with the lovely addition of a flower box and a welcoming red door.

Inside was just as cheery, with a large waiting room, where one lady sat flipping through a magazine, and a teenage girl sprawled in the middle of the floor talking into a cat carrier in a high-pitched voice.

The girl looked up, and hazel eyes widened at the sight of Ruff. Beck automatically gripped the leash, not knowing how the dog would act, if he would even respond at all.

"Ruff!" The girl popped up and threw out both arms. "It's so good to see you again!"

Ruff barked, which sounded wonderful after days of silence, coming closer to the girl, who put her arms around his neck and looked up at Beck. "You must be his new owner."

"Yes, I'm Beck. And you obviously know who Ruff is," she said on a laugh, so relieved to see the dog react somewhat normally again.

"I'm Pru." She grinned, showing braces with at least three different shades of neon bands. "Prudence Kilcannon, Aidan's niece. Everyone calls me Pru."

"Oh, hi, Pru. That's how you know Ruff."

"Yup." She gave his head a good rubbing. "He was only at Waterford Farm for a day, but it was a Wednesday, so I got to play with him after dinner that night. He's crazy, huh?"

Beck angled her head, considering how to answer. "He can be. I'm not sure he's feeling so great right now, which is why I'm here." She glanced at the empty reception desk. "Should I sign in?"

"Not on Sundays," the girl said. "We're on a skeleton staff, and my mom—that's Dr. Molly—isn't here."

"Oh, really? I was able to make an appointment on the website, and I thought she'd be working."

"It's her normal Sunday, but she's off on a special weekend with her fiancé. She got engaged last month, so my grandpa took the Sunday morning duty, which is why I'm here, keeping him company." She added a sly smile. "Got me out of church."

Beck took a seat, extremely happy that she'd get to see Dr. K. She'd called him after Ruff moved in to thank him for all he'd done, but had had to leave a message. "That's awesome, too," she said. "I wouldn't have Ruff if not for your grandfather."

"I know," Pru said. "It was all we talked about at dinner on Wednesday night. Uncle Aidan was not happy about the prospect of giving him up."

Beck gave her a look to say she was well aware of that.

Was that why Dr. Kilcannon hadn't called her back? Was he on Aidan's side about Ruff? "Then I'm glad to see your grandfather and talk to him about Ruff's health." Good to let him know she was on top of her dog-mothering game.

"Who wouldn't be?" the woman reading the magazine chimed in as she turned a page. At Beck's surprised look, she added, "As you say, he's a great vet, and I should know since I have twelve cats."

In elegant clothes and tasteful jewelry, more than she'd expect for a Sunday morning visit to the vet, the fifty-ish woman was the antithesis of a stereotypical crazy cat lady. "I've heard he's terrific with dogs, too," Beck said.

The woman smiled and brushed back a lock of long dark hair. "With everyone."

After Ruff sniffed around for less than thirty seconds, he took to his belly again, his face flat, his eyes the only muscles moving on his body.

"Oh, you're right," Pru said, studying the dog with the same intent Beck might expect from the vet.

"Something's up with Ruff 'N' Ready. He was wild when he got to Waterford."

Beck nodded. "I think he's having trouble adjusting, and I'm not sure what your grandfather can do about that."

"You'd be surprised," she replied. "They don't call him the Dogfather for nothing."

"The Dogfather?"

Next to her, the woman who owned the cat in the carrier laughed. "Your mother told me he's pulling strings like crazy now," she said to Pru. "Two of my cats have to come in weekly for allergy shots," she added as an explanation. "You get pretty friendly with the vets."

Beck smiled and nodded, but the first comment intrigued her. "Pulling strings?"

"You know," Pru said, holding up her hand as if she were working a marionette. "Like the Godfather in the movies who gets people to do what he wants. Only he's a dog guy, so we call him the Dogfather. But he does get what he wants."

"And what he wants are his kids happily married," the cat lady said. "At least, that's what Molly told me. And he's four for six, right, Pru?"

The girl laughed easily, displaying her colorful braces and a natural warmth. "Yep. And my mom got engaged at one of my uncle's weddings, which wouldn't have happened without some intervention from Grandpa. It's been wild at Waterford Farm."

Something unfamiliar tugged at Beck's heart. Regret, maybe, or plain old envy. What a place to live, where dogs were trained and rescued and Dad did some matchmaking.

"That leaves my uncle Aidan and my aunt Darcy."

Aidan was in line for matchmaking? She wondered what kind of woman this Dogfather would choose for his warrior son. Someone strong, kind, and great-looking, like Aidan, she supposed. Someone lucky, then, too.

On the floor, Pru kept petting an unresponsive Ruff. "Uncle Aidan's as miserable as you are," she said, bending over the dog to whisper in his ear. Then she looked up. "But it's okay," she said quickly, as if she realized she might have stepped out of line. "He's really your dog. We know that. Grandpa told us the whole story."

She swallowed back some guilt. "I know," she said. "I'm afraid Ruff and Aidan need to see each other."

That wasn't backing down or bargaining, was it?

"Nothing to be afraid of." A man's voice came from the doorway that led back to exam rooms, the space filled by a handsome older man wearing slacks and collared shirt, and a friendly smile.

"Dr. Kilcannon." Beck stood, but still had to look up since he was easily over six feet. She extended her hand to shake his, but he bypassed that and offered a friendly hug.

"Good to see you again, Beck."

She inched back from the light embrace. "Did you get my message? I wanted to thank you for all you did to get Ruff home to me." She added a smile. "Or to Aidan."

He sighed noisily. "It's a tough situation, and I wanted you two to work it out. The only reason I hadn't returned your call yet was overextended office hours. I'm sorry."

"No apology necessary. I'm so grateful, and happy you can see him today. But..." She turned to the woman next to her. "But I guess you're next in line."

The cat lady smiled, her pretty green eyes sparking as she looked at the vet and not Beck. "I'm in no hurry, Daniel. Rosie's shots can wait a few minutes."

"Thanks, Bella. I appreciate your patience."

The woman closed the magazine and waved a pink-tipped hand. "No problem. You can pay me back with that cup of coffee you promised."

"Of course." He took a few steps closer and crouched down next to Ruff. "It definitely looks like this guy needs some attention."

"Do you think something's seriously wrong?" Beck asked, unable to hide her worry.

Dr. Kilcannon stroked the dog's head and looked at Beck, his blue eyes startling and familiar. It was easy to see where Aidan got his looks. "Let's take him back and do an exam," he said, standing and gently bringing the dog with him. "But I'm pretty sure I have a son at home suffering from the same malaise. They miss each other."

Beck sighed. "I'm doing my best with him."

"I've no doubt of that. And you did the right thing by bringing him in."

Following him to the back of the office, Beck glanced over her shoulder to thank the woman for giving up her place in line and Pru for the help. As she did, she could have sworn Pru and the woman were looking at each other with raised brows and secret smiles.

She didn't quite know what to make of that, but if they thought she was giving up Ruff because Aidan wanted him, they were barking up the wrong tree…so to speak.

But if seeing Aidan would make Ruff feel better, she would take him for a visit in a heartbeat. She already loved the dog and would do anything for him. Even face the man who wanted to take him from her.

From the corner of his eye, Aidan saw something move, but he kept his head down, pushing the edging machine, drowning out everything with the blaring wail of a prog rock guitarist screaming in his earbuds.

Suddenly, someone poked his back, and he spun around, whipping one earpiece off at the sight of his little sister, all made up and wearing a dress.

"We're back from church," Darcy announced, like the world should stop on this news. "Where are you?"

As always, her blue eyes danced with some kind of secret, probably the knowledge that she was and always would be the brightest and most beautiful creature for miles. Her long blond hair fell in waves over her shoulders, and even the prissy sundress she wore to church looked like the latest fashion on her.

"I'm right in front of you, numskull." As the two youngest in the Kilcannon pack, they shared an unspoken bond, and though she was as pesky as that hairball she called a dog and was given to wandering the globe every time she had a chance, Aidan adored her. She knew it and gave him a toothy grin in response.

"Very funny, goober breath."

He rolled his eyes, refusing to be dragged back to

elementary school with a thirty-year-old woman. "What do you want, Darcy?"

"You. At Sunday dinner. Dad's home from covering for Molly in town, and the rest of us are back from church. You know what that means."

It meant another interminable family meal where any and all Kilcannons who were in town would gather at the house. They'd drink in the kitchen, talk family business, tease each other relentlessly, and probably finish up the day with a rousing game of Mario Kart or, if the trails were good, a late afternoon ride on the four-wheelers. And they'd all act like nothing had changed at Waterford Farm, like it was still the same place they'd grown up.

Except now it was a business and no longer a home.

Aidan swallowed and wiped his brow with his forearm, sweat stinging his eyes. "I want to finish cleaning this pen. I promised Shane I'd get it done before some buttload of trainees shows up tomorrow."

Her delicately brushed brows drew together. "You'd rather mow the lawn than drink cocktails? What's up with that?"

He shrugged and stuck the earbud back in, turning around. "I'll get something to eat later."

She snapped the thing right out again and got in his face. "What the heck is wrong with you, Aidan?"

"Darcy, let it go."

"Let go of the fact that you want to cut grass instead of coming to Sunday dinner? I guess you don't mind Gramma Finnie marching over here and knocking you upside the head. Church might be optional, but Sunday dinner isn't."

He studied her for a minute, knowing his sister's proclivity to leave home at the first sign of anything less than perfect. Yet, here she stayed. Sometimes for months at a time, before taking a trip to satisfy her wanderlust, then she came back. Lived here, actually, in a suite of rooms on the second floor. And, God knew, she was a tad old to be living at home, as Dad gently reminded her on occasion.

"Haven't you ever not wanted to be part of a big family thing every week, Darcy?"

"I travel enough to appreciate the family when I'm back." She narrowed her eyes at him. "And you've been gone the better part of ten years, big brother. I'd think you'd love some good old-fashioned family time."

"If it was the good old-fashioned family."

She drew back. "What's that supposed to mean? You have problems with the additional in-laws around the table? Because your brothers have never been happier, and Molly is positively on a cloud with Trace."

"I have problems with..." He jammed the edger into the ground and looked past her. "It's not the same as when I left."

"That's the beauty of it," she lobbed back.

His eyes widened in disbelief. "Mom's gone, Darcy."

She flinched, but lifted her chin in defense of any pain that reminder might cause. "Yes, she is, and we all miss her more than there are words to describe. But she would not want us to mope around miserable. Can't you remember her, Aidan? All she wanted was for us to be happy."

Remember her? She was all he could think about around here. "'You're only as happy as your least-happy child,'" he said, quoting the words that really should be on Annie Kilcannon's gravestone.

"So she sure wouldn't be happy seeing her big, beautiful warrior listening to…" She took the earbud and put it to her ear. "Ugh. Progressive rock. All alone in the training pen while the rest of us are tossing back Bloody Marys and Jamesons."

"She wouldn't know what the training pen is, because this used to be her old cement-floor kennel rimmed in wire for her fosters that we hosed off when we were kids."

She searched his face, thinking before responding. "Waterford has changed, Aidan, that's true. Do you think Dad's idea to turn this place into the largest facility of its type in the state was a bad one?" When he didn't answer, she leaned closer. "You were here when he came down the morning after her funeral. You heard him tell us about her dream to build a place like this and have every one of the Kilcannons and their families be part of it. It was her plan to love dogs and keep her family together. And this place is her legacy, keeping her alive forever."

He swallowed when she finished her speech. "Of course I remember that day." How could he forget that sad morning when Dad, a brand-new and broken widower, stood in front of his six grown children and presented them with a new life plan. They'd all jumped on it, upending successful lives in different cities to move here and start this new version of Waterford Farm. Aidan had agreed, of course, but he'd known he was headed for Green Platoon and thought he'd be in the Army for many more years. "But I wasn't here for it all, Darcy."

"So you resent the rest of us for making it happen?"

"No," he denied hotly. "I don't resent you. I just don't feel like I'm part of it."

"So be part of it."

"How?" He looked around, his head shaking. "Look, kid, I know this might be Kilcannon family heresy, but I'm not a dog person. I love dogs, yes. I want one or two in my life forever." Especially Ruff, but he stuffed that down, still not having come up with a way to get Beck Spencer to change her mind. "But I don't know if I want to make a living training them or matching recues with new owners. That's all well and good and honorable, but it's not me."

She nodded, listening, taking it in. "Not all of us are dog whisperers," she said. "Shane is, of course, and Liam is gifted with K-9 training, but Garrett couldn't get Lola to eat until Jessie showed up. And Molly's a doctor, not a trainer. And, in case you haven't noticed, I'm a glorified hair stylist for puppies."

"You're building a grooming business," he countered.

"One that works for me. Not *too* successful, because then I couldn't take extended vacations and scratch my itch to travel." She fluttered her fingers by her face, pretending to scratch and making a goofy face that still didn't diminish her good looks.

He ruffled her silky hair. "You're so stinkin' cute, Darcy. I'll miss you if I leave."

Her smile evaporated instantly. "You're leaving?"

Shoot. Shouldn't have said that. "No, no, I…" But his voice trailed off. "I'm restless."

"You're looking at the queen of restless, big man. Let's go hiking in Patagonia, and then we'll settle in for another six months. Want to?" Her whole face lit up like sunshine, blinding and bright.

"I don't want to go to Patagonia."

"Where do you want to go?" He heard the heartbreak in her voice and knew they'd all feel that way if he up and left.

"I don't want to go anywhere, but…" He glanced out at the property, beyond the facility outbuildings, to the rolling foothills bursting with spring green. "Back to where this was when I left."

"You know what Gramma Finnie would say."

He laughed. "'The past is yesterday's tomorrow that only happened in a dream?' Stitched on a pillow in Gaelic?"

She shrugged, not joining in the joke. "Her sayings make sense to me. And one of them is 'don't let the past steal your present.' And that's what you're doing, Aidan."

"Maybe I am, but I can't help it if I feel like I don't belong here."

"You have to find your place here," she said. "You might have to make it."

He frowned, not entirely sure what she meant, but then he glanced over her shoulder, catching sight of his father, flanked by brothers Shane and Liam on one side and Garrett on the other, all crossing the wide wraparound porch and walking briskly toward them.

"Oh man, you sent in backup."

Darcy turned to look at them. "No, but no one wants to have Sunday dinner without you, Aidan.

We've had an empty chair for too many years where you should be."

But Mom's wasn't empty. That spot had somehow been...filled. Removed. Erased. Forgotten.

"You can officially hang up your edging shears," Shane called, lifting a glass in a mock toast. "In Molly's absence, Liam made the Bloodys, and I don't think I could have done better."

"Which is saying a lot coming from that ego," Darcy joked under her breath, making Aidan laugh even though he wanted to hang on to his sour mood. And, to be fair, Shane had toned down his over-confidence since Chloe came into his life. He wasn't cocky anymore, just happy and settled. Which was exactly what Aidan wasn't.

"I wanted to finish up," he said as the four of them entered the pen and came closer. Dad was wearing work clothes, and it looked like the rest of them had joined the family for Mass. Gramma Finnie would be spewing joyful Irish proverbs of jubilation today.

"You should clean up and come inside," Dad said, the order issued with his usual ease and grace and the undertone of a general's authority. "A surprise guest is coming, and I'm sure you'll want to be there, Aidan."

"I didn't know we had a guest," Shane said. "Who's coming?"

Dad gestured toward the end of the long drive as if his mystery guest would be pulling up any minute. Who could be coming here that Aidan could possibly care about?

"You'll see," Dad said. "Someone came into the office today, and I invited her for dinner."

"Her?" Garrett lifted a brow.

"I know who it is," Darcy said. "Pru told me the crazy cat lady, Bella Peterson, was in the office eyeing Dad like he was six feet o' catnip. Dad, something you want to tell us?"

Liam almost choked, but Dad laughed. "Give it up, all of you."

"Seriously." Liam elbowed his brother. "Dad's too busy setting us all up to worry about himself."

So they were actually joking about their father dating? What the hell?

"I told you this special guest isn't for me, it's for Aidan."

"Oh yeah. Forgot the Dogfather has fresh blood," Shane cracked.

"Who is it?" Aidan asked, not really in the mood for games.

At the sound of a car coming around from the front gate, they all turned, but Aidan caught the look of satisfaction on his father's face. Whoever he'd invited, the old dog was happy about it.

He squinted at the dark red compact, not recognizing it and not able to see the driver with the sun on the windshield. But then he saw a big brown head poking out of the passenger side, and the sight literally kicked him in the chest.

"Ruff." He threw a grateful look at Dad. "Is he back for good?"

"No, but he's got the blues bad enough that Beck brought him in for a checkup this morning. We agreed it was a good idea you two have a little reunion."

"So Ruff's the dinner guest?" Garrett asked, fighting a laugh.

"Well, Beck is staying, of course."

"Of *course*." Shane's emphasis might have amused his brothers, but Aidan didn't give a crap.

He was so damn glad to see Ruff, he walked away from the four men and his sister and headed straight to the car as she parked. The smile on his face was so big, he could feel it pulling his cheeks.

When he opened the door and Ruff pounced, Aidan fell to the ground, his heart light for the first time in days. And with each lick of that stupid tongue and pounding of those relentless paws, it felt like the damn thing would pop right out of his chest.

God, he missed this dog.

"Hey, Aidan."

He managed to look over the crazy dog on top of him and up at Beck Spencer's long dark hair and big brown eyes. This was what he needed. Ruff. Beck. And another chance.

"Hi, Beck." He gave her a slow smile. *Time for round two, gorgeous.* But this time, he'd fly at a completely different altitude.

For the first time in months, he was looking forward to Sunday dinner.

Chapter Eight

No wonder her brother had spent so much time at Waterford Farm.

Beck closed her eyes and listened to Daniel Kilcannon deliver a simple prayer of grace, not fifteen seconds in length. Right before he finished, she lifted her head to capture a mental picture of a family gathered in love, ranging in age from six to eighty-six, at least four dogs around the room or under the table. Every head was bowed while the man at the head of the table asked for a blessing on the food.

If she'd gotten an actual photograph, Beck imagined she might study that shot for hours, trying to learn something about each person there and trying not to fall into an abyss that felt a lot like envy.

She'd never had anything like this, at least not in Bitter Bark, North Carolina. Today, she felt like a person who'd gotten through life on a bicycle with flat tires suddenly taking a ride in a Rolls-Royce. Overwhelmed, inspired, thrilled, and envious of anyone who got to actually live like this.

But not two seconds after "Amen," the fun kicked in. Chatter arose, and the plates were passed with as much frequency and speed as the jokes. She'd figured out the pecking order pretty quickly during the "cocktail hour"—which was essentially the entire family around the kitchen island teasing their father about his lackluster cooking skills while sipping Bloody Marys.

Aidan had disappeared for a while then, presumably to shower after running around the training pen with a very happy Ruff, and each of the Kilcannons had taken the time to introduce themselves and make her feel comfortable. Aidan had been warm—nice, even—but not overly so.

She couldn't quite get a read on how he felt about her being there, but it was obvious that seeing Ruff had made him happy. And vice versa.

So, Beck gave in and got to know the family.

Liam, the oldest, was married to a beautiful and quite pregnant Andi. They had a son, Christian, and they owned Jag, a German shepherd who was never more than two feet from the little boy. The baby was lovingly referred to as "BTB" for "Baby to Be" since they'd opted not to find out the gender in advance.

Then there was Shane, the wisecracker, married to Chloe last month. She was the mastermind behind the Better Bark campaign to build tourism in town by attracting families with dogs, including their own sweetheart, Ruby.

Garrett, the middle brother and former dot-com sensation, sat next to his wife, Jessie, who evidently had been Molly's best friend as a kid, and it was Molly's empty seat, next to her daughter, Pru, where Beck sat right now. In addition to Jag, there were dogs named Lola, Kookie, and Rusty, and one named Meatball stayed close to Pru.

And Ruff, of course, who planted himself under Aidan's chair.

"You look befuddled." Across the table, Darcy, who was about a year or so younger than Aidan, beamed a gorgeous smile at Beck. Everything about her was gorgeous, Beck mused, like all the fabulous Kilcannon genes had come together for one last hurrah on the final child.

"Just trying to get everyone's names straight."

Next to her, Pru leaned closer. "Usually when we have guests, I make little name tags in front of everyone to help out."

"You do?"

"And I like to run new people through the events of the day," she added. "So you know what to expect."

"That's why we call her General Pru," Shane chimed in.

"Someone has to keep order in all this chaos, lassie." Gramma Finnie, as Beck was instructed to call the octogenarian, put an arm around Pru and added a squeeze. "You do you, as we say."

As no other eightysomething Beck knew said, but then, hadn't someone told her Gramma Finnie was something of a minor Internet sensation herself?

"Was it difficult to start your blog?" Beck asked the older woman.

"I didn't set out to be a blogger, ye know," Gramma Finnie said. "I wanted a place to keep all the sayings and proverbs I have in my head from my old country, and this little angel..." She gestured in Pru's direction with a weathered hand with deep-violet nails. "took the time to teach me how to use a computer and the internet, and I'll be danged if I'm going to be one of those old folks they make fun of on BuzzFeed."

She knew what BuzzFeed was?

"Then it sort of happened. Before I knew it..." Gramma Finnie laughed and shrugged. "I had a following."

Beck's mouth slipped open wider. "That's amazing."

"Nothing like Darcy, though," Gramma Finnie said. "Her Insta puts us all to shame."

"And brings in a ton of business," Shane added.

Darcy waved off the compliment. "Please. I take pictures of dogs being groomed," she explained. "It's nothing. You're the real photographer, right? Dad told us you photograph babies."

"I do," she said. "I own a studio called Baby Face, and all I do is take sweet portraits of tiny little miracles every day."

"Awww." Andi put her hand on her very large belly. "Will you take one of BTB when he or she is born?"

"Of course. With Christian, if you like."

"And Jag!" the little boy chimed in with a mouthful of food.

"What a fun job," Darcy exclaimed. "Babies are even cuter than puppies, if that's possible."

"Both in the same shot would be gold," Beck agreed. "I'd love to try it."

"How did you get into that business?" Darcy asked.

"I went to art school in Chicago and majored in photography with an emphasis on portraits," she explained. "I didn't love doing adult portraits, but I discovered I had a knack for working with little ones. One of my friends had a baby, and she let me do the pictures and use them for marketing. Then I posted them in every Mommy and Me group in and around Chicago. And before I knew it, the business was booming."

"Success is doing what you love," Gramma Finnie said, her Irish brogue as thick and sweet as the bread pudding Beck had seen come out of the oven a while ago.

"You're to be commended on your determination," Dr. K said.

"Oh, she's determined." Next to her, Aidan shot her the shadow of a smile, enough that all she wanted to see was more.

"Determined to get people to tell other people about my business," she said. "And it worked. Word of mouth is everything when you're growing a small business, as I'm sure you know."

Darcy snapped her fingers like she'd had an idea. "We need a dog photographer here. Professional."

"There's a business Waterford doesn't have yet," Shane said. "I like it."

Aidan shook his head. "Don't try to get Beck to do more than a few shots of Liam and Andi's baby. She's up to her eyeballs with the pizza parlor problems. Right, Beck?"

She glanced at him, almost surprised that he'd mention her travails at Slice of Heaven. But why deny it? "It's a challenge, that's true."

"I know it's been tough since your uncle got sick," Dr. K said.

"It has. Business is slow."

"I know a lot of people tried to stop in and support the place after your uncle's stroke," Chloe said. "Did that help?"

"A little, but…" She shook her head, embarrassed to admit it was her failure in the kitchen that ended the local love. "I'm afraid my aunt is thinking about giving up, selling, and moving to Florida. She thinks Uncle Mike might do better in a tropical climate."

A collective groan rolled around the table. Not Aidan, though. He didn't moan at all, Beck noticed.

"That's a shame," Liam said.

"The place is an institution," Garrett added.

"Slice of Heaven?" Darcy asked. "I can't imagine Bitter Bark without it."

"Better Bark," Chloe corrected with a sideways smile aimed at her sister-in-law. "But I know Slice has a no-dogs-allowed policy. Any chance that might change?"

Beck shook her head. "My aunt's not a dog person."

Aidan snorted softly. "Understatement alert."

"Not everyone is," Dr. K added.

"Plus Ricardo's down the street is all about the dogs and they have a wait every night," Shane added. "Chloe and I eat there all the time because Ruby is treated like a queen."

"It's a little more than that." Beck set her fork down with a sigh, unwilling to let Aunt Sarah's decision not to let dogs in the restaurant get blamed for their troubles. "We're not going to have customers lined up until I get better at making pizza."

Most of the people around the table chuckled uncomfortably or frowned in sympathy, but Aidan turned and looked right into her eyes. "Maybe you need lessons. I'm happy to help."

For some reason she didn't know, like, or trust, her heart kicked into double time at the way he said that. Like lessons wasn't all he was suggesting.

"Aidan's pizza is amazing," Darcy chimed in.

"So good," Andi agreed. "Since he's come home, I've craved it every day."

"And oranges, Mommy," Christian chimed in. "Remember how you made Liam get you oranges the other morning when we were all still in pajamas?"

Andi laughed at her cravings and her cute son, along with the others, but Aidan leaned closer to Beck, adding gentle pressure with his substantial shoulder. "I'm serious," he said under his breath.

"Well, thank you, but I know you have work to do here."

"Actually, he's not that busy right now," Dr. K said. "Liam slowed the new K-9 unit training classes until after the baby, and that's where Aidan's been needed the most."

"So I'm free to teach and train," Aidan said. "And you do know that the testimony about my pizza skills is real, since I already worked a whole afternoon with you."

"You did?" The question came from several surprised people at the table, including Dr. K.

"I didn't know that," Aidan's father added. "Then you already know that he can help you out of this bind. And we'll do our part to spread the word among friends and clients."

Everyone agreed to do that to help out, but Beck glanced at the man at the head of the table, slightly suspicious of his motives. Wasn't he the Dogfather? The matchmaker? "Thanks, but I can get through this," she said. "I'm getting a little better every day."

"But you only need some basic lessons," Aidan said. "And if the business starts to boom thanks to my family doing a little word of mouth assistance, I'll be there to help fill the orders while you learn. It's a good solution, Beck."

She held his gaze for a moment, considering the offer. Fill orders. Teach her to make pizza. Or worm his way so deeply into Ruff's heart that she didn't stand a chance with the dog? Or was it her heart he was worming into? Based on the way those blue eyes were holding hers, she wasn't sure.

"I can help you at least until your uncle is back on his feet," he offered, so magnanimously that if she said no, she'd look like she was scared. Which she was.

No one said anything for a moment, and she felt every eye on her.

"Oh, would you look at this." Gramma Finnie held up her phone, pulling all attention to the other side of the table. "You got a five-star review on Yelp. Pru just found it. Posted on Thursday. Was that the day you were making the pizzas, Aidan?"

Yes, of course it was, Beck thought. Were they *all* in on this?

"Let me see." Aidan reached over and took his grandmother's phone, angling it so Beck could see. "Look at that. One of the travel agents raved. Huh. What do you know?"

What she knew was that not taking his offer was crazy...but taking it was dangerous. And she had the faintest feeling she was getting steamrolled by Aidan. And his family might be powering the engine.

But she really did need the help. As long as she knew why it was being offered by him.

"That's very sweet of you, Aidan," she said with a

smile. "And so nice because you'll get to see Ruff every single day." Which was probably his plan.

"And you," he said very quietly, under his breath.

Oh boy. Was that what he thought was going to happen? He'd make her fall so hard for him she gave him the dog out of...lust? Did he really think she was that weak?

"Aidan," she said, "maybe we both can learn a few lessons."

He lifted a brow. "Maybe we can."

All around the table, the silence lasted one beat too long.

"So who's up for a Mario Kart tournament during dessert?" Garrett suddenly asked, breaking the awkward moment.

The response was instant from all corners of the table, except for Aidan, who put his hand on her back.

"If it's okay with you, I'd rather take Ruff on a long walk," Aidan said to her. "Come with us?"

She should say no. She should clean up or play Mario Kart or go home. But first, Beck had to make sure Aidan Kilcannon knew that she was on to him. "I'd love to."

Chapter Nine

"I'd pronounce him cured of whatever ailed him," Aidan said as they walked toward the creek a good twenty feet behind Ruff, who bounded with joy over the trail that cut through the heart of Waterford Farm.

"He's sure better than he was a few hours ago," Beck agreed, her gaze on the dog ahead of them. "It's like he's a different dog."

"I know the feeling." He blew out a breath and lifted his face to the late afternoon sun peeking through the branches of the hickory and oak trees that lined the trail. In fact, if she hadn't been here, he might have bounded like Ruff, barked for joy, and thrown himself into the creek at the end of it all to celebrate his small success. He'd been thinking about going in to help her for a few days, but he didn't want to seem so incredibly obvious.

This had happened so naturally, he couldn't be accused of stalking Ruff or trying to finagle his way into the dog's new life. It was perfect, really.

"Are you a different dog?" Beck asked after they walked for a few seconds in silence.

"Let's just say I know how Ruff feels having been transported to somewhere strange and trying to adjust." Although his talk with Darcy had left a mark and given him much to consider.

"Are you trying to guilt me into giving Ruff back?" she asked. "Because it won't work. Or are you trying to tell me something about yourself?"

He slowed his step, looking down at her for the hundredth time that day, because he never actually got tired of doing that. "I'm not trying to guilt you into anything."

"Then why do you suddenly want to be the pizza teacher and backup cook at Slice of Heaven?"

"Look, keeping it real? I do have ulterior motives, but if you think I'm trying to work out some kind of exchange of pizza techniques to get my dog back, you couldn't be further from the truth. You have my word."

Her look said exactly what she thought of *his word*, which stung, but he let it go.

"So, what are these ulterior motives if you're not trying to take 'your' dog back?"

"Whoops. Force of habit, sorry."

She tipped her head with silent forgiveness, but was still waiting for an answer. He took a few more steps, thinking about his motives and how much to share. Enough so that she believed he was genuine and Ruff wasn't the only reason he'd suggested the arrangement.

"I've been trying to…don't laugh now…find myself."

She didn't laugh, which he appreciated, but studied him for a moment. "I didn't know you were lost."

He shrugged. "I'm like Ruff. Having a hard time adjusting to this place."

"Yeah, 'cause Waterford Farm is sheer hell. What with all the big happy family, adorable dogs, inside jokes, and a precious porch-wrapped farmhouse filled with love and laughter. Who'd want to be here?"

"That's the outsider's view," he said.

"Because the outsider doesn't see the world's cutest grandmother who blogs and the three newlywed older brothers on the inside?" She gave him a gentle elbow in the ribs. "You live in a Norman Rockwell painting, big guy. Dogs included."

He heard a whisper of pain in her voice, and it hit him somewhere deep. Somewhere relatable. "I know that," he said. "You should also know that the person who made that family, who started fostering precious dogs, who encouraged those inside jokes, and who filled that yellow house with love and laughter is MIA in a big way."

She was quiet for a long time, the only sounds Ruff's occasional bark and their footsteps on the path.

"Do you mean because she's passed away, or because they don't, you know, have her portrait over the dining table?" she asked. "Because that might bring down the festive family mood your father obviously works very hard to maintain."

He swallowed. "It's like they prefer to act like she was never there."

"Aidan." She drew back and frowned at him. "They do not. I heard your mother's name mentioned, but not in sorrow. They don't wallow in grief. There's a big difference between living your life with loss and wailing with helpless misery all the time. And don't forget, you're talking to a person who's lost…all of them."

Good God, he had forgotten. What a jerk. He put his arm on her back, adding pressure. "I'm sorry."

"It's okay," she assured him.

He waited a moment, guiding her to follow Ruff to the creek. "But I am out of sorts, Beck, and working with you at Slice appeals to me. So, if that's the 'ulterior' motive you are looking for, there it is."

She didn't respond to that, looking around slowly at the picturesque creek, babbling over stones and rocks, bathed in a mix of sunshine and shadows, the edge of this forest thick with a hundred shades of green.

"And Norman Rockwell morphs into Thomas Kinkade," she said softly.

He laughed at that. "Yeah, this is definitely one of my favorite places on the whole hundred acres."

Ruff was halfway in the water when they reached him, soaked up to his belly and drinking from the cold spring.

"For good reason," she whispered, still looking around in awe.

"I used to come here when I was a kid." He led her to a large flat rock that was worn and warm and incredibly familiar to him. "Just me and my little Doxie."

"Your dog was a dachshund?" she guessed.

"Yes, and I named her Doxie because I lacked originality."

"Please, I named a dog Ruff."

He laughed again. "True. Well, Doxie was a foster, but we kept her because my mother was the original Foster Failure. She'd keep the dogs, every time, and then we'd each get one of them sort of 'assigned' to us to be sure they were clean, fed, exercised, and such. I got Doxie, and she was with me for years." He shook his head, remembering her pointed nose and tiny legs and how she'd sleep right on his pillow, curled into a circle, staring at him until he'd wake up. "And, you know, being the youngest brother has its challenges, so I'd bring her here."

"Why?"

He gave in to a smile. "Because when I wanted to cry about something, Liam and Shane and Garrett gave me crap. They'd tell me to buck up and be a man. They'd say, 'Kilcannon men don't cry.' And I'd have to swallow it all and man up. When life didn't go my way, I brought Doxie down here and bawled like a baby where no one would see me."

"Aww." She pressed her hand to her chest as if the admission touched her heart. "I can't imagine you crying, Aidan."

He shrugged. "I did, some. Right here at my crying creek with my wiener dog."

That made her laugh softly. "And you always had a family setter, right?" she asked, getting comfortable on the stone next to him. "Your grandmother told me she and her husband had one with them when they came from Ireland and that there's always been a setter in the house."

"I was in the shower, what? Ten minutes? And she got that story in?" He chuckled. "Gramma Finnie is a piece of work, man."

"She *is* special." She put her hand on his arm, her fingers as warm as the rock they settled on, facing the water. "They all are, Aidan."

"I know." He picked up a stone and tossed it toward the creek, waiting for the splash before he continued. "I'm not saying they're not the greatest family, but..." He hesitated, rooting for the right words.

He didn't have to dig too deep. After the conversation with Darcy and the long family dinner, all the feelings were right under the surface. "I've been gone for ten years, Beck. And after my mother died, they—all of them, without me—built this...this place. I don't have any skin in this game."

"You have a name in this game. And this place is really incredible."

"But it's not a home anymore."

"You don't live here, do you? Your grandmother said only she and your dad and Darcy still live there."

"I'm renting a house Shane and Garrett bought and shared before they got married and moved in with their wives. But I'm working here, and I'll be honest, I'm not loving it. Not yet." He had a snowball's chance of fitting in and finding a home here with Ruff. But now? His sister's words came back to him.

You have to find your place here...

"I haven't found how, or if, I belong here. I miss flying. I miss having a purpose. I miss"—*my mother*—"the way things used to be."

"So you want to make pizza and figure it out?"

He glanced at her and smiled. "I want to help you make pizza and figure it out."

She lifted her chin and looked at him, probably unaware that at that very moment, he could see the resemblance to her brother as strongly as ever. It was something in the color of her eyes. More than the color. The spark. In Charlie, it had been fun and warm and a precursor to something that would make Aidan crack up.

In her, it was pretty and feminine and a precursor to something that made him want to find out what it would feel like to kiss her. A lot. Often. And for a really long time.

"What's the other one?" she asked.

Frowning, yanked from his fantasy, he shook his head. "Other what?"

"Ulterior motive. You said 'motives,' as if there's more than one."

"Isn't that one enough? I just bared my soul."

She shrugged as if unimpressed with his bare soul. "I want to know them all. Why would you offer to come to Slice of Heaven, teach me how to make pizza, and work there when we need help?" When he didn't answer right away, she leaned her whole shoulder into him. "I knew it. I *knew* it."

"Knew what?"

"You think you can..." She looked away as she searched for the words, her gaze drifting to Ruff, who was still splashing around in the shallow water and having the time of his life. "Con me."

"*Con* you?" He snorted. "What about me has said 'con artist' to you? Was it when I was fully honest about Ruff being home? When I brought him to you because you have a claim on a dog I believed was mine? When I helped you out of a lunch rush, or offered to watch him at any time, or was nice to your aunt, who'd rather I disappeared forever and acts like Ruff is about to eat her for lunch? Which one was the con?"

With each beat in his speech, he saw her expression change until she lost the hardness and distrust in the angle of her jaw. "I know, you're right. But you don't ever give up until you get what you want. I know that, and it's daunting."

He wanted to argue, but couldn't lie. "Look, do I still want Ruff? Hell yeah. But if that happens, it would have to be organic and natural. No, I don't give up easily, if ever, but I'm also not going to be a jerk about it. And whether you understand it or not, I want a break from this place. Right now, I need it."

"You're not going to infiltrate and try to make him love you more than me? Although," she added with a dry laugh, "not sure how he could love me any less."

"He misses me, and it'll be good to transition him from me to you," he told her. "It's really better for him. For all of us. I promise I'll help you win him over."

She gave him a dubious look. "Why would you do that?"

"Because I loved your brother and want to respect his very specific wishes."

"As I do," she shot back. "And I have the—"

"Letter, I know." He put his hands on her shoulders, momentarily surprised by the small but taut muscles he felt as he turned her to face him. "Listen to me, Rebecca Spencer."

She blinked at the use of her full name, but didn't look away.

"Can you fathom that I might actually want to help you? That I care about the family of my best friend and the pizza parlor he wanted to own and run, and that I do not want to see it sold, folded, or out of business? I also care about the well-being of his dog, no matter who he calls master or mistress." He added some pressure to his touch, wanting so much for her to believe him, because this was the absolute truth. "I owe that to Charlie, too, you know," he added. "I owe him genuine care for the dog he adored, the business he wanted to inherit, and the family he loved."

She searched his face, her eyes moving back and forth, and he could see she was weighing her opinion of him and trying to decide if he was a risk worth taking.

"Okay," she finally agreed. "So it's a few pizza lessons to help me learn and working some shifts to start to build a customer base again. That's all it is?"

"That's all it is." But he could still see the doubt lingering in her eyes, and he leaned closer. "What are you afraid I'll do?" he asked softly.

Her lower lip slipped under her top teeth. "I'm not sure."

The sudden increase in his heart rate surprised him, along with a low, slow heat in his belly and the need to get even closer to her. "I won't hurt you."

"It's not you hurting me that scares me," she said, her voice reedy as if her throat was suddenly as bone-dry as his.

"What scares you?"

She didn't answer, taking a deep breath, letting her gaze drop from his eyes to his mouth, linger for a moment, then slide back up again. "I'm not afraid. I'm..." Her eyes shuttered for a second. "I feel things."

He gave in to an easy smile, enjoying every second of this unexpected intimacy. "Things? What kind of things?"

"The kind of things that derail plans and complicate life and make even the strongest woman change her mind."

"Oh." The smile gave way to a chuckle. "*Those* kind of things. Yeah. I feel them. I'd have to be dead not to." He leaned closer. "You're beautiful, funny, and now you own my dog. But I'm pretty sure Charlie would send the hounds of hell after me if I made a move."

She lifted one brow. "He's not in hell, Aidan."

"That's for sure." He added a squeeze to her shoulders. "But you don't have to worry. I'm not after your heart."

"Promise? Because it's...closed for business."

"Is that so?"

"Too much loss," she explained. "I can't risk any more. So, promise me you won't..." She couldn't finish, and all that made him do was inch closer to find out what he wasn't supposed to do.

But she stayed silent, and he knew that, as much as he ached to close the space and kiss her, that would be her tipping point. One mistake, and he wouldn't get his escape, or to be with Ruff, or get to know her even better.

And he wanted all those things more than he wanted to kiss her. Which was a lot. So he held her gaze and said the words he knew his best friend would hold him to in this life and beyond.

"You have my word, Beck."

Chapter Ten

Beck woke Monday morning with the first glimmer of real hope for Slice of Heaven since she'd arrived two months earlier. She got up early and took Ruff on a long walk around Bushrod Square to tire him out, knowing he'd be cooped up in the apartment most of the day.

Exhausting him with exercise was key, she'd learned yesterday. And all of the Kilcannons had given her tips and tricks for training, though they all agreed Ruff didn't respond well to treats. He loved Aidan, that much was clear, and the visit seemed to have done him some good.

Although, he'd still paced the apartment last night, looking out the window as if he longed for another life.

Maybe he'd like Chicago, Beck thought as she dressed for the day. If she ever got back there. With Aidan coming to teach her how to make better pizza, maybe they'd build up the business while Uncle Mike got better and then she could go home.

It was a slow process, but what other option did she have? It might mean staying the better part of the summer, but by fall, she could be back in Chicago, knowing she'd done everything to help the two family members she had left.

Thinking of Mike, she made a silent vow to visit him that afternoon. She'd missed him since he'd had that stroke. The doctors said over and over again that it was mild, that he was lucky, that he could be back to normal in a few months, but he had to *want* to be back to normal. And he didn't want anything.

Just like Ruff didn't want the kiss she planted on his forehead before going down to the kitchen to break the news to Sarah about Aidan.

"Oh, well," she said with a sigh of resignation. "You'll love me eventually, Ruff. Little Miss Sunshine says it will be so."

Downstairs, Beck pushed open the kitchen door and all that hope, optimism, and clear thinking disappeared at the sight of Aidan working the commercial stand mixer. It was replaced by something more…primal.

The same thing that kept her awake and knotted up last night as she replayed the conversation by the creek and tried to reconcile how much she'd wanted him to kiss her. But he hadn't. And that was good.

Right?

Wrong. Look at him. He wore a simple white T-shirt under a Slice of Heaven apron, his features set with the calm concentration that she imagined he'd wear when flying Black Hawks into war zones. Steady, strong, working the mixer like it was a toy, not a massive, cranky, old piece of crap that almost chewed off her hand twice.

He handled it with the same confidence she had with a camera and a baby.

And there went all the stuff that made her a woman, churning into an achy lust that tightened things that hadn't been tight for a long time and set off little fireworks in her chest. It was natural, this attraction to a man who not only looked good enough to eat, but was actually making pizza that *was* good enough to eat.

It was normal to—

The dining room door thwacked open and damn near hit her in the face.

"Oh!" Beck jumped back as Aunt Sarah bounded in, a tray of condiments in her hands that she nearly dropped. "Sorry."

"Oh, Rebecca. There you are. Can we talk?" She angled her head in the direction of the dining room. "Now."

Beck glanced at Aidan, who'd watched the exchange, but hadn't missed a beat with the mixing blades, turning the bowl with ease and finesse.

"Thought I'd get started on a batch of dough for tomorrow," he said, lowering the speed on the mixer to talk over the sound. "And I can't get the oven to turn on, which will be a problem."

"You need to set it to almost 650, but don't let the dial actually hit 650. Stop at the red line we marked in Sharpie. It's actually 647."

He lifted both brows. "Seriously? What happens at 650?"

"It complains by turning itself off. I'll get it going if you gimme a sec." She slipped into the dining room, followed by her aunt, who set the tray on one of the tables with enough force to jostle the salt and pepper shakers.

"He's *working* here?" she asked.

"Not until he learns how to turn on the oven."

"Rebecca."

"He's only come in to help me learn how to make great pizza, Aunt Sarah. And that means we'll have great product for a while. Isn't that—"

"Why?"

Beck blinked at her, the force of the question throwing her. "I know you have out-of-date accounting systems, but the numbers are bad whether you've done them on a computer or by hand. You know that. We have to increase business."

Sarah crossed her arms, tightening them protectively. "We don't have to do anything that drastic."

"Maybe we have different definitions of drastic," Beck replied. "I'm trying to learn how to make pizza that actually doesn't taste like my favorite handbag slathered in ketchup. He knows and has offered to help."

"Can't you find someone else?"

"For the whopping sum of zero dollars? No."

Sarah shut her eyes, fighting frustration. "Someone who's not a constant reminder of Charlie."

Beck's shoulders fell. "Honest, Aunt Sarah, he doesn't remind me of Charlie. He's very different and his own man. And I think being here might be helping his own grief. Have you ever thought of that?"

Sarah shook her head. "I can't think beyond this store and my husband." She glanced around the undersized room, her gaze skimming the half-dozen chipped Formica tables and the counter where orders were placed and filled. Finally, she focused on the wall of awards, the twenty-four brass plates almost covering the seafoam-green mistake. "He wouldn't even get out of bed this morning."

"All the more reason to bring business to this place," Beck said. "That will give Uncle Mike the incentive to come back to work."

Her lips turned down. "Honey, I don't think he's ever going to come back."

"Please don't have a defeatist attitude," Beck pleaded. "I know from experience that there's nothing to gain from that. He needs to see you're certain this is temporary and that we're doing everything possible to keep his business healthy while he heals."

But Sarah's whole face strained at that impossibility, her eyes darkening to a deep green. "It's hard to be optimistic when you're married to someone who gives up hope. And..." She glanced toward the kitchen. "I can't help it. He lived and Charlie died. In the same helicopter. I know my feelings are wrong, but they're real."

"Of course they are." Beck put a hand on Sarah's shoulder, acknowledging the confession. "But he's an old family friend who loved Charlie, too. And the man can make amazing pizza, which is a lot more than you or I can do."

A smile, the first one in ages, flickered over Sarah's lips. "We sure could use some amazing pizza around here."

Beck instantly reached out to hug her. "You can't give up hope," she said. "Uncle Mike can't sense that you've given up, either. He needs to know we're here fighting for his business every day. That will give him the will to live again."

She sighed as if she didn't buy a word of Beck's optimism.

"Let Aidan stay, and be kind to him, Sarah. He's hurting, too."

She nodded slowly. "You have a good heart, Rebecca. So much like your mother."

Warmed by the compliment, she gave her aunt another hug. "Why don't we both go see Uncle Mike after lunch and tell him how Aidan is helping? Really let him know we're holding this place together for him."

"I'm going to meet with a physical therapist to see if there's some way they'd come to the house," Sarah said. "It's really expensive, but I'm pleading our case. She agreed to do a conference call with the insurance company, so I can't miss it. It's a great day for you to visit him, though, since I'll be gone for a few hours."

"Then I'm definitely going," Beck said. "Can I take Ruff? Uncle Mike likes dogs, Aunt Sarah."

Her face crumpled like she was about to cry. "And I've denied him a dog all these years, and now he's going to—"

"Shhh." Beck gave another squeeze. "He is not going to do anything but get physical therapy, recover, and come back here to make pizza. You understand?"

Sarah patted her cheek. "I want to believe that. And yes, you can take the dog."

"Thank you." She slid her arm around Sarah and led her toward the door. "Now let's go be nice to the man who's going to save this business."

She eased out of Beck's touch. "Let me do the condiments first. And you can work closely with him."

"I think it'll be fun."

Sarah eyed her, making Beck think that response might have been a little *too* positive. She lifted her brows. "He did get even more handsome, didn't he, Rebecca?"

"Yeah, I guess, I mean…I never noticed."

Sarah smiled. "That's what I used to say about Uncle Mike. Then he made me pizza, and I was a goner."

Beck managed a shrug. "Well, no chance of that happening, then, since I don't eat pizza."

When she went back into the kitchen, she heard Sarah snickering, an actual chuckle that could soon be a laugh.

And as much as Beck wanted to disavow her of any ideas about Aidan, she sure as heck didn't want to put a stop to a sound she hadn't heard in two months.

Beck lifted the dough and held it between Aidan's face and her own, making a squeaking sound of joy. "Windowpane!" she announced, inching her head to the side to look him in the eyes. "We did it!"

"You did it," he corrected, gently taking the dough from her hands. "Ready to shape it?"

She considered the request, then puffed out a breath, feathering the bangs that covered her forehead. "Can we work on that before dinner?" she asked, glancing at the clock. "I have an errand to run."

An errand? Aidan tried not to let his disappointment show. "Don't you work all afternoon?" He was fully prepared to spend the day here. Was looking forward to it, in fact.

"Sometimes, but I wanted to go see my uncle Mike today. I'm taking Ruff with me."

"To your aunt's house?"

"She gave her blessing, and I think my uncle needs company."

He turned his attention to the dough, flipping and rolling it back into a ball. "I could go with you," he suggested, glancing at her to gauge her reaction, surprised at how much he wanted her to say yes.

But Beck was looking at the doughball in horror. "What are you doing? That was my first and only windowpane."

He laughed. "There'll be more. But we can't store it like that." He tugged at the dough, testing it. "It'll lose all the elasticity by dinner."

"How do you know?"

He shrugged. "Intuition."

"I'm afraid that's like strong hands," she said, reaching back to untie her apron. "Something I'll never have."

"You're not going to give up, are you?"

"Pffft. I finally made a windowpane." Still struggling with the knot in the back, she looked up at him. "Would you really like to see Uncle Mike?"

"Oh yeah. I always liked him, and your aunt wouldn't let me see him when I went to their house."

She nodded slowly, coming around to the idea. "I think it's a great plan. It can only help him to see more people. And a dog. And..." She made a face. "I can't get this."

Without a word, he put a hand on her shoulder and turned her around so he could work on the knot. She'd pulled it hard, and he couldn't get his big fingers into the knot, forcing him to lean closer to see it. And get a whiff of something that smelled more like flowers than tomato sauce in her thick ponytail.

He tried not to inhale.

"You really don't want this thing to come off," he said, fighting the tight weave of the fabric. "Can I cut it?"

"Nope, we can't afford new aprons."

"All right, hang on." He had to crouch down lower, close to her back and rear end, clenching his jaw so his body didn't go into desperate teenage-boy mode. Her back was narrow, the cotton of her T-shirt clinging to every curve and sweet muscle.

"Aidan, what are you doing?"

Admiring the landscape. "A really lousy job of undressing you," he joked, making those muscles tighten with a quick laugh. Finally, he got a hold of the string and pulled it through the knot, reluctantly standing to turn her back around.

But then he got slammed again by the brightness in her eyes and the soft flush in her cheeks.

Uh oh. They were both...what had she called it? Feeling things.

"You get the dog," he said, his voice husky and thick.

She held his gaze for a second, no warning or fear or anything he could interpret in that look. Except...yeah. Things.

"Okay," she said, taking off her apron as she rushed out.

As he took off his own apron, he looked skyward and pictured Charlie. "I gave my word, dude."

And that should be enough.

Chapter Eleven

Less than twenty minutes later, after a ride in the open-air Waterford Jeep with Ruff happily bounding from one side of the backseat to the other, Aidan pulled up to a simple two-story tract home in Pine Woods Grove, a place he'd been to a thousand times in high school.

Beck unlatched her seat belt and turned to Ruff, who, as always, ignored her.

"You want to go in and warn Mike that we're here?" he asked. "See how he's feeling?"

She thought about that, then shook her head. "I think we should surprise him. Anything to kick some life back into him."

"Only if you're sure. I mean, he can talk and everything, right? He's responsive?"

"If he wants to be. But he claims to forget things. Simple things like words or names of movies or even what month it is. The doctor said that's temporary. His stroke was on the right side of his brain, so left functions were the most affected, like the use of his arm, his facial muscles, and logic, reasoning, and words."

Aidan nodded, aching for the old man.

"But creativity and emotion are on the other side, and they shouldn't be affected," she added brightly.

"Then let's go make him happy and remember how creative he is." They got out, and he leashed Ruff. "You have got to be good," he said sternly, taking the dog's face in his hand to make his point. "No crap out of you, hear me?"

He gave a few quick barks as if to say, *Who, me? Crap from me?*

"I mean it. Do it for Charlie."

His ears perked at the name, as they always did. Aidan had stopped saying it to him because it was clear that *Charlie* didn't mean *Charlie is here*. Even now, after all these months, Ruff missed his real master.

"I miss him, too," Aidan said, adding a good neck rub to ease the disappointment. "But you gotta man up now and be perfect. 'Kay?"

One more bark gave him hope, so he walked around the Jeep to meet Beck.

"I think I should hang on to his leash," Aidan said. "In case he goes ballistic."

She agreed, but bent over to pet him. "He's a good boy. Good boy."

And Ruff looked away, which gave Aidan an unexpected kick in the gut. "Come on, Ruffer," he said in a harsh tone. "Give the girl a break."

"It's okay," she said quickly. "He'll come around."

"Unless you get tired of trying."

She looked shocked. "I will not ever stop trying to win him over."

He put his free hand on her back. "Charlie would

be proud of that attitude," he said softly. "I'm sorry that Ruff keeps rejecting you."

"Are you?" She nudged him with her elbow to turn the question into a tease. "Or are you feeling smug that he only loves you?"

"Maybe both," he admitted.

That made her laugh as they reached the door. She unlocked it and went in first, gesturing for him to follow with Ruff. He did, but two steps inside and he had to stop. The faint scent of something like cinnamon and coffee, and the sight of a familiar blue sofa in the living room on the right, and on the left a formal dining room that was more of a catchall for business files than a place to eat, stopped him cold. The gray slate floor, the wooden staircase railing, the light coming from a long, warm kitchen that ran along the back of the house…it all crashed over him with memories of teenage years and Charlie.

Even though his best friend had lived here for only about three years before they went to college, Aidan was transported to the past, to the anticipation of a high school baseball game or a night out with girls they'd met from Chestnut Creek or Holly Hills. He slipped back to the laughs, the video games, the sheer comfort of hanging out with his best friend.

He tried to shake off the punch of grief, but Ruff pulled him hard, barking and sniffing with intention.

"Oh God, please don't pee on Aunt Sarah's floor," Beck said in a harsh whisper.

"No, that's not a pee sniff," Aidan said, transferring his attention to the dog. "He smells something." Maybe the same thing Aidan did—memories of a good friend.

Ruff pulled him to the steps, sniffing furiously, nose in every corner and against the carpet.

"Or some*one*," Beck said softly, looking up at Aidan as she came to the same conclusion. "Is that possible?" she asked. "After all these years, can he smell him?"

Charlie had been home many times on leave in the last decade. And who knew if her aunt had dragged belongings up and down the stairs recently?

"Dogs' noses are amazing things." Ruff yanked him up the stairs, and Aidan gave Beck a questioning look. "Can we?"

"Yes, that's where Uncle Mike is. Top of the stairs on the right."

Ruff bounded up, adding a bark, stopping to sniff at the top stair, then made a sharp left into the hall, heading straight for Charlie's door. He stuck his nose in the corner of the closed door and all but ate the paint off of it.

"Oh." Beck put her hand on her chest. "He does smell Charlie." She reached to pull Ruff back from the door. "I don't think you should go in there."

Aidan clipped his hand around Ruff's collar to hold him back. "Come on, Ruff." But he fought hard, sniffing and barking.

"Wha's all da ruckus?" The gruff voice broke over the noise, making Aidan turn and finally quieting Ruff.

A man he barely recognized stood in the doorway down the hall, wearing pajamas, his salt-and-pepper hair sticking up straight, his left arm dangling at his side.

Good God, he looked half dead.

"Mr. Leone," Aidan said, stepping forward, holding the leash so Beck could take it from him. At that moment, everything was silent, even Ruff. Thanking God for that gift, Aidan closed the space and stopped just short of a manly embrace. "I'm Aidan Kilcannon. Do you remember me?"

Mike stared at him, his expression blank, no warmth or response in his gray eyes. "No."

"Of course you do, Uncle Mike." Beck came closer to where they stood, putting a hand on her uncle's shoulder. "Aidan was Charlie's friend in high school. And this is Charlie's dog, Ruff."

"Aid'n." His voice was little more than a gravelly struggle. Then he looked down at Ruff, and only then did Aidan realize the leash was loose. And Ruff was down on the ground, head flat, as close to submissive as Aidan had ever seen him.

He glanced at Beck, who looked as stunned as he was.

"Yeah, yeah," Aidan said. "This is Ruff."

"Charlie found this dog in Afghanistan, Uncle Mike." Beck eased down to pet him, and for once, he let her. "Aidan brought him back for me," she said, looking up with sheer joy on her face. "And I'm so glad."

Aidan smiled at her and the animal who'd suddenly transformed. It was like Mike had some supernatural dog-whispering capabilities, because Ruff didn't so much as bark. He stayed low, waiting for a command.

"Do you want to get back in bed, Uncle Mike?" Beck asked, standing up to give the same kind of loving attention to the older man.

"With the dog," he said.

Beck chuckled. "We might push Aunt Sarah right over the edge if we do that."

"Bring him." Uncle Mike turned toward his room, giving Aidan and Beck a moment to exchange looks of total bewilderment. After a second, she shrugged, and they followed, including Ruff, who trotted into the room, leaving the scents of his former owner behind.

Mike got himself into a large recliner that was positioned so he could reach a table with his right hand and also see a TV hanging on the wall, giving Aidan a chance to see that he wasn't incapacitated completely. He was slow, unsteady, but Beck was right. With good physical therapy, this man could be back in the game.

Yes, he'd had a mild stroke, but he was also suffering from grief and denial. It was almost like PTSD, which Aidan had seen. Something had to get him charged again. And once again, Aidan had that surging need of wanting to do something for Charlie, who had deeply loved his uncle.

"Come!" Mike ordered, patting his thigh with his good hand.

Instantly, Ruff was up and over, sniffing at the pajamas, the chair, and the hand that stroked his head.

Beck's mouth opened to a shocked O shape. "How did you do that?" There was no small amount of envy in the question, but Mike didn't answer her. Instead, he rubbed Ruff's head, currently nestled between the armrest and Mike's leg.

"Goo' boy," he muttered, closing his eyes with each move of his arm. "Goo' boy."

Staring at the exchange, Aidan dropped slowly onto a corner of the bed, trying to think of any time he'd ever seen Ruff that docile. Never. Not with Charlie, not with anyone.

Finally, after a good long pet, Mike looked up at Aidan and gave a smile that lifted only half his mouth. "Always wanted a dog," he said simply, the words slightly garbled but forceful enough to be understood. "But...Sarah."

Aidan nodded, some military training rising as he sat erect and faced the man. "Yes, sir. I grew up with a lot of them."

A tiny spot of drool trickled from the left side of Mike's mouth, and Beck immediately reached for a tissue to dab it. Mike looked up at her, a question in his eyes.

"Charlie wanted me to have the dog," she said again, as if he hadn't picked that up at first. "I'm keeping him."

He grunted and nodded. "Sarah said...bad dog."

Beck laughed again. "Ruff can be willful," she said. "But you have the magic touch, Uncle Mike."

"Love dogs," he muttered.

"I know." She took a step closer and crouched down so she was at eye level with her uncle. "That's why I brought him in here today. Sarah said it was okay."

His hand still moved rhythmically over Ruff's head. "I like this one."

"He likes you," Aidan replied, noticing that Ruff's eyes were at half-mast, content and bordering on ecstasy. "It's like he was made for you."

"So, guess what Aidan is doing, Uncle Mike?" Beck asked, staying low to hold his gaze. As she looked at the old man, something twisted in Aidan's heart.

What a remarkable woman she was, he thought, suddenly struck by her selflessness. She was sacrificing everything for these people, wanting to do her best, trying to make the business succeed, and bringing this dog over just because she knew it would make her uncle happy.

"He's helping at Slice of Heaven," she told him. "And he's so good at making pizza, you wouldn't believe it."

Mike eyed him. "How good?"

"I learned from the best, sir. Charlie taught me everything he knew."

"Everything?" There was a strong and undeniable challenge in the single word.

"The customers love his pizza," Beck added, deflecting the question.

"Do you love it?" Mike asked her, the question surprisingly pointed.

She looked at him, silent.

"Well?" he prompted, one bushy brow raised. "Then you can't say."

Aidan leaned forward, confused. "You can't say what?"

"Bet she never tasted your pizza." Another challenge, this one issued with force in his voice.

Come to think of it, she hadn't. There'd been two extra pies today, and Aidan had sampled both, and even Aunt Sarah had taken a slice before she left. But not Beck.

"She won't," Mike said. "Won't eat pizza."

"Uncle Mike." She waved her hand to quiet him. "That's not important."

"Crazy."

"The important thing is Aidan is teaching me how to make it the way he does, and that's going to help the business so it's nice and strong and healthy when you are."

"Can't make it if you can't eat it." At the harsh tone, Ruff lifted his head, sensing discord. "Right, boy?"

Ruff barked once and dropped his head back down. Aidan didn't know what was more remarkable—the change in Ruff or the fact that Beck didn't eat pizza. Was Mike serious?

"I'll figure it out," she said vaguely.

His hand still on Ruff's head, Mike turned to Aidan. "How can she figure it out?" the old man asked suddenly, totally throwing Aidan.

"Good question."

Beck narrowed her eyes at him, but Mike shook his head as if bewildered. "How can she figure out the secret ingredient if she doesn't taste the pizza?"

"Excuse me?" Aidan choked the question. Had he understood that? "There's a secret ingredient?"

"A secret in the sauce." Mike's brow furrowed, then lifted. "Sarah. Sarah is the secret."

Aidan and Beck looked at each other, both confused. Was this the loss of logic and reasoning she'd mentioned? Because, from what Aidan had discerned, Sarah couldn't cook her way out of a pizza box.

"I know how Charlie made sauce," Aidan said. "I know every single step and ingredient."

Mike dropped back against the chair. "He was sworn to secrecy."

"Come to think of it, his sauce *was* better than

mine," Aidan admitted on a laugh. "It had...something. I thought it was technique."

"The secret wins every damn year," the old man muttered. "But..." He shrugged.

"You won't share it?" Aidan added, really confused now.

"I can't," he said, the words so broken that Ruff sat up and checked on him again. Mike heaved a noisy sigh and curled a thick finger around Ruff's soft ear. He tipped his head, and his eyes filled with tears. "I forgot it."

"What?" Beck came closer to him. "Are you sure? You never wrote it down?"

"Nope. Never told anyone...'cept Charlie."

"Not Aunt Sarah?" Aidan asked.

"But you just said the secret is Aunt Sarah," Beck said.

He shook his head. "That's all I can remember. That Sarah is the secret. Without it, I can't make pizza. I won't even try."

What? For a moment, he and Beck were dead silent, staring at him, then at each other.

"That's why you won't go to PT?" Beck guessed. "That's why you don't want to come back to work? Because you can't remember some ingredient so obscure even I don't know about it?"

He looked down, still petting Ruff. "If I can't do it right...I can't do it."

"But you would?" Aidan urged. "If you had the secret recipe or ingredient or code word?"

The old man managed the closest thing to a laugh Aidan had seen. "Sure. Yeah. Probably."

Not much of a promise.

"Then why don't you get better so you can get in there and figure it out?" Frustration made Beck's voice rise, but Aidan leaned forward, reaching for her hand.

"We can help him," he said. "We can figure out a recipe or ingredient. We can do it together, Beck."

Beck stared back at him, her eyes widening, then softening as the offer seemed to hit her heart.

"Would you know it if you tasted it?" Beck asked Mike without taking her eyes off Aidan.

"When it touches my lips, I'll know if it's my pizza or not."

They shared a quick nod of agreement.

"On one condition," Aidan added, directing the comment to Mike. "While we work on it, you do your physical therapy."

Mike stayed silent, his eyes downcast, but his hand stopped stroking Ruff's head. Finally, he met Aidan's gaze with an old, gray, watery one, but it was direct and unwavering.

"I remember you now," he said. "Used to say you were born in light. Lucky kid. Touched somethin', and it turned to gold."

He smiled, remembering his childhood nickname of Golden Boy, which was for his platinum blond hair as a kid as much as his seeming good fortune as he got older.

"And I'm going to touch everything in your kitchen, Mike, until we strike gold."

That brought a slow, crooked smile to the man's face.

Beck took her uncle's hand, forcing his attention to her. "But you have to promise, Uncle Mike. If we find it, you'll come back. While we try to figure it out, you'll do physical therapy and get strong and get back into that restaurant. Do you promise?"

He nodded slowly. "You have my word." Then he gave a sly wink to Aidan, which told him all he needed to know. This man was made of the same stuff as Charlie, and his word was his word.

They could do this. They had to do this.

Aidan put his arm around Beck and realized that this plan meant more time with Ruff...and Beck. And that suddenly felt very right to Aidan.

Chapter Twelve

Beck closed the cover on her tablet and dropped back on her pillows, exhausted after hours of combing the Internet for pizza sauce secret recipes.

Aunt Sarah had been no help at all, sadly. Yes, she'd heard Mike joke that "she" was his secret ingredient since they'd won the first Best of Bitter Bark award a few weeks after getting married and had won every year since. But she had absolutely no idea what this so-called secret ingredient was, if it even existed.

But they did have one small victory. Sarah arranged for in-home physical therapy, and Mike finally relented to work with the woman, so that was progress. Now if they could just figure out—

A loud, sharp, insistent bark interrupted Beck's thoughts. Sitting up, she blinked into the dim light of her room, surprised to see Ruff at the doorway, since he'd yet to show any interest in sleeping in her bedroom.

"You okay, bud?" she asked.

He answered with another loud woof, coming close to prod her bed with his nose.

"What do you need?" She still couldn't figure out how to interpret this dog's barks. She knew *happy*, because it was when he saw Aidan. And *sad* was when he was alone with her. Other than that, he remained a mystery.

She put the tablet on the nightstand and reached for him. "You hungry? Lonely? Scared?" She patted the bed in invitation, but he just jabbed his nose, this time at her leg, adding another bark. "Pee?" she guessed.

That made him turn in a circle and trot to the door.

"We can handle that," she said, climbing out of bed. "Hold your horses, Ruffer. I'll take you out."

Grabbing a hoodie to pull over her T-shirt and sleep pants, she ushered him into the living room and glanced out the windows toward the square, surprised to see a few people out dog walking, visible by the soft white lights strung over all the trees. But then, Bushrod Square never closed, and it was the favorite gathering place for the many dog owners and tourists who visited Better Bark.

At the door, Ruff gave a noisy bark.

"All right, I'm coming." She grabbed the leash from the kitchen counter, latching it on to his collar. "See? I know what you want." She rubbed his head, but he looked down, as if it pained him to have eye contact with her. He'd been better since the visit to Mike, but he still didn't show any signs of wanting to connect with Beck.

"I'm gonna win you over, kiddo," she promised him—and herself. "Let's start with a midnight walk to pee in the park. What male wouldn't like that, huh?"

She stuffed some treats, her phone, and keys in her pocket, and he barked a few impatient times, certain now of where he was going. Which could have been interpreted as, *Shut up and let's go*, or, *You're the greatest dog mom ever*.

Little Miss Sunshine chose the latter.

He led the way down the stairs and out the back door, turning on Ambrose Avenue, not stopping to sniff or check out his surroundings, since he must have known there was nice Bushrod Square grass in his near future.

"See? You're getting the hang of your new home. Now if you could only love your owner."

He walked faster toward the crosswalk, staying a few steps ahead of her the entire way. At the intersection to get over to the square, he suddenly pulled on the leash, trying to take her the other way.

"No, we're going to the square, Ruff. This way."

He was strong, though, taking control and heading in the opposite direction. Bitter Bark was a safe town, but it was now a full-blown tourist town. And the street Ruff headed to was lined with busy restaurants, a few bars and cafés, all of which would be open. She didn't want to head into the business district when there was essentially a city park with plenty of other dog walkers right there.

"Ruff!" She gave a sharp tug and led him in the other direction. "This way."

He relented, but not easily, making her fight the leash all the way across the street. Okay, not the relaxing night stroll she'd had in mind, but she wouldn't give up.

By the time they got to the square, her shoulder was sore, her arm muscles were stretched, and the leash had practically cut her fingers. Finding a bench right near the entrance and under a bright light, she sat down and switched the leash to her left hand. Again, he pulled—hard.

"Hang on a sec, Ruff." Sliding the strap under her thigh to hold it, she used her left hand to rub the right, massaging her aching fingers to—

The leash snapped out from under her leg as Ruff launched into a full run. *Damn it!*

"Ruff!" She jumped up and started after him, horrified that she'd let him get away. He was fast. Wild. And no matter how much effort she put into the run, that dog was twenty, thirty, fifty feet away, out of the square, bolting down the street like a racehorse out of the gate.

She kept running, her blood pumping so furiously she could barely hear the air singing in her ears.

"Ruff! Ruff! *Ruff!*" As he ran out of sight, she slowed her step and looked around for help, but the people she thought she'd seen out here were too far away. Every second took Ruff farther. She was going to lose him.

With a grunt of frustration, she stuffed her hand in her pocket, grabbed her phone, and called the only person she could think of who might be able to help.

For all she knew, Ruff was headed to him right now.

The soft buzz of his phone pulled Aidan out of the deepest sleep he could remember in weeks. He woke in a fog, his throat parched, his bare body damp with sweat and that low-grade state of arousal he'd felt all day.

Taking his phone from the nightstand, he peered at the screen and two words.

Beck Spencer.

And that did nothing to quell his arousal. "Hey," he said after tapping the phone, his voice barely a sleepy rasp. "What's—"

"He ran away! Ruff ran away!" The words almost didn't make sense, they were so loud and panicked and high-pitched. "I took him to the square, and he ran away. Please help me, Aidan."

He was up before she finished her plea, stomping around his floor in search of clothes. He grabbed a pair of jeans and held the phone with his shoulder as he stuffed his legs into the pants with the same speed and agility he'd use in a military drill.

"Which direction?" he asked, pulling up a mental map of where she lived.

"He shot out of the Ambrose Avenue entrance of the square not two minutes ago, heading north." Her voice cracked with fear and tears. "Oh, Aidan, I'm sorry. I'm so scared. Please don't take him away from me. Please."

"Beck, honey, chill. We'll find him. And you'll keep him." His mind flipped through a dozen possibilities and, in a matter of seconds, landed on one. "I think I know where he might be going."

"You do?"

He grabbed whatever shirt was on the top of a pile of clean laundry, but didn't take the time to button it or find shoes as he ran toward the front of the house, snagging the Jeep keys on the way.

"Maybe," he said. "But just in case, I'll call in some backup to search."

"Where do you think he is?"

"My guess is he went to see his new best friend, Mike." He slammed the door behind him and jogged to the Jeep, so grateful his brother Garrett had lent him the wheels until he could buy his own.

"My uncle?"

"Or where he thinks Charlie might be, which is the same place."

"He's gone to my aunt and uncle's house?" Her voice rose with disbelief.

"A guess, but that's where I'm headed."

"I'll meet you there," she said.

"No, stay at your place." He stuck the key in the ignition and fired up the noisy engine, knowing that the sound of the Jeep should get Ruff's attention if Aidan got close enough. "Search the square once, then go home, because the most likely place for him to go is where he's familiar and where he knows he'll be fed. So you need to stay close to your apartment and the pizza parlor. I'll text you the minute I get to Mike and Sarah's house."

"Okay." She sounded devastated and defeated. "Aidan, I'm sorry. I'm so sorry."

"Hey, I know that dog. The blame for running away falls squarely on his shoulders. You sit tight. We'll find him. I'll give a call to the sheriff's office and see which one of my cousins is on duty at the fire station tonight. Ruff is not getting out of Bitter Bark, I promise you."

He heard a whimper that was as sweet as it was desperate. "Thank you."

It didn't take Aidan long to drive toward Mike and Sarah's, scanning every inch of his surroundings on the way. Ruff wouldn't go all the way back to Waterford Farm. It was too far. But he might try to get to Mike.

While he drove through the darkness, he called his cousin's cell phone, happy to find Captain Declan Mahoney on duty at the fire station that night.

"Pine Woods Grove?" Dec asked after Aidan told him what was going on. "I can't send a truck unless the dog is in need of a rescue, but I have a top-notch volunteer who lives there who's got three dogs of his own. Bet he'd jump in his truck and take a look around."

"That'd be great."

"And I'll give a call to the sheriff, Aidan. They can get a cruiser in the area, circling the Bushrod Square area and widening out a search from there."

"Awesome, Dec," he said. "I owe you one."

"Hey, not a problem. This is a Waterford dog? You think he'd head back there?"

"He wasn't at Waterford long," he said. "He's been living with Mike Leone's niece upstairs of Slice of Heaven, so she's waiting there in case Ruff returns."

"Okay, keep me posted."

"Thanks, man."

By the time Aidan disconnected, he'd reached the street that led out of town and up to Mike and Sarah's neighborhood. At the intersection, he slowed to a stop, put on the brights, and sat up to get a good look around the area. The streetlights were rare this far out of the heart of town, and at this hour, most lights, even porch lights, were off.

"Ruff!" he called, listening for any response.

Even in the dark, he could find his way to Charlie's house, he'd been there so many times. Good thing, since he barely looked at the road in front of him.

Instead, he peered into driveways and lawns, searching the shadows and bushes for a lost dog. He called his name so many times it was a wonder a neighbor didn't come out and complain.

A few dogs barked from inside houses, making him wish that Disney folklore was true and they really did have a barking hotline from house to house. But this wasn't *101 Dalmatians*. This was real, and if they didn't find that dog...

It would be like Charlie had died all over again.

The thought was all he needed to rev the engine, call out some more, and finally make the last turn to the two-story clapboard home, which was completely dark at this hour. As soon as his lights hit the house, he saw the dog sprawled on the front porch.

Relief made him groan as he turned off the engine.

He wanted to text Beck, but he had to get Ruff out of here first, before he barked and woke up Sarah and Mike. Ruff didn't even look up when Aidan climbed out of the Jeep, bypassing the door for the sake of a sneak attack. He stealthily headed up on cold, damp grass, his gaze locked on the target.

Ruff was asleep, snoring loud enough for Aidan to hear as he approached. All he had to do was grab the leash, then slide his arms under Ruff's belly, and airlift his ass to the car. Quick and quiet. An easy mission.

He was two feet from his target, ready to launch into his rescue, when six billion watts of lights came on, followed by a screeching siren. Ruff jumped two feet in the air, spun around, and started howl-barking like a wounded water buffalo.

Damn it!

"Ruff!" Aidan leaped toward the dog, but Ruff vaulted in the other direction, spinning around with deafening, staccato barks of fear and desperation. Seconds later, the front door flew open, and all Aidan could do was pray Aunt Sarah wasn't packing.

She stood in the doorway, her hair in wild tufts, a cotton bathrobe hanging over her shoulders, a look of sheer horror as she backed away from Ruff as he pawed the screen door.

"Ruff! Down!" Aidan ordered.

Sarah touched something on the inside wall that silenced the siren, but Aidan was still bathed in high-intensity light like a prison inmate caught making a break.

"Sorry, sorry, Sarah." He snagged the leash and tugged hard. "He...ran away."

"And came here?"

"To see—" Ruff fought him, trying to get to the door, barking desperately, sniffing at the screen, then clawing at it to get in.

"Stop him!" Sarah screamed in abject fear.

Aidan hoisted the beast and draped Ruff like a mantle around his shoulders. "Really sorry. We're out of here."

"Why would he come here?" She sounded positively bewildered by the idea.

He took a few steps back, not sure how to answer that. As he did, he noticed a light had come on upstairs, and there, in the window that Aidan knew from memory was Charlie's room, was the clear silhouette of a man, slightly hunched, one arm hanging at his side.

"Maybe to see Mike," he suggested. "They hit it off today."

She hugged herself, then tied her robe. "Okay." She started to close the door, then added, "See you tomorrow, Aidan."

Well, that was progress.

He marched Ruff, hanging like a corpse around his shoulders, back to the Jeep and slid him into the back without a fight. Instantly, Ruff dropped down and started doing the whine of repentance and shame.

"Don't even think about an apology, brother. You're in so much trouble, it hurts. Now I got to take you all the way back to Beck. In the middle of the night. And see her in pajamas."

He grinned at the dog and gave his head a good rub.

"You're the best, Beasto. Know that?"

Chapter Thirteen

Beck waited for Aidan on a bus-stop bench on Ambrose Avenue, her hands shoved into the pockets of her hoodie while she tried to get her emotions under control even after Aidan called with news that Ruff was safe.

She failed, though, churning inside as the full weight of what almost happened tonight hit her hard.

She almost lost someone again.

It had taken the better part of her life to really put a balm on the loss of her parents. That wound had finally healed, and she had been taking the baby steps to make the kind of connections she'd known she needed, and then Charlie died.

Everything had collapsed again, but she'd held it together, and wham. Uncle Mike had a stroke. It was like she held on to loved ones with feeble fingers and no grip. The same way she'd held that leash. No, wait, she hadn't held the leash at all—she'd carelessly slipped it under her leg.

Lost in guilt and self-pity, she didn't hear the Jeep rumble close until Aidan was whipping into a parking spot not far away. Ruff was in the back, head out the window, quiet enough that she suspected he knew he was in trouble. But she didn't care.

She launched off the bench and jogged to greet Ruff with a big hug, which he accepted without a fight.

Aidan got out, the proof of how quickly he'd gone to rescue Ruff evident in his unbuttoned plaid shirt and bare feet. His hair was still a sleepy mess, and she wasn't even sure the fly of his jeans was snapped.

She tried not to stare or hug him with something even stronger than relief as he came around the car to her.

"Mission accomplished," he said, gesturing to Ruff. "I give you one very, very bad dog."

"I'm glad he's safe."

In front of her, he tipped her chin, the contact of his finger warm on her skin. "You okay? I wouldn't take you for the crying type."

"I was scared I'd lost him," she admitted, reaching to pet Ruff. "I'm so glad we found you, Ruffer."

Ruff turned away, making her straighten with a sigh. As if he sensed that hurt her, Aidan pulled Beck into a silent hug, pressing her against that bare chest and wrapping a strong arm around her. "Might have told me Aunt Sarah has a screaming motion detector."

"Yikes, I forgot." She eased back, biting back a smile. "Was she mad?"

"Not very. But that alarm scared the crap out of me and my dog."

"*My* dog," she corrected, then sank into his arms. "Unless you changed your mind."

He didn't answer for a moment, but held her tight, the granite of his chest making a warm and welcome place to fall. "It's not my mind that has to change," he said. "And your dog-care skills are not being judged. Damn beast is difficult to manage, not going to lie."

"Not for Uncle Mike," she said, sliding her arm around his waist as they started to walk, the move too natural and nice to question. "Did you see him?"

"Up in Charlie's room," he said softly.

Her eyes flashed. "I didn't know he went in there."

"It might be why Ruff reacts to him like that. He smells like Charlie."

She let out a long sigh, the very idea of Mike in there making her sad. "So, how can I thank you?"

He was silent for a beat, long enough for a slow tendril of heat to wind its way through her and make her wonder if he was thinking of all the same ways to say *thank you* that she was. A longer hug. A stroke of fingers. A sweet, sweet kiss.

"Food," he said.

Okay, maybe they weren't on the same wavelength after all.

"After a successful mission, I like to eat," he said. "A lot."

Not as exciting as a kiss, but doable. "We happen to have some of that right here. I hope you like pizza," she added on a laugh, leading him to the side door on Ambrose Avenue, because it was easier and faster than the dining room entrance.

"Who doesn't like pizza? Wait. You. Is that true, by the way, or is your refusal to eat pizza some kind of urban myth you keep up for Uncle Mike?"

She gave him a sideways look as they walked in and headed toward the kitchen. "It's true."

He snorted a dry laugh, slowing his step. "Seriously? He wasn't rambling or joking?"

"Uncle Mike would never joke about pizza." She paused as they reached the kitchen door, glancing up the stairs. "I don't want to leave Ruff up there alone, no matter how bad he's been."

"Bring him into the kitchen," Aidan said. "Dogs belong in kitchens. It's where the scraps and people are."

"My Ruff liked the kitchen, too." She unlocked the door and inched it open to a very dark kitchen, the lingering smell of basil and tomato drawing Ruff like a magnet. "C'mon, boy. Let's test the scraps of one of those recipes we've been googling all night."

"Test as in taste?" Aidan asked.

"*You* can taste it. And Ruff can, too."

"I'm pretty sure that I've lived thirty-two years on earth and never met a soul who didn't eat pizza. Man, woman, child, or beast."

"Sorry to break your streak," she said, flipping the switch for the softest lights around the perimeter so the kitchen wasn't too blindingly bright.

"No wonder you're struggling with making it."

Was that the reason? Because she wasn't going to start eating it now. "You can make something you don't eat," she told him.

"Not well."

She looked up at him and smiled. "Which is why I need you, remember?"

He tapped her nose playfully. "That and my Night Stalker midnight rescue mission skills."

She laughed at that, mostly to hide the silly thrill that went through her when she thought of this man and the heroic things he'd done at war. "Charlie always played the Night Stalkers down," she said. "He said he was a glorified bus driver for the much-higher-profile special ops guys."

"He didn't want you to know how important we were."

"Well, I think what you guys did over there was amazing. Especially that last tour."

She saw Aidan's shoulders rise and fall as he moved through the kitchen with the familiarity of someone who'd worked there for years, not a few days. "To be fair, there are sexier flying gigs in the Army than taking those monsters up to give rides to the guys who everyone thinks are the real badasses. But it was hard work, very rewarding, sometimes sickening, and a ton of fun." He stilled for a moment behind the counter, then added, "Until it wasn't."

Before she could respond, he paused behind the counter, locked his fingers, and stretched out his hands like a virtuoso getting ready to pick up his instrument.

Even in the dim light, she could make out the shadow of his whiskers and the deep indigo blue of his eyes, the exact color of the plaid shirt he'd yet to button. Under that shirt, chiseled muscles moved as he inhaled and exhaled.

And he hadn't buttoned the damn jeans.

He studied the dough-rolling counter like it was a chess set and he was the master...and she studied him like he was the only thing for miles she wanted to taste.

"So if you were to try pizza, what's your topping choice?" he finally asked, opening the proofing drawer to get a doughball they'd made earlier today. "Traditional pep and shrooms, or would you be adventurous?"

"Cheese would be adventurous for me, so make what you want. I'm not hungry." Her gaze slid down over his abs again, counting the cuts and appreciating each bulge line and vein and that dusting of hair. Not hungry for pizza, anyway.

He looked up, caught her, and his lips slid into a smile as sexy as everything she was ogling. She braced for a tease, an invitation, even a look as smoky as the one she was guilty of giving.

"Please tell me you have beer in this place," he said.

Oh, Beck. Let it go, girl. She cleared her throat and headed to the fridge. "Uncle Mike has a secret stash behind the blocks of Parmesan in the walk-in," she said. "I'll get us some." Along with a nice chill to take her temperature down to where his was. Cool.

When she came back with two bottles, he was prepping the counter for the dough, sprinkling cornmeal so he could roll out a pie. Cornmeal, not semolina, she noted, determined to use this as a lesson in pizza making...and not anything more lustful than that.

He walked to the oven and peered at the old-school dial, Ruff right at his side. "Six forty-seven, or the pizza gods will cry."

"You're learning the ways of Slice of Heaven," she said, scooting up on the edge of the counter to watch him work. Ruff, finally subdued after his latest escapade, rolled up by the side sink, his gaze glued to Aidan.

Beck sipped a beer as she took in exactly how Aidan folded and rolled and stretched the most perfect circle of dough she'd ever seen.

"How do you *do* that?" she asked as he worked the edges to make sure they were thicker and would puff up when baked.

"It's easier now that I made the dough in the mixer. Want to try?" Before she could answer, he curled the edges and rolled the whole thing back into a ball, making her moan for the loss.

"It was perfect, Aidan. Why did you do that?"

"Next one'll be better 'cause you made it. C'mere." He took her hand and slid her to the floor, turning her around so she was between the counter and him. Taking her hands in his, he placed them on the dough. "Now...knead."

Need. That was exactly what shot through her at the sensation of his muscular, hot chest against her back. Her limbs went heavy as if she'd downed the whole beer instead of two sips, and she could barely breathe.

She pressed her fingers into the dough, pushing and prodding until he added his hands to the mix. His powerful fingers massaged the dough, rolling it once, then pressing it with a competent, easy touch that was somehow both powerful and tender.

All she could think about was what those hands would feel like...on her.

"Let's spread it out now," he whispered into her ear, making her knees wobble and her stomach tighten.

"You do it," she said.

He chuckled softly, and she could feel the rumble of his laugh in his chest, and then he used those big, capable hands to cajole the dough into yet another thin, round, perfect pie.

"Now the edge," he said, taking two fingers and squeezing his way around the circumference, like an artist putting the finishing touches on a sculpture. "Make it a little rough around the edges..." He whispered the words into her ears, fluttering her hair and waking a thousand butterflies in her stomach. "That way the pie crisps up real nice in the oven."

Transfixed, she put her hand over his, lightly touching his knuckles, following each move, feeling her eyes shutter as the contact danced through her from fingertips to toes.

"See? That wasn't so..." He stepped back. "Hard."

Oh boy. "Well, now we need a recipe for sauce," she said.

Not a recipe for *disaster*, which was exactly where all this kitchen play was headed.

Swallowing, she slipped away from him and boosted herself back on the counter like the physical connection had had no effect on her at all.

But she did take a deep drink from the beer bottle, trying to quench her desert-dry throat. "Want to hear some of the secret stuff I found?"

Aidan shook his head. "There's no secret, Beck. Charlie would have told me. It's in the making, not the ingredients." He'd already started a pot with some red sauce. Dipping a ladle in, he brought it to his nose and sniffed. "This is exactly how Charlie made it, every time. I know every ingredient, and I followed that recipe to the letter." He reached his finger in and took a tiny drop, offering it to her. "Taste?"

"You think you can fool me into tasting pizza?"

"A drop of sauce?" He rolled his eyes and popped the finger into his mouth, moaning as he licked the sauce. "That's good. I wish I had a second opinion, though."

She pulled out her phone and tapped the link she'd texted to herself. "This guy says sugar is the trick. And another one says anchovies. Claims they add umami, whatever that is."

"It's a flavor profile, like salt, bitter, sweet, and sour. Maybe all three. And it's an essence, too. Kind of like something you really want but don't know it until you taste it."

"That sounds promising for a secret sauce."

He made a face. "Charlie never put anchovies in his sauce."

She leaned closer and added some edge to her glare. "If it gets Uncle Mike back in here, we want to try it."

He conceded with a tip of his head. "All right. We'll try sugar, since that'll be easy to add to this. How much?"

She held the phone out to show him the recipe, which he studied for about two seconds, nodded, and went for a bag of sugar to stir it into the sauce.

While she watched and appreciated his every move, he took the pan off the burner, let it cool, then loaded up a fresh ladle to pour it over the pizza dough with the same fearless strokes she'd seen her uncle and brother do so many times when she'd had to be in this kitchen. She plopped the stuff on the dough, every time, never even and smooth like that.

He scooped up some cheese and held his hand over the pie without even looking, his gaze on her for a second. Long enough to make her stomach flip and send little jolts of attraction down to her toes. Silent, concentrating, he added some pepperoni slices and a quick dash of dry oregano and glided the cheap aluminum peel under the masterpiece.

Carrying it with one hand, he turned and took a few steps to the pizza oven, pulled the door down with a familiar squeak, and slid the pie into place. Only after he closed the door, put the peel down, wiped his hands on a dishcloth, and took a long pull on his beer, did he talk again.

"So what was it?" he asked, coming to stand right in front of her so that his hips touched her knees. "Found a bug in the dough? Got sick on pepperoni? Allergic to tomatoes? Or maybe you've been too close to the stuff your whole life that it's lost the magic?"

Oh no. She didn't want to go down that particular rabbit hole. "Doesn't matter," she said, purposely picking up her phone to distract him. "Will you try the anchovies tomorrow? I want to taste umami. This guy says it's the essence of life. That's extreme."

"You know what else is extreme?" He gently eased the phone out of her hand and set it down, removing the barrier so that they were eye to eye with her on the counter. "Not eating pizza."

She angled her head. "Ha ha."

"Did you ever like it? Have you tried it? Burn your mouth on it?"

"Aidan."

"I want to know." He got even closer, his hips making her legs spread to accommodate him. She should change her position or jump off the counter or give him a soft nudge in the other direction.

But she did none of those things, because he happened to be right where she wanted him at that moment.

"Why do you want to know?" she asked.

He searched her face for a few seconds longer, those crystal-blue eyes traveling over every inch, openly assessing what he saw. "You look like him, you know," he said softly. "You have some of his expressions and mannerisms, and phrases. But…"

"But Charlie ate pizza."

"Voraciously."

"Then moving here didn't affect him the same way it did me," she admitted softly. "Maybe because he was older. Or a boy. Or…" She lifted her hand and let her knuckles graze his jaw, enjoying the scrape of his whiskers and the shape of his bones. "Had you as a friend."

"Maybe," he agreed. "It sure didn't make him stop eating anything. Did you *ever* eat it?"

"Of course. I loved it."

"Until you moved here?"

"Until…" She took a slow breath, willing herself not to get emotional. He wasn't going to quit until she told him, and honestly, she wanted to tell him. If anyone would understand, it would be someone who knew Charlie and their childhood history. "Until my life got turned upside down and I went to bed one night with two parents and woke up to find out I had none. Then I had to move, *without my dog*, away from my home, from my friends, and my nice little sixth-grade class at Piedmont Elementary in Allentown, Pennsylvania, to live with my aunt and uncle in someplace called North Carolina…" Her voice trailed off as he cupped her jaw, his hand rough but still so tender and warm.

She closed her eyes and angled into his touch before continuing. "And then my lovely little existence evaporated into…pizza, which will forever be associated with that sorrow. The smell, the taste, the touch, the screech of that thirty-year-old oven door opening and closing. It's all one big bad memory of a very dark time in my life."

He used his thumb, that clever, talented thumb, to stroke the skin right under her lip. Slowly, carefully, tugging at her lower lip like he could coax it open. "We should get you over that."

"Not necessary." She barely breathed the words since her chest was so tight that her pounding heart felt like it could crack a rib.

"Yes, it is. You can't do this job until you do, Beck. You gotta bite the bullet. Or the pepperoni, as the case may be."

She tried to laugh, but the sensations going through her made it impossible. Heat and need and a burn so deep it felt like nothing could ever douse it.

Well, something could. *He* could.

"Don't you want to figure out that stupid secret recipe?" he asked, his finger moving over her lip, searing it. "Don't you want to conquer this shortcoming?"

"Shortcoming? Not eating pizza hasn't kept me from living to my full potential."

"Really?" His eyes glinted with a challenge. "'Cause I think it's paralyzing you. And it's not helping your aunt or uncle, either."

She stared at him, hating that, deep, deep inside,

she knew he was right. And instead of moving away, changing the subject, or somehow protecting herself, she was...inching closer.

"I don't want...pizza." Or trouble, heartache, and loss. But she sure as heck wanted to kiss him.

"Mmm." Unexpectedly, he stepped away, leaving her cold and achy and wishing he'd come back. He walked to the oven and pulled down the door very slowly, exaggerating the ugly noise.

"Whoops. My bad," he joked.

"You're mocking me."

"I'm helping you." He peered into the oven. "Look at that beauty. One more minute and we'll have bubbles and perfect coloring with an unparalleled flop and fold. You're going to love it."

"Aidan." She pushed off the counter in frustration.

"Don't come over here, Beck." He held up his hand. "Aroma alert."

She didn't smile, even though he did. "I'm glad you think my misery is funny."

"I don't think it's funny, but I do think it's something you could beat."

"And making fun of it will beat it?"

He slid the peel in and maneuvered it under the pizza, easing it out with a familiar sound of metal scraping stone, followed by an equally familiar aroma. "Remind me to get this place a legit wooden peel."

She didn't answer, but braced for the visceral reaction, but this time, none came. Probably because every cell in her body was too busy battling lust to worry about old memories.

Carrying the peel to the counter, he studied his work, letting it set.

"This is a good pizza, Beck. Maybe a great one. But any chef is going to tell you that you cannot cook if you don't taste your food." He picked up a cutter and slid it through the gooey cheese in one easy stroke, then did the same thing sideways. Soon, he had six perfect slices.

Then he closed his hands around one of them, tenderly easing it out of the pack, holding it with his index finger making the fold. The very end flopped a bit, enough for her to know that the dough had been perfection.

"Here it is," he said, waving it in front of her.

She stepped closer, almost ready to take the dare. "Would it be enough?"

"For what?"

"To shut you up and make you try every single combination of umami and sugar and pancetta and...magic until we have it?"

"It might, yeah."

She reached out her hand, embarrassed that it was shaking. "'Kay." She could do this, right? She'd been making the stuff, handling the food, kneading dough, and cooking up sauce for two months. How hard could it be to bite it?

She opened her mouth...and handed the slice back to him. "No, I don't want it."

He blinked in surprise, but nodded. "'Kay. I would never force you to do something you don't want to do."

Relief washed over her as he stepped away, taking his pizza to the other side of the kitchen to eat it. Still silent, he crouched down and tore off a few bites to share with Ruff.

Following the relief came a low bubble of anger. Fury, actually, at herself and her stupid, stupid hang-ups.

"It's not that I don't want to," she said softly. "It's that I can't. Big difference."

Very slowly, he straightened and brushed off his hands, studying her while he chewed the last bite. "Why don't you start small?" he asked after swallowing.

"Just one piece?"

His tongue flicked over his lips as he came closer, his gaze burning right through her. "Just one taste."

Her whole body tightened as she walked toward him, holding his gaze, each step closing the space between them and ratcheting up a low-grade hum in every cell.

In front of him, almost touching, she looked up at him and the tiny dot of sauce on his upper lip. She'd taste that.

"You have a little sauce on your lip," she whispered.

"Perfect." He slid one hand around her waist and used the other to lift her face toward his. "You want it, Beck?"

She practically swayed in his arms, her lips parted with a surprisingly ragged breath. "Yeah." She breathed the word, her eyes already closing in anticipation.

"You know what's going to happen, don't you?"

She sure as hell hoped so. "Mmm. What?"

He lowered his head. "You're going to want more."

The sexy words rolled over her, pooling her insides to hot liquid as he barely brushed her lips with his.

The kiss was more like air over her mouth, a teasing, torturous test of her strength. Still trembling ever so slightly, she reached out both hands and set them on his shoulders, adding pressure, bringing him closer.

His lips were soft and tender, warm and sure. At her soft moan, he opened his mouth and let their tongues touch, and then she tasted it. Tangy and earthy and peppery and delicious. The taste of...Aidan.

He broke the kiss, easing back, opening his eyes to hold her gaze. "Well?"

"That must be umami."

"How can you tell?"

"Because...that's something I really want but didn't know it until I tasted it."

He used his thumb to stroke her cheek, smiling at her. "Tomorrow? Anchovies."

"I can't wait."

Chapter Fourteen

The first thing Aidan heard when he reached the open kitchen door at Waterford Farm a few days later was a sudden outburst of laughter and a few hearty barks. He paused on the patio, listening to it, sizing up whose voices he heard, and waiting for that twist of discomfort he'd felt for the first month at home.

Shane, Garrett, Darcy, Dad...and no twist. Not even a quick punch in the gut. Just a nice desire to go in, drink some of the coffee, and maybe eat whatever smelled like fresh-baked buttery perfection. That pleasant change made him smile as he entered and got hit with a noisy greeting as sweet as the croissants they were all chowing down on.

"Aidan, good to see you." Dad came right over to give him a bear hug, and Rusty followed, taking a sniff. "Liam's not here today if you were planning to do some K-9 training with him."

Aidan raised a brow and absently reached down to pet the setter's deep-red fur. "Andi feeling okay?"

"She's fine, but remember he's slowed all his work until after the baby's born."

"S'okay. I just came over to say hi."

"Everything going well at Slice of Heaven?"

"Yep." In fact, "well" was an understatement. Ever since the night in the kitchen, there'd been a constant buzz of electricity between them, though he hadn't kissed her again.

He was enjoying the work as much as the company, laughing a lot, and feeling better than he had in weeks. Months. Maybe more. But the biggest surprise of all—he'd been missing his family, which was why he got up and came over here this morning.

Dad gestured toward an open box in the middle of the island. "Grab a croissant. I managed to snag them the minute Linda May brought them out of the oven this morning."

"You've already been in town today?" It wasn't even eight thirty.

Dad shrugged and unhooked a white mug for Aidan's coffee. "I was outside with some new rescues howling for attention at five in the morning. So, I ran in early and got us some breakfast from the bakery since Crystal isn't coming in until ten today."

"Plus, the bakery is owned by..." Darcy, seated at the island counter, leaned into Shane. "Linda May."

"Oh, Linda May." Shane drew out the baker's name in a low tease. "But then again, she may not."

Garrett, a phone in one hand and a mug in the other, chuckled. "Good one, Shane."

Good one? "Don't you guys get tired of pestering Dad?" Aidan asked. "It's not like he's out there on the hunt for a new wife."

"Thank you," Dad said, handing him a steaming cup. "It's like a blood sport around here."

From the counter, Shane, Garrett, and Darcy looked up, feigning innocence.

"We want you happy, ol' guy." Shane lifted his mug. "Like we are."

"Who's old?" Dad lobbed back. "I'm busy running this place and on damn near every committee in town. Plus, I've been working at both vet offices because Molly's planning her wedding and going off with Trace half the time—"

"I heard that." Molly came through the same door that Aidan had just used, her reddish-brown curls wild and her eyes bright. "And I'm here all day, so you don't have to cover for me anymore, Dad."

His sister breezed into the kitchen, giving a wave to Shane, a high five to Garrett, and leaning over to plant a kiss on Darcy's head. "Hey, gorgeous."

"Where's Trace?" Darcy asked. "I saved him the last chocolate chip."

"What a dear sister-in-law you'll be. He went to see Tashie and Boris, of course," she said, referring to the service dogs Trace was training. "But he'll join us soon. And speaking of joining us..." She turned to Aidan, arms outstretched. "Where have you been?"

"In town, mostly," he said, hugging his sister with almost as much fierceness as she did him.

"Oh yes, I've heard! I know all about Ruff and how you gallantly handed him over to Charlie's sister. You are truly a hero, little brother." She got up on her tiptoes and brushed his cheek with a kiss. "Also heard Beck's a ten and that you two took a long walk with the dog and that you're practically inseparable at her uncle's pizza parlor, with your heads together in the kitchen trying to re-create the perfect pizza."

He drew back, not sure whether to laugh or cry. "Pru or Gramma Finnie?" he asked, already guessing the source of all this ridiculously accurate intelligence.

"Both. The dog part was Pru, but Gramma pronounced her a ten. Actually, I think the expression she used was 'a dime,' because, well, Gramma."

"And the pizza part?"

Darcy raised her hand. "Guilty. Carly, the part-timer at Slice of Heaven? I groom her golden, and the girl likes to chat." She grinned. "'Inseparable' is a direct quote, so if you want to keep that stuff on the DL, remember the walls have ears and eyes."

"And, apparently, a mouth."

"Isn't it good to be back?" Molly teased, slipping by him to get the coffee Dad poured for her.

Was it? No doubt, Molly's question was rhetorical, but he sure didn't feel quite as suffocated in this kitchen as before, so maybe he had just needed some time away.

"Yes," he answered. "It's good to be back, but Beck and I are hard at work trying to discover her uncle's secret recipe, which was forgotten with his stroke."

"Oooh. Secret sauce. Is that what they're calling it now?" Darcy cooed with about as much subtlety as an Uzi in target practice.

"What does that mean, Darc?" he shot back, purposely playing dumb.

"It means..." She looked around for help, but didn't get any as the rest of them were maybe a tad more chill or mature than his little sister. "It means I hope you'll share whatever you two are cooking up. Maybe next Wednesday night dinner. Where were you last night, by the way?"

"Making pizza, like I told you."

"So, any luck in the kitchen?" Shane asked. "With the pizza, not Beck."

Aidan rolled his eyes. "We've made more than a dozen different recipes and taken slices—along with Ruff—every afternoon to Mike Leone. The good news is he's done two sessions of PT. The bad news? No secret recipe."

But, damn, they were having fun trying.

"So you're not back here for good?" Garrett asked, a hopeful look in his eyes.

"You need me, Bro?" Aidan asked without a second's hesitation. He couldn't do much for Garrett's rescue operation, but the two were close in age and spirit, and Aidan would do anything for his older brother. Anything but leave Beck right now, so he braced himself for the response.

"Nothing anyone can do to help." Garrett set his coffee cup on the counter with added force. "I got more dogs than families, is all. Couple of purebreds, a few puppies that aren't going into service dog training with Trace, and Marie wants to send fifteen more next week."

"Fifteen?" Aidan blinked.

"Some asshole—excuse me"—Garrett shot a look at Dad—"had fifteen damn dogs locked in vans in a garage."

A collective groan rolled around the room.

"Do we have room for that many dogs?" Aidan asked, picturing the packed kennels.

"More or less. If I can find the ones I have the right homes."

Garrett was picky as hell about rescues. These

rescues would be loved, healed, and trained to perfection before he sent them out, and when he did, he had to be positive the family on the receiving end was worthy of the gift.

"I keep finding people who are too far away. But I'll take the dogs," Garrett assured Aidan. "And you keep doing what you're doing. You look…happy."

There was a millisecond of silence in the room, but Aidan lifted his mug at them to cover the awkward beat. "Like Gramma said, Beck's a dime."

That made them all laugh, while he drank his coffee.

"Well, I understand Mike Leone's desire to remember his recipe," Shane said. "Chloe had a bunch of tourism stuff out yesterday, and I saw that guy's won Best of Bitter Bark in the pizza category every year for, like, twenty-five."

"Twenty-four," Aidan corrected, and Dad let out a low whistle.

"Twenty-four years? I remember the first time he won like it was yesterday. Jeez, I am getting old."

"Not old, Dad," Molly interjected. "They're calling it 'seasoned' now."

Gramma Finnie came into the kitchen, her white hair coiffed, her cardigan du jour buttoned neatly up to her throat. "If he's seasoned, then I'm cooked to a crisp."

"Stop it, Gramma," Darcy chimed in, scooting off her seat so her grandmother could have it. "You're eighty and outrageous is what you are."

While the jokes flew fast and furious, Aidan settled in on another barstool, eating one of Linda May's famous croissants and soaking up the relaxed atmosphere. Maybe all he'd needed was some time away. With Beck.

"Yikes, I'm late." Darcy popped up in the middle of the conversation, looking at her phone. "I have a bichon coming in at eight forty-five." She snapped her fingers. "Kookie! Let's move it, luv."

Darcy's tiny white Shih Tzu, with gray and white fur brushed nearly to the floor and adorned with a ribbon between her ears, shot out from the dining room, followed by Rusty, who loped over to Dad as if he'd suddenly realized he wasn't next to his master.

"Speaking of seasoned." Dad put his hand on the old dog's head and stroked him. "There's my boy." Then Dad nodded to Aidan. "Before you leave, can we talk? In my office? I have something I want to show you."

"Be right there." He cleaned his mug, polished off another pastry, and headed out of the kitchen to the other side of the rambling house where Dad's office was at the end of the long hall. There, he found his father seated at his oversized desk, the sun streaming through a window behind him.

Next to him, Rusty was curled in one of his favorite beds, but he got up and took a few steps closer to Aidan, looking for the affection that every person who entered this room offered the dog. Aidan rubbed his shiny red fur and got down so that he was eye to brown eye with him before dropping into the guest chair across from Dad's always neat and shiny desk.

"What's up?" Aidan asked.

He didn't answer right away, but slowly opened a manila file folder, taking his time as Daniel Kilcannon often did when he had something of importance to impart.

A lecture on not being around enough? A change in schedule that would mean he'd have to stand in for Liam? Or some fatherly advice that he so often handed out freely whether his kids wanted it or not?

"I've discovered something...*interesting* in Charlie and Ruff's papers."

Aidan leaned forward. Didn't see that coming. "Interesting?"

Dad blew out a slow breath, lifted a sheet, and moved it to the side, then picked up another. "Cilla was given an exhaustive file from the Army representative who ultimately handed Ruff over to her."

He frowned, imagining what could be in such a file about a stray Charlie found wandering about a bombed-out hospital north of Kabul. He certainly had no papers and hadn't been chipped. No one had ever tried to claim Ruff by making contact with the Army. What else could be in that file? He waited as Dad scanned a piece of paper, then lifted his gaze to meet Aidan's.

And his heart stopped. He knew that look, knew it meant that what was about to be said might be life changing.

"There's a copy of Charlie's Record of Emergency Data," he said.

"His DD93?" That form on file for every deployed soldier, stating next of kin. That person was responsible for doling out any specific items and honoring any additions or personal requests. It was also not something the Army usually sent out unless someone asked to see it. So, why include it with transport papers? "It names Beck as next of kin, right?"

"Yes, it does."

Aidan shifted in his seat, stretching out his legs, trying to wrap his head around this loss of a dog he wanted so much. He'd begun to accept that Ruff was staying with Beck. No, he'd more than accepted it. He understood it. And that made each day with both of them even more precious.

"So, as next of kin, her claim to Ruff is really cemented. Is that what you're saying, Dad?"

Because all he had was the pain-swathed mutterings of a dying man.

"Not exactly." Dad extended the paper over the desk to hand it to Aidan. "Just the opposite. In fact, I believe this was included in the package because this is the single document that made it possible to get Ruff transported in the first place. The Army couldn't ignore this request."

Aidan peered at the words on the form, skimming the typed text down to an addendum at the bottom, dated early summer of last year. The words typed into the box punched him as he read.

In the event of my demise, my dog, Ruff, is to be officially transported to Waterford Farm in Bitter Bark, North Carolina, by contacting the owner, Daniel Kilcannon, who will arrange transport. The dog is to be kept there until which time Major Aidan Kilcannon returns home, when he will become Ruff's rightful owner.

It was signed by Charles John Spencer in distinct handwriting that Aidan instantly recognized.

The whole page seemed to move in front of him, maybe from the unexpected tears of sheer disbelief. And he couldn't speak for a minute.

"Sort of shifts the momentum, doesn't it?" Dad asked.

Aidan finally tore his gaze from the document. "It's not a game or a battle."

Dad conceded with a nod. "But you both want the dog. This addendum, which was signed by the CO and officially added to Charlie's file, offers compelling and, some might say, indisputable proof that you are the owner Charlie selected."

He waited for that kick of victory, but all Aidan could see was the sorrow he'd have to face in Beck's pretty brown eyes. The light would go out. The lips would turn down. Her narrow shoulders would fall in defeat...and he'd...oh *man*.

"This is going to destroy her."

Dad dropped his elbows on the desk and rested his chin on his knuckles, saying nothing as he stared at Aidan.

"But if I ignore it," Aidan said, "then I'm not honoring Charlie's specific last wishes."

His father nodded thoughtfully. "Maybe there's a way to work something out. You'll want to move the dog in the least-disruptive way, since he's already having a bit of a struggle."

"You know that?"

"Dec was at dinner on Wednesday and told us you called him at the fire department when Ruff got away from Beck."

"That wasn't her fault," he said, sitting up straighter to make sure her dog skills were fairly defended. "Ruff isn't easy. I told you he's essentially untrainable. Although he is like a different dog with her uncle, but no one else."

"I knew he needed to find his purpose." Dad picked up a different paper from the file. "He could very well be a therapy dog. Maybe not officially trained, but since he was found at a hospital and has responded to a sick man? Comfort might be his job, and when he's doing it, he's happy."

"I bet you're right, but…" Aidan stared at the paper again, hearing Beck's voice the night Ruff ran away. *Please don't take him away from me. Please.* "Would it be wrong to ignore this?" he asked, praying to hear the answer he wanted.

But his father didn't answer, narrowing his eyes. "Regardless of what you decide to do, Son, this is Charlie's official statement about who should have the dog. I thought you'd be all over this."

Except now…he cared about Beck. More than Charlie? More than Ruff? He didn't know. "It's a dilemma," he said. "Do I do what Charlie wanted, or give Beck what she wants?"

"What do you want?"

He stared at his father, unable to answer the question any way but honestly. "I want her to be happy." The words slipped right out and betrayed him. Shocked him, too. But nothing fazed the Dogfather, who nodded as if he totally understood that sentiment.

"Could she have seen this?" Aidan asked.

"Does the Army copy next of kin, or did we get it because of Ruff?"

"Not unless the NOK sends a specific request. She might have, if she thought I was going to push it with the dog."

"But you're not going to push it with the dog." It was a statement, as if Dad already knew the answer.

Aidan exhaled softly. "I don't know."

"The longer you wait, the more she and Ruff bond. It'll be hard for her and the dog to separate."

And the longer he waited, the more *he* and Beck bonded. And it would be even harder for him to let her go. "I'll figure it out," he said, pushing the paper back across the desk. "Don't you think that Charlie's real last request was that Beck be happy? Whether she has the dog or not, he only wanted her to be happy. Ruff safe, of course, but Beck happy."

Dad steepled his fingers and leaned his chin on the tips, eyeing Aidan with open scrutiny.

"Your mother would be so proud of you," he said finally, making Aidan draw back.

"That's not what I asked."

"But the question you asked would make her proud. No 'Aidan' in the mix of who is happy, just others. You know that would make her proud."

"It's hard to be around here without her," he admitted.

Dad's laugh was mirthless and quick. "Don't I know it."

"And why do you let those goons tease you about dating, anyway? You're not going to meet a woman like Mom."

He smiled. "Let them have their kicks, Aidan. They're all in love, and they want to spread the joy."

"But you won't, will you? Date?"

He angled his head. "Am I asking you personal questions about Beck?"

Which wasn't an answer, but Aidan understood. "Well, I guess you don't have to, based on the way I'm responding to this news."

Dad laughed. "Garrett's right. You seem happy." He picked up the DD93. "But you do need to do the right thing about this, whatever that may be."

He looked at the paper. It could give him Ruff, but lose him any chance with Beck. Was that a risk he was willing to take?

Chapter Fifteen

S arah sailed into the kitchen, her eyes brighter than the sun that streamed in the windows over the sink. "He lifted his arm!" she exclaimed. "He lifted it all by himself."

Beck lowered the dough she was working on to surprise Aidan before he got there, her jaw dropping. "That's amazing, Aunt Sarah."

"The therapist is good, but Mike's...motivated. Really, honey. Is this because of the work you and Aidan are doing? I could kiss you both."

Beck came around the counter and hugged her aunt, giving a kiss instead of taking it. "Truth? You might want to kiss Ruff."

She leaned back and started to curl her lip, but the look on Beck's face must have stopped her. "You think the dog does that much for him?"

"Ruff sure likes him more than he likes me, and Uncle Mike dotes on that creature."

Blowing out a breath, Sarah moved to put her purse in a cabinet and find an apron. "I should get him a dog."

"That would be the ultimate act of love on your part."

Her back to Beck, Sarah dropped her shoulders. "That's a big commitment, honey. I'm not sure—"

"Wait, I have an idea." Beck came closer to turn her aunt around so she could gauge her response to this. "Let me take Ruff over there during the lunch hours. Then I'll bring him back, but Uncle Mike can have Ruff from, say, ten to two. Every day. He has a dog for more than a visit, both of them are happy, and you don't have to wallow in guilt for what you're not ready to do."

She knew instantly from the warmth in Sarah's green eyes that it was a good idea. "The therapist is there today," she said. "And Carly's coming to work for me so I can be home at the end and she can show me more exercises we can do every day, but..." She bit her lip. "Yes. I think that's a great idea. Just not today."

"We'll start tomorrow." Beck gave her another happy squeeze. "And before you know it, Mike will be back and everything will be normal again. I'll go home with Ruff, our mission accomplished."

"Oh, hello, Aidan."

At Sarah's greeting, Beck turned to see him standing in the kitchen, taking in the whole exchange. His smile faltered a bit as he met her gaze, then he turned his attention to the pizza counter.

"Look at you, Beck. Five doughballs, and you used the mixer." He gave a laugh. "Guess pretty soon we'll *all* have our missions accomplished. Whatever they might be."

She studied him for a minute, weighing this man

against the one she'd said good morning to for the last few days. Something had changed. Was it her mentioning going home?

"You're going to be proud of me, young man." Sarah sashayed closer to him, hands on her hips. "I'm letting Ruff stay with Mike during lunch rushes starting tomorrow. That's progress, right?"

He smiled at her. It didn't quite reach his eyes, but it was a smile. "That's great. My dad thinks Ruff might have been a kind of therapy dog in another life, which really explains their connection."

"And Mike lifted his arm," Sarah added.

This time, his smile was genuine. "Excellent news. You're right, Beck, your job may be finished here soon."

"Soon…ish," she said, still trying to figure out what might be bothering him. Was he sick of the job? Restless again? Jealous of Ruff and Mike? Or…not happy she was leaving?

For some reason she didn't understand, that sent an absolutely unnatural thrill through her.

"But in the meantime, we have work to do, Aidan Kilcannon." She gestured to the counter. "You will not believe the treasure trove I found on the Internet last night. A chef in Rome who swears by sour cream. That's something we've never tried."

He frowned with nothing but doubt. "Sour cream?" He shrugged. "I guess."

"I'm starting to think Aidan's lost his enthusiasm," Sarah said, possibly in tune with his change as well. "What you two need is a day out of the kitchen."

"Not until Sunday," Beck said.

"How about today?" Sarah asked. "Carly's coming

in, the pizza is essentially made, at least enough that I can handle this. Ricardo's is having their personal pizza BOGO, which means we'll be dead. Why don't you two do me a huge favor and take a drive to our restaurant-supply store in Chestnut Creek? They have that lovely wooden peel you asked for, Aidan, and you can poke around and get back in the groove."

A rush of gratitude filled Beck, who loved the idea.

"I'm in the groove," Aidan said. "But I know the area. I used to go out to the Foothills Regional Airport with my dad for vet house calls when I was little, and when I got older, I'd go there to watch the private planes come in. I have a favorite spot in the hills off the highway that's so close to the runway you can see inside the cockpits."

And there it was—the spark in his eyes. And all Beck wanted to see was more of it.

"Can we go?" Beck asked.

"If it's not going to cost us lost business," he said. "I'd love to, but I don't want to leave you in the lurch, Sarah."

"We're fine, and like I said, I'm celebrating the raised arm," she said on a laugh. "And honestly, ask Beck. We really don't get customers when Ricardo's has a BOGO."

"Then we should change that and have a BOGO of our own, but..." He looked at Beck, his gaze direct and meaningful. "I think you and I could use some time alone. There's something I want to talk to you about."

"Oh," Aunt Sarah said with an embarrassing tease in her voice. "Maybe I'll have more to celebrate soon."

Beck blinked at her, not sure how to respond, but Aidan gave an easy laugh. "You sound like half my family, Aunt Sarah. Matchmakers, all of them."

And Beck didn't know which surprised her more—that his family was talking about them, or that he'd called her aunt *Aunt* Sarah.

Or maybe it was how thrilled she was to spend the day ahead with him. Yeah, that might be the most surprising thing of all.

Aidan couldn't remember the last time he'd laughed so much. Maybe with Charlie, after they landed the same tour in Afghanistan. They'd actually celebrated. Hard. But that had been a different kind of fun from wandering around a sleepy North Carolina town that was, in many ways, a carbon copy of Bitter Bark. Not as many tourists and not nearly as many dogs, but the same brick buildings, the same hickory-lined residential streets, and the same feeling of comfort, ease, and home.

Ruff was the source of most of the humor, barreling across a restaurant-supply warehouse like the proverbial bull in a china shop until Aidan took him outside and Beck picked up the Slice of Heaven order. Then he went powering through the heart of town, barking, jumping, trying to pee on every lamppost and bush. They took a quick break in a park off the main drag. Then, both of them starving as the afternoon wore on, they attempted a sandwich shop, but Chestnut Creek wasn't as dog-friendly as Bitter Bark.

After a battle with a rambunctious Ruff, Beck waited back in the park with him while Aidan got them something to eat.

But it wasn't only the dog who kept things lively, Aidan mused as he waited in line to order sandwiches. The party in a person was Beck, who had seized the day out of the kitchen and in the fresh air with as much gusto as Ruff had. Her laugh was infectious, her optimism endless, and her hand, when she slipped it into his and looked up at him to share something, was perfection.

Carrying the bag, he headed out and found them halfway down the street with Ruff sniffing around a small craft brewery.

"Beer might help him," Beck joked.

"Not him, but it's just the ticket for our picnic."

Her eyes widened, big, brown, and bright. "We're having a picnic?"

"On a pretty hill with endless space for Beasto and a perfect view of the runway." He angled his head toward the brewery. "And two craft beers to go."

Forty-five minutes later, the picnic was exactly as he'd planned. Sunshine, rolling hills, homemade beer, an exhausted dog, and the prettiest girl he'd taken out in...ever.

Beck lay on her back, staring up at a cloud, her dark hair spread over the blue-and-black checked blanket he'd found in the back of the Jeep. She held her beer on her stomach with one hand, and it rose and fell precariously with every breath.

The only sounds were the occasional bird and Ruff's relentless snoring once he collapsed behind them.

Aidan tried to concentrate on the runway and skies around it, waiting for the next little joyride to come in, but his gaze slipped right back to the woman next to him. In nothing but the plainest white T-shirt, jeans with some holes in the knees, and Converse sneakers, she was certainly a *dime*.

Thinking of Gramma Finnie saying that made him chuckle, and Beck opened one eye in his direction. "What's funny?"

"Oh, nothing. Something my grandmother said."

She rolled over on her side, propping her head up, totally unaware that the V of her shirt fell, revealing the soft flesh of her cleavage and forcing him to take a deep drink of a now lukewarm beer.

"She's so adorable," Beck said. "All my grands are gone now, but my dad's parents were near us when we lived in Allentown, and I loved going to their house."

"Why didn't they adopt you and Charlie?"

"My parents had left clear instructions that if anything should happen to them, we should go to my mother's sister."

The only thing he really heard in that sentence was *left clear instructions*. Like Charlie. In his DD93. Which he'd conveniently forgotten about for the last few hours, but had intentionally planned to talk to her about out here.

"And it was probably harder for Sarah than us," she said, oblivious to the direction of his thoughts. "I mean, she and Mike had been married six or seven years, but they hadn't planned on kids and still lived like newlyweds." She smiled up at him. "Did you know you called her *Aunt* Sarah today?"

He shook his head. "Because that's what you call her."

"You two are making progress. And Ruff and Mike."

"Making it even harder when you take him to Chicago," he said, hoping that would start the conversation, but realizing how it sounded as soon as he saw the look on her face.

"You won't quit, will you? Still trying to lure him away."

"Not lure."

"You're luring." She flipped around on her stomach to offer him yet another incredible angle of her body. "C'mere, Ruffer." She reached her arms out to him. "Come to your sweet owner."

Ruff opened one eye, snorted, and went back to sleep.

And damn if she didn't roll around again, onto her back, the whole time gracefully holding that beer bottle out so a drop didn't spill.

"You think it's funny that he hates me, don't you?"

"No, that's not what I'm thinking," he said. *At all.*

She turned her head, let her hair fall over her face, and studied him. "What are you thinking? What did Gramma Finnie say? And what was it you wanted to tell me this morning?"

Easy things first. "Gramma said you're a dime."

She frowned, then choked a laugh as she realized what he'd said. "She's hilarious. Tell her thank you. She's a quarter."

"Damn near a dollar," he joked. "And as for what I'm thinking…" He leaned over, giving in to the need to get closer. "I'm thinking that she's right."

As they held each other's gaze, he brushed that

lock of hair off her cheek, letting his fingers graze her skin.

"And what you wanted to tell me?"

Just then, he heard the hum of propellers and turned to spy the small plane coming overhead. "It's a Beechcraft Bonanza 36," he said without even getting a good look at it.

"How can you tell?"

"Shape of the fuselage. That bright sound of the propeller. Hear that whine? Some good history in that bird."

"Sounds like a..." Her voice faded as it flew right overhead, making Ruff jump up and bark at it as it cruised toward the runway. "Plane," she finished.

He watched the pilot make a picture-perfect landing, feeling the grinding touch of wheels to concrete as clearly as if he sat in the cockpit. He let out a grunt, perfectly timed, and smiled. "Nice."

"Have you always loved planes?"

"Always," he said without hesitation. "Anything that could fly."

"Why didn't you go into the Air Force?"

"Because you can fly in the Army, and I liked the ROTC program at Wake Forest."

"And why helicopters and not planes?"

He shrugged. "Doesn't matter to me. I want to be up there defying gravity, making the machine soar." He glanced down, unaware that she'd moved again, on her side now, head on hand. Her other hand lightly rested on his leg.

"Then you should fly."

He drew back. "I just left that job a while back, remember?"

"What can you fly besides a helicopter?" she asked.

"What can't I fly is a better question. I got a pilot's license in college. No, I can't land a 747, but anything that size?" He jutted his chin toward the taxiing Beechcraft. "That's a breeze."

She sat up. "You should fly," she said again.

"I don't want to fly commercial, Beck. It holds no appeal to me."

"But when you find your passion, you have to pursue it."

He let out a sigh. "Easier said than done when I have the weight of the Kilcannon family business and my father's expectations on my shoulders."

"You're a grown man," she said. "No one has made you sign a contract to work at Waterford Farm. Go get a job flying planes. I bet there are hundreds of them."

He eyed her, considering the idea for a moment, and then remembered the look on his father's face when he'd walked in the door that morning. "You make it sound simple."

"Passion is simple."

"Nothing is simple where my family is concerned," he said. "It's done right and well and for the good of mankind and all dogs."

She inched closer. "Is that a bad thing? I mean, you're military. Doing the right thing and doing it well is ingrained in you."

"From childhood, not only the military."

"I know. I can tell by the way you make pizza. And don't start me on how much you love dogs."

He plucked a blade of grass, trying to decide if he wanted to have this conversation or not. Mostly not, but he trusted her judgment. She was the closest thing to Charlie he had, the closest thing to a best friend right now.

"No one seems to get this when I say it, but I don't feel like I fit there. They look past me like I'm temporarily insane. But I miss it when I'm not there. I don't want to be…suffocated by Kilcannons, you know? For the past few days, I'm as content as I can remember being since I left Afghanistan. In the kitchen of a pizza parlor."

"There's a lot of Kilcannons," she agreed, lightly rubbing her thumb over his hand resting on the blanket. "And they're big personalities who love hard and strong. They all look at you like you hung the moon, too."

He gave a dry laugh, but let the idea rub into his conscious, like her light touch. "The luck of the Irish being last," he said. "Liam's king, of course, being the oldest male. But the youngest male carries a lot of expectations, too."

"But you are feeling content," she reminded him.

He turned his hand in hers. "Maybe I'm content because of the company I keep."

"I make you content?"

"You make me…" *Hungry. Weak. Achy.* "Want to kiss you."

"Then you better do that, Aidan. While you've got the chance."

He closed the space between them easily, lightly placing his lips over hers and getting the bone-deep thrill of feeling that sweet bow under his mouth. Lifting his hand to slide his fingers under her hair, he angled her head to deepen the kiss, opening his mouth to taste her.

Their tongues touched, making them both groan softly, adding mutual pressure and pleasure to the kiss. Threading the silky strands of her hair, he inched her back just as the whine of a plane screamed in the distance overhead, coming straight at the runway. As it got louder, he eased her all the way down and slid next to her.

Breaking the kiss, he stayed on his side but turned her face to the sky as the plane flew over. He studied her profile, her lashes, her sweet skin, and delicate bones. Then he leaned close to whisper in her ear, "That's a Cessna 175, single-engine four-seater. Sweet ride."

She smiled as the noise hit its maximum, then faded. "You didn't even have to look."

"Didn't want to. This view is prettier."

She turned to him, locked gazes, the only sounds Ruff's soft snore and their heartbeats. "You still can't have my dog," she whispered. "We can kiss for hours, but you can't have my dog."

Except there was a paper that said he could.

But right now, with heat rolling through every vein in his body? "I'll take the 'kiss for hours' option."

"Good call." She rolled one more time, lying on her side, lining up their bodies for another long, wet, easy kiss.

Aidan stuffed his problems into some mental compartment, added the issue of a piece of paper that sat on his father's desk, and locked it all away. Right now, he wanted to explore the next kiss, touching her face, her neck and sliding his hands down to her waist.

She sighed with pleasure, taking her own trip over his arms, shoulders, and neck. Blood coursed through him as he rose above her, feathering kisses on her throat and hearing a slapping sound and the pressure of—

A paw?

He popped open his eyes to see one massive brown tongue bathing Beck's cheek as Ruff's front paw batted Aidan's arm to move him out of the way.

Beck started laughing, wiping her face.

"What the hell, dude?" Aidan said, sitting up to move him off. But Ruff barked once, loud, and gave Beck a huge face-lick again.

"Aidan!" She shot up, her eyes bright from joy as well as arousal. "He likes me! He's protecting me!"

He barked in full agreement, smacking Aidan one more time with his paw.

"Move over, Rover," Aidan said, giving the dog a nudge in the chest. "This is my girl. Find your own."

"No." Beck slid her hands around Ruff's neck. "This is the nicest he's ever been to me."

Ruff took the love, rolling his head from side to side, then lifting it so she could have the ultimate intimacy of scratching his neck.

"Oh, Ruff, you do love me." She pressed her face to his and made a completely different kind of whimper of joy, as sweet but not as sexy as the ones Aidan had been listening to. "I love you, too, big boy. I do. I love you."

Aidan sat up completely, unable to do anything but smile at the exchange.

"Oh, Aidan, I've waited so long for this." She turned to look at him, nothing but ecstasy in her expression. "I'm sorry he's interrupting, but…"

"Oh no. Have your moment," he said on a laugh.

"I'm happy I could push him over the edge."

She laughed at that, loving on the dog with the same infectious, enthusiastic, wholehearted affection he wanted to be getting right then, but he couldn't resent the beast. The woman was irresistible.

"Finally!" She hugged him with one arm and used the other to bring Aidan in and include him in the moment. "Thank you, Aidan. Thank you for making him love me."

"Not sure that was exactly what I was going for, but…"

Another laugh bubbled up. "But you did anyway. And…" She leaned into him. "We'll pick that up later. Right now, I want to enjoy the moment that my dog finally decided he loved me."

Her dog. Her dog loved her. Except…

"So, Aidan, what did you want to tell me?" she asked again, but her attention was on Ruff, delicate forehead to monstrous brow, bonding so hard he could practically feel the connections forming.

"I wanted tell you that…" His voice faded into a strangled silence.

"What?" She finally looked at him. "What was it?"

He couldn't do it. He couldn't steal this joy from her. "Just how much I wanted to kiss you."

A slow smile broke over her face like sunrise on a North Carolina morning. "That's it?"

"I know I promised…" *To honor Charlie's last wishes.* "What exactly did I promise that day down at the creek?"

She touched his cheek. "You promised to respect the fact that my heart is not open for business, if I recall correctly."

"I did?" He inched back. "So I didn't promise to not kiss you?"

"Not in so many words, no."

He dropped his gaze over her face, taking his time to count a few freckles and study the bow of her lips. "Then I wouldn't be breaking a promise if I kiss you again? And again. And maybe a few times after that? Would that bring your heart into the equation or only...the body it resides in?"

She studied him for a moment. "It's dangerous ground, Aidan Kilcannon, but..."

"But what?"

"I really like the way you kiss."

"So keep your heart out of it and kiss me some more."

"Let me think about it," she said, giving Ruff a rub on the head. "For now, we better get back and hunker down for the dinner rush."

As they packed up, another Cessna flew over, and on the way home, while Beck leaned against her window and took a nap, he thought about that plane and his passion and place in the world.

He was still restless and lost, but he didn't feel nearly as alone as he had before Beck showed up.

Chapter Sixteen

For the next week or so, Beck's world kind of dissolved into pizza and kisses. Most of the time, simultaneously. Since they'd taken the day trip to Chestnut Creek, something had changed in this relationship, and it wasn't that she and Aidan held hands, hugged, and found ways to press up against each other and swap spit every chance they had.

Beck could feel herself slipping close to a very dangerous edge. Much more of this, and she'd end up in Aidan's bed, or him in hers. And that would be the end of everything, because once they were intimate, she'd be a goner.

So she let the fire get stoked, kept his advances to the heavy make-out kind, and managed to say goodbye at the end of every night.

But it was getting harder and harder each time.

And tonight would be no different as they worked side by side, late into a Friday, long after yet another busy night. But it was as much fun as she could ever remember, certainly in this kitchen.

Aidan hooked up a speaker to his phone, so they had music. Ruff was wandering about and getting way too many scraps. And the last of Uncle Mike's secret beer stash was being polished off by two very cozy pizza chefs.

Beck even brought her camera down, ostensibly to take pictures of each pie they made, but really to capture Aidan in all his golden glory as he bit his lip in concentration, rocked his mighty shoulders in time with the music, and rolled out perfect little test pies, each an experiment of every obscure recipe she could scare up on the Internet.

"Hold that," she said, focusing on his face and not the roll of dough he lifted to shape.

He looked right into the camera, a gleam in his wild blue eyes and a half smile teasing lips she absolutely loved to kiss. And she did. When every pizza came out, he tasted it, and then Beck tasted him, and they pronounced it…close but not good enough.

Because all this kissing and touching and laughing and wanting was good, but not good enough. That low-grade ribbon of desire tightened in her belly, making her palms damp and her heart pound. She couldn't remember an attraction so primal or a need so real.

"Oh, that one with the ground mustard seed is ready," he said, tossing the dough on the counter. "It'll make a nice picture."

She glanced in the viewing frame of her camera and admired the last shot. "This is a nice picture."

As he passed, he leaned over her shoulder and looked at it. "A man making dough? Who'd want to look at that?"

She smiled up at him. "Me."

He kissed her nose, then headed to the oven. "You're crazy."

About you. "You're photogenic." She leaned back, lifting the camera to fire off a series of shots while he slid the new peel under the little pie and produced it with a flourish.

"Hey, Beck, c'mere and smell this."

She popped off the counter and headed over, Ruff right on her heels, where he'd been pretty much nonstop since their day-trip. At least when Aidan was around. Alone, in her apartment, he was still not the loving pet she dreamed of. Maybe he was just protective, since he seemed to come close whenever Aidan did. Which was most of the time.

A whiff of sauce that was much tangier than the last batch hit her nose and got her attention.

"Oh, that's good." She sniffed again, coming closer, smiling up at Aidan and not at all surprised at the craving that seized her stomach. She didn't want pizza. She wanted him. She took one more inhale and accepted the truth: She wanted both.

The aroma of melted cheese and tangy basil wafted toward her, making her mouth water as Aidan lifted the first slice to his mouth. She watched as he bit into it, as he closed his eyes and made that sexy moan of pure delight.

She couldn't help putting her hand on his chest to add the sense of touch to this overload of pleasurable feelings. Under her fingers, his heart hammered harder than she'd expect for a man who was doing nothing more strenuous than making pizza.

When he opened his eyes, chewed, and swallowed, he stared right at her.

"You're ready, aren't you?" he whispered.

For anything. Her gaze moved from the pizza to

his mouth, and back. "I'm ready for my taste." Standing up on her tiptoes, she kissed his lips, waiting for him to tip his head, open his mouth, and share the taste as he'd done every time.

But he stayed still, his eyes open.

She dropped back down. "You're going to make me eat the pizza, aren't you?"

"I'd never make you do anything." He set the slice back on the peel and put his hands on her shoulders. "But I'd love to get you over this, Beck. I'd love to help you escape the prison of your past."

Her eyes filled unexpectedly, the tenderness almost overwhelming her. "Why would you want to do that?"

He looked surprised. "Because I care about you? Because you're Charlie's sister? Because..." He lowered his head and whispered in her ear, "I want you to kiss me for more than a taste of pizza."

"I did," she said. "I do."

"More than kiss. Like...all night."

She knew exactly what he was asking her, and chills danced over her whole body, and she nearly melted into him. "You think I won't because of my past? That you are like one big piece of pizza I can eat and forget all my old issues?"

"You could try," he teased. But his smile disappeared as he leaned back to look at her. "I'm pretty sure you're not going to get there with me until you unload some of the things that make you scared of losing people."

She drew a line with her finger under his lip. "Maybe you should be a shrink, Aidan Kilcannon."

"Maybe I should be." He turned her, easing her back to the counter to lift her up into her favorite perch. "Let me examine you," he said in a thick fake accent. "Tell ze doctor when ze last time you have good pizza experience."

She giggled at the voice.

"No laughing, or I vill make you lie on ze couch."

Which might be very nice. But she played along, sighing, closing her eyes, and taking a trip down memory lane.

"I used to eat pizza," she said. "Before my parents died. But, as I told you, being forced to move here and live my life around pizza magnifies the memory of their loss."

"But you must have one good pizza memory." The accent was gone now as he set his large hands on her thighs, holding her in place, eye-to-eye for this examination.

"Probably."

"Can you remember it? Take another whiff and try. They say the sense of smell is the strongest trigger for memories."

She followed the order, vaguely aware that she put her hands on top of his and gripped as she let herself go back. Far back. "I was six or seven, I think. Charlie was ten or eleven. It was a winter night, a weeknight, I remember, and school had already been canceled for the next day due to a snowstorm. Dad came home early from work—"

"He was a lab technician, right? At a pharmaceutical company?"

She nodded. "Yes, a chemist, actually. And my mother was a substitute teacher at my school, but mostly she was home with us." A smile tugged at her lips, as it so often did when she thought about

John and Karen Spencer. "We were the most average family in the world."

"Nothing about you is average, Beck. Or Charlie."

She tipped her head to acknowledge the compliment. "That night, Dad brought home pizza because it was all he could find, and Mom had been snowed in and couldn't get groceries for dinner. I don't know why, but it was a big deal not cooking on a school night. It was exciting. Different, you know? Oh, and he'd picked up *Toy Story* at the video store." The smile grew. "I'll never forget that. It was my first introduction to Woody and Buzz."

He chuckled at that, listening intently. But the way he looked at her gave her the confidence to continue what was probably a boring story, and one she'd never told another person, not even Jackie.

"We sat in the den and ate around the coffee table—another thing that was different and fun—and all I remember was the pizza was so good. It didn't burn my tongue, and it was gooey and great. After I finished, I stayed on the floor, with my head against my mother's legs, and she..." Her throat tightened unexpectedly, as she remembered the sensation of Mama's hands in her hair, the sound of the movie, the noisy laughter from Dad and Charlie.

All of them, *gone*. And she was only twenty-eight years old. A wave of grief rose up, unexpected and strong.

"She what?" he asked softly, reaching to stroke her cheek.

"She braided my hair," she managed to say. "And I remember having that awareness, even as a little kid, that this was the way it was supposed to be. This was security, stability, home. I don't know what to call it, but it's...emotional umami," she added with a sad smile. "The essence of something you want, but don't even know you want."

"That's probably more the reason you hate pizza than this place," he mused. "That moment is ingrained in you, and you're associating that smell with happiness, not pain. And you know you can't feel that happiness, not that particular one, with those people, ever again."

She stared at him for a long moment, letting that all sink in. "You might be right." It certainly made sense.

"Then what you need to do is replace that moment with another really good one, one that feels like..." He grinned. "Emotional umami. You should trademark that, by the way."

She searched his face and felt her whole body sink. Felt her defenses crack and her heart roll around in her chest until it practically fell into his hands. "Aidan."

"Yeah?"

"You're doing it."

"Cheap armchair psychology?"

"Breaking that promise you made."

He inched back. "I know, I know. Closed for business, Beck. I know." He rubbed his thumb along her cheekbone, making the hairs on her neck stand up and sending little bolts of chaos and desire though her chest and into her stomach. And lower. "It's like Sarah's No Dogs Allowed sign." He slid his hand down and tapped her chest. "No Aidan allowed in here."

"It's a dumb sign," she said on a laugh.

"It's killing business."

"I should throw that sign away."

"And let me in."

She held his gaze. "And then what?"

He stared at her, silent, his mind whirring by the look in his eyes, but he offered no ideas.

"I mean, I'm going back to Chicago," she whispered. "With Ruff."

His eyes shuttered, making her wonder which of those two statements bothered him more.

"And you're…"

"I'm falling for you," he admitted on a whisper. "And all that does is make me feel even more lost."

"Oh."

He stepped away suddenly, throwing a glance at the pizza on the counter. "This might have been forgotten in the past few minutes, but that pizza? I think we nailed it. We should take that one to Mike next time we go over for a taste test."

She put her hands on his shoulders and drew him back, refusing to let him change the subject. "Why does it make you feel lost?"

"Because I don't even know who I am, or what I want to do for a living. The last thing I need to do is try to drag you into my mess."

"What if I want to be dragged?"

"To bed?"

"That's where you want to drag me."

He considered that before answering. "I'm not going to lie. It's keeping me awake at night, and the showers are getting long and cold."

"So no-strings, no-suffocation, no-seriousness kind of pleasure? That's what's on the table? Can you promise that's all it would be?"

He flinched ever so slightly, almost imperceptibly, but she saw it. "No."

"Then I can't—"

"There would also be some surprisingly good mustard-seed-in-the-sauce pizza on the table."

She wasn't sure what he was offering, but she was sure of one thing—falling for Aidan scared the daylights out of her. So she clung to that and shook her head. "I'm going to pass on both," she said softly.

"Gotcha." He gave a quick smile and turned back to the pizza.

"So I did the right thing?"

"Define right." Jackie added a dry laugh. "I mean, if that picture you sent counts for anything, I might say…you're freaking crazy, Rebecca Spencer. That man is smokin'."

Beck curled deeper into the sofa, tucking the phone against her neck as she lifted a cup of warm coffee to her lips. Sunday morning phone calls with Jackie had become an unspoken part of their schedule, and today was no different.

Only, it seemed they had much more interesting things to talk about than how many clients Baby Face lost the previous week.

"Yes, he's gorgeous, but do you want me to fall head over heels in love and never come back to Chicago?"

Jackie didn't answer for a moment, and Beck suspected it wasn't because she was drinking her coffee.

"You *do* want me to come back?" Beck urged.

"I want you to be happy."

"By having a fling with Charlie's best friend?" she asked with a snort. "How is that going to make me happy?"

"He gets you, Beck. That whole analysis of your pizza problems? That's not casual."

"Well, the sex would be casual." She sipped her coffee and closed her eyes. "Not to mention amazing."

Jackie laughed. "You've made bigger mistakes."

So true. She'd never been in love, but she'd tried a time or two. Invariably, the relationship had left her far lonelier than when she started. "I'm meant to be single," she said. "But not completely. I have Ruff now."

At the mention of his name, the dog, sprawled on the other side of the sofa, lifted his head and stared at her with something she wished looked more like love. This was...tolerance.

"You won him over? Talk about burying the lead."

Beck laughed. "He doesn't like when Aidan and I kiss. He's my great protector."

"Then you don't need the copy of Charlie's letter to wave in front of Aidan in order to keep the dog? Unless you want to use it as a white flag of surrender, if you get my drift."

"Your drift is clear. No, I don't..." But maybe there was an explanation in that letter, something between the lines that she'd missed when she read it so long ago. "Yeah, send it to me with the accounts payable stuff and your last timesheet."

"I don't have many hours logged," Jackie said. "The calls have slowed since the coupon in the ad expired."

"Slowed to a halt?"

Her friend sighed. "Not going to lie. Your books are taking a hit. But you'll bounce back. You always do. Is Mike ready to come back to work?"

"Soon, I think. He's really responding to therapy and actually took Ruff for a short walk yesterday. The only person who loves that dog more than Aidan and I do is Uncle Mike. And Aunt Sarah pet him the other day. Did you hear the angels sing?"

Jackie laughed. "It sounds like everything is good over there in Bitter Bark, baby."

"Could be better if I...you know." She made a face. "Should I?"

"You'll know when the time's right, Beck. Something will click, something will change. I promise you, it will be completely obvious that you're ready."

"You're always so wise and logical." Beck sighed. "Thank you."

"Anytime, but now I gotta run to brunch. What's up for your Sunday?"

"Taste testing," she said. "Aidan and I are cooking for his family Sunday dinner today and letting them pick the best pizzas to take over to Mike. We think we might have discovered the secret ingredient."

She chuckled. "Sounds fun. Does he have any brothers?"

"Three, each better-looking than the next, but all married courtesy of their matchmaking father."

"Oh, that's right. The Dogfather. Bet he has his sights set on you and Aidan."

"Me?"

"You never thought of that?" Jackie asked.

"I don't think anyone ever thought we'd be so attracted to each other. All I think about is the next time I'm going to see him."

"Then maybe you should think about moving back there," Jackie said, all joking gone from her voice.

"Why would I do that? I spent half my life trying to get out of Bitter Bark. This town represents nothing but misery for me."

"Yeah, sounded like that night in the kitchen with the music and the kissing was miserable. And the long drive in the country. And the fun walks with the dogs. And the big family, and pizza project, and helping ol' Mike get better. So much misery."

Beck laughed softly but couldn't really argue with Jackie, who was always the voice of reason.

Chapter Seventeen

When he got to Waterford Farm that morning, Aidan poked his head into the grooming studio, checking for Darcy. He was surprised to find her with a packed house on a Sunday, up to her eyeballs in dog fur and barking hounds.

"Is this your creative way of getting out of church?" he asked as he walked into the sunny room she'd managed to turn into the girliest pet-grooming studio in the known world. It had a chandelier, for Pete's sake, along with walls the color of Pepto-Bismol, furniture that looked like it was stolen from Versailles, and fancy silk boxes overflowing with ribbons, clips, and all manner of dog décor.

The place even smelled as sweet as Darcy herself.

"Garrett begged," she said. "We finally got the famous fifteen, and they all need work."

"Oh, right. The rescues that Marie had." He hadn't seen their old family friend since his return from the Army, but Marie Boswell had been a fixture in and out of Waterford since he was a teenager, maybe younger. She'd been a friend of his mother's and was the woman who first started Annie Kilcannon on the path of dog fostering. "The dogs that were locked in a garage?"

He took a few steps farther into the studio, eyeing a skinny dog that had the ears of a basset but not much else to help identify its breed. "They're bad, Aidan," she said, all of her usual sunshine missing from her voice. "Look at this poor little lady."

The dog was flat on Darcy's worktable, eyes up and wide and sad while Darcy clipped her nails.

"What's her name?" Aidan said, coming closer to pet the sorry little thing.

"Oh Lord, Marie was in charge of naming."

He laughed. "So, if she was watching ESPN, it's probably the Yankee roster or something. Don't we have her to thank for Boris and Natasha after a Cartoon Network binge?"

Darcy smiled and switched paws, tapping her own fuchsia nails on the little dog. "Don't forget Petunia, Rosie, Lily, and Dahlia when she took a gardening class."

"So, who's this?"

"Mammy."

"Mammy?" He scowled. "What kind of name is that for a dog?"

"As good as Rhett, Ashley, Scarlett, Melanie, Carreen, Pa, Ellen, Charles, Belle, and Bonnie Blue." At his look of total confusion, she grinned. "*Gone With the Wind* repeating on cable."

He rolled his eyes and shook his head, glad to know that when they got to a forever home, they could get normal dog names. "And you're grooming them all."

"Garrett wants to get pictures and start lining up

homes for the healthy ones. A few of them need TLC, and two are with vet techs now, waiting for Molly and Dad to get back from church." She looked up at him, her blue eyes full of sadness. "How could someone stick fifteen dogs in vans with almost no food and water? What is wrong with humanity?"

He rubbed her shoulder, nodding. "You know what Liam says."

"Dogs, because people suck," she answered, knowing, as they all did, their oldest brother's favorite motto.

Aidan wandered over to one of the waiting crates to where a wretched-looking Yorkie was rolled into a corner, shaking. "Who's this?"

"Bonnie Blue, and she is."

Without asking, he flipped the latch and reached in, moaning when he felt her tiny body vibrate with fear. "Oh, baby girl. C'mere." She practically fit in his hand, still curled in a ball and terrified. "Don't worry. Darcy's going to cut your hair and make you look like a debutant's dog."

"I wish," she said. "I'll be lucky if she lets me trim her. She literally howls at the sight of scissors. I don't want to think about why."

"Oh." He stroked the dog's wee head, over and over, which made her stop quivering for about three seconds before she started up again. "A few weeks here and they'll be good as new."

"If we can find homes. It's getting harder and harder, you know." She leaned over and kissed Mammy's forehead. "Don't fret, love," she whispered. Then, to him, she said, "I hear you and Beck are the chefs du jour. That's a nice change from 'I don't wanna eat Sunday dinner.'" She imitated him with a high-pitched whine that amused and embarrassed him.

"Yeah," he said on a laugh. "It's been a good few weeks."

"Like her, do ya?"

He looked over the little ball of shaking fur at his sister. "I'm afraid I do."

"Afraid? What's to be afraid of? Other than giving Dad another W on the scorecard."

"You better hope not," he joked. "Then you'll be all he has left."

"He has himself," she fired back.

"Darcy, do you seriously want Dad to date? First of all, he's sixty."

"And handsome as hell, not to mention smart, funny, successful, and owner of a heart of pure gold."

Holding the dog carefully, he eased onto a velvet-covered sofa-like thing that had no place in a grooming studio, but somehow it fit Darcy's perfectly. "And that doesn't bother you?"

"Not at all. And it shouldn't bother you."

"But it does," he said.

"You know what I think?" she said, pointing her nail clippers at him. "I think it's Dad you have issues with."

"Dad? I don't have issues with Dad. Hell, I broke the bank and a few rules to come home at Christmas 'cause you guys said it's such a bad time for him. I'm here, aren't I?"

"Not for the past few weeks and before that, not mentally." Her pretty brows drew together, making him notice that, for once, she wore no makeup and was still perfect. "Yeah, that's your problem, Aidan. It's Dad."

"Dad." He shook his head. "You're wrong. I love Dad. He's the best. He's perfect. He's the man we all aspire to be."

"Not all of us," she quipped. "But you do come from a long line of exceptional men, and he's at the top. Maybe you don't like pressure."

He stood up, scowling at her, but careful not to squeeze the pupper. "I flew Black Hawks into war zones, kiddo. I thrive on pressure."

She shrugged. "Then you come home and you're the youngest brother again, trying to fit into a business you didn't create."

"And your point is?" He heard the edge in his voice, but didn't care. Darcy's armchair psychology wasn't as good as his had been the other night with Beck. It sucked, actually.

"My point is Dad can put a lot of undue pressure on us, even if he does it with the best of intentions. You should talk to him about that. As far as him dating? He's not interested, so you can stop fretting about it."

"I don't *fret*," he shot back. "But I don't like it."

"Why? Don't you think he deserves a love in his life?"

"He had a love in his life, Darcy."

She stepped back and eyed Mammy critically. "I think you're done, missy. Treat time!"

Mammy looked up, and her stubby tail knocked back and forth as Darcy offered a tiny strip of fake bacon. She gobbled it up in one bite.

Finally, Darcy looked up at him, her blue eyes misty. "Aidan, we all miss her, okay? It's not just you. We all had a place in our heart that belonged to no one but Annie Kilcannon. And one by one, my siblings are finding another way to fill the holes in their heart. And, like it or not, Dad deserves that hole to be filled, too."

He stared back for a long time, with a mix of affection for his wise little sister and resentment that he had that hole at all. "What about you? You've hit the big 3-0, Darc. Is there a man who'll abide by velvet chairs and glitter bombs in his life?"

"Pffft. Not for years, my friend. I'll marry after I've seen every square inch of this globe."

"I can tell you a few inches to skip."

She smiled. "Thanks. Now, give me that little bundle of cuteness and then put Mammy Jammy in the crate for me, 'kay?" When he handed the Yorkie to her, Darcy made a squeal of delight. "You calmed her down, Aidan. What a touch you have with the ladies."

He snorted softly. "The four-legged kind."

"Not working your magic on Beck?" she asked.

"Must you pry?"

"Must you make comments that require prying? Plus, you don't come over here unless you need a shoulder to cry on or a woman's opinion. Which is it?"

"Maybe I wanted to see my favorite sister."

"You do seem like you're doing better. Has it been that good to be away from all of us?"

"It's been great," he said, not even trying to deny it. "I'm sorry."

"For what? Enjoying your time? I don't take it personally that you don't want to be at Waterford. Dad's another story, though. He takes it *very* personally."

He sighed and picked up the end of a crystal-encrusted leash. "Kill me if I ever put this on a dog."

"That's Kookie's. Hands off." She picked up a tiny silk handkerchief and carefully tied it around Bonnie Blue's head, covering her eyes. "Okay, Bon-bon. You pretend you're that horse in the movie you were named after who didn't want to run past fire."

The trick worked, calming the dog while Darcy clicked and clipped and brown hair fell like autumn leaves around the little dog. Then something caught his eye in the window behind her.

"Well, look at that," Aidan said, stepping closer. "Is that Beck taking pictures?"

"Oh, yeah, she's been at it for a little while. That's Scarlett and Rhett. Didn't they clean up nice?"

He barely glanced at the two dogs Garrett had on leashes, or Ruff powering around the pen like a lunatic. His attention was riveted on the woman working the camera. Her dark hair loose, she wore jeans and a flowy yellow top that fluttered in the breeze. He couldn't hear her, but when she moved the camera and threw her head back, he knew exactly what that laugh sounded like.

"Take Mammy out there for me, Aidan. She's ready for her close-up. And tell them I'll have Bonnie Blue ready in about twenty minutes."

He got up to retrieve another leash—not sparkly—and open the crate door to get Mammy. As he did, he threw a look at his sister.

"I'd say thanks for the talk, but I'm not sure I wanted to hear it from my little sister."

She smiled at him. "Out of the mouths of babes..." She nodded toward the window. "And speaking of babes, I think yours is looking around for you. Go get 'er, tiger."

He laughed and led Mammy outside, where Beck was bathed in sunshine and laughter. And all Aidan wanted was to bathe in both with her.

Beck crouched down as far as she could without falling on the grass, waiting for that split second when her lens would capture emotion in the eyes of her subject. "C'mon, baby. Come on. One look. One—oh, that's good."

She snapped, then gave in to gravity and let her backside hit the ground, laughing when the bug-eyed pug named Rhett lumbered over to sniff her. She held the camera over her head to give him some love and praise.

"That's a great shot."

At the sound of Aidan's voice and the sight of Ruff bounding over to greet him, she looked up to find him bent over and sneaking a look at her image screen.

"Thank you." She reached her free hand up, and he took it, gently pulling her to her feet. "Garrett hit me up for some pictures as soon as I got here."

He didn't answer right away, looking intensely at her, a quizzical expression she couldn't interpret on his face.

"Is that okay?" she asked.

"Is this?" He leaned closer and stole a peck of a kiss. "I missed you."

Butterflies fluttered in her stomach as she whispered back, "Same."

They'd spent most of yesterday together at Slice, except for a quick trip she'd made to pick up Ruff from Uncle Mike. Lunch and dinner had been as busy as she could ever remember, and they'd said good night after cleaning the kitchen and making plans to meet here today.

And she'd thought about him every waking moment since then. In fact *missed him* was an understatement.

"It's more than okay," he said, but she wasn't sure if he meant taking pictures or missing him. "These dogs need homes."

"Fifteen, Aidan." She shook her head in disbelief.

"That's a lot in one day, even for Waterford."

"And the way they were treated." Her shoulders dropped as she thought of what Garrett had described to her. "One was in the trunk of a car. I can't stand how wrong that is."

"Marie Boswell, our friend who deals with rescues all over the state, is part of a forensics team that works to bring people like this piece of crap to justice. And after a few weeks at Waterford, the dogs will be strong and healthy."

She smiled. "You sound as optimistic as I do."

"I guess it's contagious." He couldn't help it. Still holding her hand, he brought it to his lips for another kiss. It was like he couldn't stop himself, and she knew exactly how that felt. "You want to start the pizza or continue taking pictures of the dogs?"

"Are we in a rush? I'd love to take pictures and meet all of the Fabulous Fifteen."

He laughed at the nickname and nodded toward his brother, walking in their direction with the cutest yellow dog with ears that stood straight up like triangular antennas with a bright red bow between them. "Look at that Pommie. Insane."

"That's a Pomeranian?" she guessed.

"More or less. And she has Darcy's fingerprints all over the grooming job."

"Scarlett's kind of wild," Garrett said as he reached them, holding tight to a squiggling dog. "Not sure I can get her to settle down long enough to pose."

"I don't need a pose, just an expression." Beck reached over and playfully flicked one of the stand-up ears. "You are a cutie, know that, Miss Scarlett?"

The dog barked once, sharp and loud.

"Take her, Aidan," Garrett said, handing over the furry package. "I'll get the other one back in and go round up a few more. And then hit Dad up for a huge Waterford investment."

Aidan drew back. "You want to build more kennels to house them all?"

"I want to buy plane tickets to get at least some of them to families who've been wanting rescues from us but aren't in state." Garrett clipped a leash on little Rhett at the same time that he slipped a treat into the dog's mouth. "Come on, Red. Even though you're brown."

"Rhett," Beck corrected. "As in Rhett Butler, handsome hero of *Gone With the Wind*."

Garrett rolled his eyes. "Marie's whack. But right now, I don't care what we call these dogs. If you make them look appealing and we get them healthy, maybe those families will be willing to pony up the cost of picking them up. Good luck with Scarlett."

Aidan put the squirmy dog down, and she instantly

took off, making it a good ten feet before he caught up with a few long strides. Knowing from experience with babies that the window of opportunity could open and close in a split second, she raised her camera and watched him through the viewfinder, making a quick adjustment to the f-stop to control the depth of field.

He got his arms around her little body and hoisted her up, turning and stopping and giving her a glorious shot. But she was pretty sure the potential adoptive parents wouldn't want Aidan in their picture. Although...who wouldn't?

He looked as golden as the Pommie in his arms, a lock of hair over his face, his smile as natural and wide as she could remember, his heavenly body moving like a man in complete sync with his environment.

She took another shot, and another.

"You do belong here," she whispered as he came closer. "You look more at home at Waterford than anywhere else."

A flicker of surprise glinted in his eyes. "Because I can catch a dog?"

She turned the camera to him to show him the last shot. "That's the face of a happy man."

"'Cause you're here," he shot back.

She gave him a sly smile. "Hold the dog as still as you can and lean away. I can change the background and photoshop you out."

"Ouch. So easily wiped out of your life."

"Just the picture. Come on, now. We can do this. It's exactly like shooting a baby. They can't follow directions, so you have to work to get that millisecond of emotion in their expression. Like...that." She snapped a few when Scarlett stopped moving. "In fact, hold her like a baby. And crouch down, then lean back."

He did, flipping the dog in his arms with the ease of someone completely familiar with them. Beck stood over him and focused on Scarlett's precious face. "There we go, little girl," she cooed. "Look at me. Look at me. Look..." She centered the shot and took three in rapid-fire succession that were all gorgeous. "Sorry if you don't agree, but I think you're right where you belong. You just haven't figured that out yet."

He squinted up at her, but she didn't look at him, too intent on getting Scarlett's attention again. "For some reason, I like this place better after I've been gone for a while. Too much of a steady diet makes me uncomfortable, but yeah, I love the dogs. I love the concept. But I don't—"

"That's it!" She got the perfect shot and lowered her camera, easing herself down to his level to look at him. "You know, when I was first brought to Bitter Bark, I felt a lot of the same way. I loved my aunt and uncle, I appreciated that they made a home for us, and I could see that it was the greatest little town. But I didn't belong here, not at all. So I squirmed until I got to Chicago, and then I made my own way. I found my passion, built a life, and figured out a way to belong. What could you do here that would make you feel that way and allow you to come and go frequently enough that you didn't feel suffocated?"

"Fly."

She inched back.

"That's when I feel free. When I'm airborne."

She looked hard at him. "Then get yourself a plane and…" She reached over to rub Scarlett's head. "Fly these dogs to their homes."

She actually heard him take in a soft breath, then he blinked at her. "Rebecca Spencer. I could kiss you."

She smiled. "Don't let one little Pommie in your arms stop you."

He leaned close and put his mouth on hers, and instantly Ruff barked from a few feet away, tearing over to slam a paw between them. That sent little Scarlett into a frenzy of squirming and barking. And then out came a big black-and-white dog tearing across the grass like a kid who'd been told it was his turn to pose for the camera and he couldn't wait.

They just laughed and shared a look that said, *Later*. But before it was gone, Beck took one more picture of Aidan in case she ever needed to remind him of what a man who belonged where he was actually looked like.

Chapter Eighteen

he fifteen rescues took up everyone's attention that Sunday. Dad and Molly were in full vet mode, with help from Liam who was bringing dogs back and forth from the kennels for individual physical exams. Darcy finished grooming the last of them while Shane, Garrett, and Trace exercised and fed the healthier ones. The kids, Pru and Christian, helped clean and prepare kennels by doubling up some of the current residents. Through it all, Andi rocked on the porch with a belly so distended she could barely stand, and Jessie and Chloe flitted in and out of the kitchen, refilling cold drinks for everyone.

That left Gramma Finnie as an audience of one for Aidan and Beck's pizza making that would feed the hungry troops. She made herself comfy at the kitchen table, her laptop open in front of her, chatting easily with Beck, who was making a more elaborate salad than they normally served at Slice.

Aidan only half listened to their conversation as Gramma told Beck about her background and life. He'd heard the stories a million times, and his head buzzed with a whole new set of vibrations that felt an awful lot like…possibilities.

Beck was a genius. Why hadn't he thought of it? Garrett had mentioned flying rescues in and out of Waterford years ago, long before Aidan ever seriously considered getting out of the Army, but it hadn't been brought up again in the time he'd been home.

He'd need a plane, that was all. Which would take a loan, possibly from Dad, or maybe an investment from the business. There wasn't much money in the rescue end of the business, but there was heart. And that's what Dad had in spades.

Eager for his father to come back and essentially finished with all the prep they could do before actually getting the pizzas in the ovens, Aidan grabbed a Bloody Mary refill and slid into the bench side of the kitchen table next to Beck.

"Don't worry, I'll eat it," she was saying to Gramma Finnie, who'd remarked on the size of the salad. "Man cannot live by pizza alone," she teased, making his grandmother's old blue eyes light up and her fingers move.

"I can use that for tomorrow's blog. I like each entry to start off with a proverb or quote, and I'm running out."

"I can help you there," Beck said. "My mom was a big 'sayings' person. She liked them on pillows and mugs and hanging on the wall."

"I love her already," Gramma chimed in, making them laugh. "What was her name?"

"Karen. Karen Fitzgerald Spencer."

Gramma Finnie actually gasped. "Fitzgerald? Oh my saints above, lassie. Ye from the same part o' Ireland."

Beck laughed lightly. "Many, many generations ago, Gramma Finnie. Not like you. I'm afraid the history is lost and I don't know where those Fitzgeralds are from."

"Well, I can tell ye. There were Fitzgeralds in County Kilkenny, where my family was for hundreds of years. And another clan right over in Cork, with Waterford between the two of us." She beamed. "It's like we're already related, lassie."

Beck smiled right back, maybe not catching the *already* part that the sneaky old lady slipped in with Gaelic flair. If she did notice, she laughed it off, as bright as the sunshine through the window accentuating the gold in her eyes and in her hair.

Oh, Kil. You've got it so damn bad.

The problem was, Aidan didn't care.

"Maybe we are related," Beck quipped. "I certainly feel at home around this family."

"Ah, that's the Kilcannon magic," Gramma Finnie said. "Now, tell me about your mother, lass. What was her favorite saying?"

Beck didn't hesitate. "'Turn your face to the sun, and you won't see the shadows.'"

"Oooh." Gramma Finnie drew out the response, her voice actually cracking with delight. "That's a good one." She pointed her ancient fingers over her not-ancient keyboard and gave Beck a questioning look. "May I use it?"

"Of course," she agreed. "I have tons more in my memory banks."

"I want them all," Gramma Finnie said with a playful, greedy laugh. "Tell me, but not too fast. These old fingers don't type as quickly as they cross-stitch." She looked over the laptop at Beck. "Which I do quite well, but it's so low tech."

"Okay, let me think." Beck closed her eyes for a second, unlocking her memory, but Gramma Finnie used the moment to jab Aidan's shoulder.

I love her! she mouthed, raising her brow with a very obvious question. When he stared at her, her eyes widened in a silent demand.

He lifted a shoulder and gave a slight nod. Did that count for *like* and not *love*?

He couldn't communicate more, because Beck's eyes popped open. "She liked to say, 'The happiest people don't have the best of everything, they make the best of everything.'"

Gramma Finnie fell back against her chair. "Oh yes. We're related. I bet if I go through my Ancestry.com files, I'd find a Kilcannon or a Brennan—that's my maiden name—married to a Fitzgerald. In fact..." She started clicking away at the keyboard. "I seem to recall—"

"Um, you guys?" Andi opened the kitchen door and held the doorjamb, looking from one to the other with eyes that were uncharacteristically wild.

"Are you okay, lassie?" Gramma was up with a speed that belied her years.

"Maybe. I think so. No. Oh my God, my water broke."

They were all up, then, instantly coming to hold her and guide her to the closest chair. She clung to Gramma Finnie the most, as all the women in this family did, half laughing and half moaning with anticipation or fear or whatever women felt when they were about to give birth. "I need..."

"Liam," Aidan finished for her. "I'll get him."

He didn't wait for a response, tearing out of the kitchen door, across the drive, around the pen, bolting into the kennels, ignoring Darcy as she rushed closer holding a dog, all the while calling his brother's name.

"What's up?" Shane shot out from around the curve.

"Is everything okay?" Garrett popped into view, holding one of the new dogs.

"He's in the vet office with Molly and Dad," Chloe said, coming into view next to Shane. "Is it Andi?" she guessed.

He nodded, turning to go back out. "Water broke," he called on his way.

He could practically hear the stampede behind him. They all tore across the path toward the vet building. His brothers nearly caught up with him, but Chloe and Jessie broke off to go see to Andi, who by best calculations was on the early side for delivery.

He thrust open the door and powered through the tiny waiting area, pushing the door to the back exam rooms. "Liam!"

The big guy was out in the hall in a second. "Is it Andi?" he asked.

Before Aidan could answer, Dad and Molly showed up through another door, in scrubs. And behind him, the cavalcade of Kilcannons practically mowed Aidan over. For one split second, they all stood in the hallway in silent shock.

"Her water broke." At least three people, including Aidan, said it at the same time.

"Holy..." Liam turned from one side to the other, blood draining from his face. "She's early."

"It's okay," Molly assured him. "Two weeks."

"Babies come early all the time," Dad said, giving him a nudge. "And if it goes too fast, we can handle it, right, Molls?"

Molly shot Dad her best *you've got to be kidding me* look, but it wasn't nearly as vile as the one he got from Liam.

"My child isn't going to be born in a vet hospital."

"There are worse places," Shane cracked.

"Like in the kitchen, if you don't get her to a hospital," Trace added.

Liam held his hands up, then dropped them, his chest heaving. "Yeah, yeah. I gotta go. I gotta drive. I can't drive."

"I'll drive," Garrett said.

"I'll follow," Darcy promised.

"Molly and I are in minor surgery, but then we'll be right behind."

Liam started to bolt, then stopped, frozen. He looked from one face to another, his dark eyes crazed, his face pale, his mouth actually quivering. "I'm having a baby."

"Technically, your wife is." Shane gave him a tug. "And if you don't want Gramma Finnie pulling that child into this world, *move*."

Liam nodded again and again, making them all fight smiles. "I'm having…" He turned to Dad. "Does it always feel like this?"

And Dad, the old softie, was already in tears. "Every time, Son. Every single time."

Liam let out a hoot and headed off, leaving them all in his dust once he finally got his act together. There was one more beat of silence, then it all broke loose. The hollering, high fives, laughter, and plans of who'd go where and who'd stay with Christian and how they'd all pull together to support Liam and Andi as they started their family.

When it died down, Aidan's adrenaline dump was replaced by something he hadn't felt in a long, long time. A bone-deep, rock-solid, impossible-to-deny love for this clan and their ability to rally around each other with the precision and focus of a finely tuned military unit. For the first time since he'd left his comrades-in-arms behind in Kabul, he felt grounded.

And a little bit jealous of Liam.

Despite the chaos of the rescues and excitement of a new baby, the family certainly didn't lose its appetite, Beck noted. Once Andi was officially admitted to Vestal Valley General Hospital for delivery, everyone agreed the taste test should continue at least for those who stayed behind.

They'd divided into shifts, and right now, Dr. Kilcannon, Darcy, Garrett, Jessie, Shane, and Chloe were at the hospital, sending home reports, mostly of how nervous Liam was and how well Andi was doing.

Christian had already been well prepared that he would not be at the hospital when his brother or sister was born, but the arrival of all the new dogs and the constant love and attention from his family kept him in great spirits. He did stay close to Gramma Finnie, Beck noticed, who was clearly one of the solid rocks of this family.

As Aidan pulled the second pizza from the oven to oohs and aahs, Beck explained to the group gathered around the kitchen counter how they were working to find a secret ingredient, but nothing her uncle had tasted so far met his very high bar.

"This smells so good," Molly said. "Maybe you've invented your own secret recipe."

"But you're missing pineapples," Pru said, up on her tiptoes to check out the toppings. "We like pineapples, don't we, Trace?"

"The only way to eat pizza," he agreed.

Beck caught the quick, shared smile between the teenage girl and her father, their affection for each other palpable even to a stranger. Aidan had told Beck the story of how Molly had raised Pru alone for thirteen years before a man, recently out of prison, showed up at Waterford Farm looking for help for a sick dog. Not just any man, Aidan told her, but Pru's father, long thought to be dead. Once again, Daniel Kilcannon was credited with pulling the strings to make that romance happen.

"No pineapple," Beck said. "But we have Version A and Version B, and we want you to taste each and pick your favorite."

"Is it a battle?" Molly asked.

"And if it is, I hope you weren't so obvious as to make A for Aidan and B for Beck," Pru teased.

"And C for Christian!" The little boy came zooming in, ready to grab a slice, but Aidan adeptly snagged his hand before he touched the steaming pizza.

"Why don't you wash these things?" he suggested, turning the little fingers over for an examination. "While we set up for dinner in the kitchen."

"Sunday dinner in the kitchen?" Christian looked horrified and thrilled at the same time. "Grandpa wouldn't like that."

"Grandpa's not here." Gramma Finnie moved in to guide the little man to the sink. "Let's wash up, laddie, and eat wherever we want tonight."

The screen door opened as Christian let out a wail of "Yay!" but his expression changed as he saw Shane and Chloe enter. "Is there a baby yet?" he demanded, dinner forgotten.

"Not for a few hours at best," Chloe told him, wrapping the child in a hug and planting reassuring kisses on his cheeks. "But your mama told me to tell you she loves you *sooooo* much."

"At this rate, she may finish those last two weeks in labor," Shane said softly to the adults. "Apparently, nothing moves fast except our family in a crisis."

And they sure did that, Beck mused.

"You're just in time to eat," Aidan said, greeting his brother with a man hug and pat on the shoulder, one of the warmest exchanges Beck had ever noticed between the two.

Was it the pending birth? The pizza? The day of new dogs and life-changing ideas? Something had Aidan very chill, very happy, and very…settled today.

When he stepped away from Shane, Aidan caught her looking at him and gave the quickest wink, which did crazy, stupid things like curl her toes and make the hair on her neck dance.

Maybe it was…*her.*

Shane came over to the counter to examine the pizza and inhale noisily. "Bro, you are gifted."

"One of these is Beck's."

"Then you're an awesome team. And I am so hungry, I do not know what the rest of you are going to eat."

"There are two more in the oven," Beck assured him.

"We can't all fit at the kitchen table," Christian said, calling over all of them from the other side of the room. "So I have the best idea ever in the world."

"Three...two...one," Shane whispered.

"Mario Kart," Trace, Molly, Pru, and Aidan all said quietly at exactly the same time.

"Mario Kart!" Christian yelled, cracking them all up.

Still laughing, they all took off to set up in the family room and left Aidan and Beck to cut and serve the pizzas.

"I've never seen anything like it," Beck said, watching as they streamed from one room to the next, leaving a wake of laughter and love.

"What I can't believe is that kid used to be shy, at least to hear Andi tell it. Now, he's the loudest one in the bunch." He concentrated on making perfect slices with the pizza cutter.

"Because he's so comfortable here." She sighed like a kid at Christmas. "This place is wonderful."

He smiled, his gaze on her as he came closer and put his hands on her cheeks. "And it's all better with you." He kissed her forehead, then her nose, then stole a kiss on her mouth that tasted as sweet as the exchange. "Andi's baby had bad timing, though," he added.

"Ruined our pizza party?"

"Ruined my chance to talk to Dad." He inched back and added some tender pressure, his fingers grazing the nape of her neck in a way that made her feel breathless. "About the plane."

"You like that idea?"

"Mmm." He smiled. "I do. I like that idea a lot."

"Aidan!" She wrapped her arms around his waist and gave a squeeze. "That's awesome."

"So are you." He kissed her again. "I'm starting to think *you* are the secret ingredient."

The compliment warmed her right down to her toes.

"We're hungry out here!"

"Mario's ready to race!"

"Bring the 'za or get a room." That was Shane, in the doorway, who might have been standing there the whole time. Who knew? Not Beck, and she didn't care. She couldn't remember the last time she'd felt so...at home.

They delivered the pizzas to more showers of compliments, but it was Chloe who practically jumped out of her seat on the first bite.

"You guys could win for sure. This pizza is that good!"

"Win what?" they asked in unison.

"Best of Bitter Bark. It's coming up in three weeks, you know."

Aidan and Beck looked at each other, silent.

"You didn't know," Shane presumed.

"We're living in a pizza bubble," Aidan shot back. "We could win," he whispered to Beck. "For Slice of Heaven. Number twenty-five."

"Only if Uncle Mike actually makes the pizza," she said. "He wins the awards, not the restaurant. We could win, but it would be number one for you or me."

She turned to the group. "Which is better? A or B?"

All of them threw different answers, including Christian, who offered up a cheesy mouthful of "C!" and fell onto the floor, giggling.

"Doesn't matter," Trace said, holding up a slice. "They're both the best pizza I've ever had."

"And because it's the Best of *Better* Bark this year," Chloe added, "I managed to attract a dog-loving producer from Food Network who's enamored of our town's tourism campaign."

Shane gave her a look. "Pretty sure that guy's enamored with our town tourism director."

She flicked off her husband's tease. "He told me on Friday that he's going to include two of the restaurant winners in the *Best Kept Secrets* show they're doing on North Carolina small-town restaurants. Linda May is killing herself to win the Best in Baked Goods. You guys have to get pizza. Ricardo's is the only real competition. And maybe that new guy who opened a delivery business. There's no one else who can compete."

Beck stared at her, the words floating around, almost making no sense. "Food Network is coming to Bitter Bark?"

"*Better* Bark." At least three people, none of them Chloe, corrected for her.

"They sure are. And you better believe if Slice of Heaven wins, I'll get that producer to feature the restaurant on the show."

"That'd send sales through the roof," Molly said.

"I watch that show every week." Gramma Finnie scooted closer on the sofa and put a hand on Beck's leg. "They do like the history, lass. If your uncle is a twenty-five-time winner, that host will gobble him *and* the pizza up. And you'll have a line out the door for a year."

Beck fell back against the sofa, speechless.

But no one else was. The room exploded with ideas, suggestions, and words of support.

"Plus, it's Aidan," Molly said, beaming at her brother. "I've never seen you fail at anything you put your mind to."

"Thanks, Moll." He held a slice of pizza up in a mock toast. "To *Best Kept Secrets.* I hope we found one."

While they ate and Beck settled onto the sofa and picked at a salad, she couldn't think about anything but Uncle Mike and not only getting him to taste the pizzas and pick one, but also convincing him to come back and make the pizza so he could win.

Could he do that in three weeks? Enough time in this house, and Beck was beginning to think anything was possible.

Next to her, Gramma Finnie patted her leg. "I do think ye could win, lass," she whispered under the ruckus of the racing game.

"I hope so."

"You know what they say about hope," she said.

Beck drew back. "Hold On, Pain Ends?" she guessed, pulling out the old acronym her mother used to use when Beck had a boo-boo.

"Walk with hope in your heart, and ye never walk alone."

Wow. She tried to smile and react normally to that, but a flutter in her chest took her breath away. It was exactly what Mama would have said. Exactly. It wasn't the sentiment or silly saying that got her, it was the...familiarity.

Slowly, Beck put her salad bowl on the table, eyeing the remaining slices of pizza on a tray. But a shout at the TV stole her attention, as Trace nearly beat Pru on the animated racing course, but she slid ahead of him at the last second.

"Mr. Bancroft!" Pru yelled. "You let me win!"

"Umproo," he fired back, making everyone laugh at a joke Beck didn't get. "You won fair and square."

Gramma Finnie leaned forward. "There are a lot of inside jokes in this family, lass."

"I noticed."

"If you stick around long enough, you'll make a few." She put her arm around Beck, somehow the most natural move in the world, fluttering a few strands of her hair. "I'd like that," Gramma added softly.

"I'd like that, too," she whispered back, closing her eyes as crooked, aging fingers slid through her hair tenderly.

And just like that, this old woman's touch sent Beck back a few decades, a hundred miles, and a lifetime into the past.

"You should try your pizza," Gramma Finnie whispered. "The one you made is better."

"You think?"

"I know."

Beck swallowed and let the sensations of the moment roll over her. A tender older woman. A happy, solid family. The smell of food, the sound of laughter, the knowledge that everything, in that moment, was secure.

"I think I will." She leaned forward, slid a slice onto a napkin, and brought it to her lips, completing the memory with the first bite.

It was so delicious she had to close her eyes to fully appreciate it. When she opened them, she glanced to her left and caught Aidan looking at her. They held each other's gaze, not needing to speak a word, but both of them sharing a moment as intimate as any kiss they'd exchanged. He knew. He understood. He got what this meant to her.

She could have stayed in that place forever, except Shane jumped up and thrust his cell phone in the air and yelled, "It's a girl!"

And then there was nothing but Kilcannon chaos, which tasted almost as good as the pizza.

Chapter Nineteen

Aidan followed Beck home even though they'd kissed good night in the Waterford Farm drive at ten o'clock on Sunday night. A slow drizzle had increased to a heavy rain, and that was all the excuse he needed to make sure she got home okay.

He slipped into his usual parking spot on the street, hustling around to the back of the building, where she parked, to meet her before she even got out of her car with Ruff. She didn't seem the least bit surprised as she turned off the ignition and opened the door, but Ruff barked mightily in greeting.

"It's raining," he said, as if that explained his decision.

"And I ate pizza." She slipped out of the car and stood, wrapping her arms around him, not caring that the rain splattered all over her. "So we should celebrate."

"With more pizza?" he suggested, already knowing that was not what either one of them had in mind.

"With more...this." She tilted her head back, inviting a kiss that he wanted to take, but he had to look at her instead. The rain dribbling down her cheeks could easily be mistaken for tears, but he knew better. This was not an unhappy woman. This was joy. Pure joy, and he was holding it in his arms.

"How long do I have to wait?" she asked without opening her eyes.

"Long enough for me to memorize the way you look right now, all wet from rain and lit by the moon and streetlamp."

That made her smile. Laugh, even, but she didn't open her eyes or change her position or speak.

"Long enough for me to brace myself for how hard it's going to hit me when I kiss you, and how much I am not going to want to stop."

"Mmm." The little moan was her only response, but it told him she felt exactly the same way.

"Long enough for me to tell you that I can't remember the last time I felt that good at Waterford Farm. And it's all because you were there."

Finally, she opened her eyes. "Really?"

"Really."

"I felt the same way. I mean, at home and at peace and secure. It's been a long, long time since I felt that way, or..." She bit her lip, as if trying to stop herself from what she was about to say.

"Or..."

"It's been a long, long time since I've felt this way about anyone," she admitted on a whisper. "I don't know what your secret ingredient is, Aidan Kilcannon, but I can't seem to get enough."

A raindrop hit her nose, and he kissed it off, then moved to her lips. "Same," he murmured. As he intensified the kiss, Ruff started to bark ferociously.

"Oh no you don't, buddy. Not this time." He

grabbed hold of the dog's collar with one hand and guided him out of the car. "Can we go inside, Beck?"

Silent, she took his hand and led the way.

The hallway was dark, but she didn't put on a light. The minute they stepped inside, she turned, embracing him again and taking another kiss. Ruff's barks echoed in the tiny space, loud enough to cover up their noisy heartbeats and already ragged breaths.

Each kiss grew hotter, deeper, and more desperate. They managed to get up the back stairs, fish out keys, unlock, and slide inside, but there, all he could do was lean her against the closed door and move his hands everywhere.

She did the same, hungry and greedy to touch him.

Ruff circled, barked, and finally accepted that he was being ignored, the room finally quiet except for their soft groans and the occasional sweet whimper from Beck's throat.

"We're sliding to the floor," he murmured into the kiss.

"Really? Feels more like floating on air to me."

Yeah, that, too. "If we go in your room, Ruff can't see us."

"You think he cares?"

"I think he'll eat my face off if I try to undress you."

"Then I better do it for you." She slipped away from him, tugging him along by the hand. "He should sleep on the sofa if we're quiet."

"Or bark outside the door if we're not."

Laughing, she brought him inside her bedroom and closed the door firmly. The room was dim, lit only by a yellowish cast from the ridiculous Christmas lights they never took out of the trees in Bushrod Square.

But it was enough for him to see the dresser, a rocker, and the bed. Enough for him to see the promise in Beck's eyes. Enough for him to drink in the sight of her gorgeous body as she backed away and gathered the hem of her T-shirt in loose fists.

"Undress, did you say?"

He tried to swallow, but his throat was bone-dry, and his head got light as blood rushed out of it to be put to better use than thinking. "Beck."

She lifted a brow in question.

"Let me." He took a few steps closer. "I haven't thought about much else since I met you."

"Not pizza?"

"Pizza's just a way to be around you." He hadn't realized how true that was until he said it. But from the first, his desire to be in that kitchen was grounded in his desire to be with this woman. Not Ruff. Not away from Waterford. *Her.*

"Then…" She looked up at him, arching slightly into his body to invite more under-the-shirt exploration. "I love pizza."

"That didn't take long." He laughed, but it disappeared into the first real kiss in this room, and then everything melted away. Everything.

Her top and little white sneakers. His shirt and far too heavy boots. Her silky bra came off with one easy snap as he laid her on the bed, trailing kisses while she fumbled with his shirt buttons.

But more than clothes disappeared. It was like he could feel walls tumbling down, brick by brick. Old hurts and new problems. Deep wounds and surface cuts. Everything smoothed out until it was as silky as the skin on her belly, warm and feminine under his lips. He unzipped her jeans and helped her tug them off, snagging his wallet and a condom he'd been optimistically carrying for weeks, then kicked off his khakis.

And finally, almost completely undressed, they lay all the way down, breathing like a couple of racehorses in anticipation of the starting bell. It was time. This was it.

She splayed her hand on his chest, circling her palm as blood thrummed through his body, making him ache with need. He traced a line with his fingers over her hips, sliding into the lace strap of an itty-bitty thong he could rip if he wasn't careful.

And finally, they kissed again. Once, gently. He held back, wanting to relish every moment, every sensation. Wanting to be sure she was ready. He was, of course. Hard and certain and as ready as a man could be. But this was Beck, not some hookup, not some easy, feel-good, meaningless fling.

This was not meaningless. They were forever connected by Charlie. By Ruff. And now, by this.

"You having second thoughts?" she whispered, searching his face with her eyes and her fingertips.

"I'm having first thoughts," he admitted.

"What's that?"

"The first time I realize just how much you mean to me."

"That's what this is for, right?" She kissed him on the lips. "To show me how much. And let me show you."

He sank into that kiss, then, openmouthed and fully ready to give himself like he never had before. He wanted to be completely lost in Beck, so far gone that he couldn't think or see or feel anything but her.

With one move, he did away with her panties, and she dragged his briefs out of her way. Her touch was sure, hot, and insanely good.

"Show me, Aidan," she whispered in his ear. "Show me what it means."

Nothing had ever been easier. Sex was effortless, glossy, sweet, and slow. They fit perfectly, no matter how many times they rolled around, assumed new positions, and laughed, kissed, touched, and connected at the deepest level.

When her nails dug in and her pleas grew desperate, when his body clutched and refused to obey his mind, and when they were both absolutely at the peak of pleasure, everything else disappeared except the two of them and the pure pleasure they gave each other.

As Aidan moved and Beck rocked and they both fell into complete release, Aidan reveled in those long, drawn-out, crazy seconds of being totally and utterly lost.

Except, when Beck collapsed on him, soaked and spent, Aidan wrapped his arms around her and realized he wasn't lost at all.

He just got found.

The bed rumbled. Low, loud, like a freight train coming to life and vibrating, then whistling as it flew right by Beck's ear. Her eyes popped open in shock, and she stared at her wall, then blinked to full alertness when the train backed up, roared again, and blew so hard she felt the bed vibrate.

Aidan snored that loud?

Shame, because everything else he did in bed was beyond perfection.

She slowly turned and came face-to-face with Ruff, on his back, paws up, snoring like a bear in hibernation.

She bit back a laugh at the hilarious sight, feeling relief the snoring wasn't Aidan's. Then surprise, because Ruff had never shown any interest in sleeping in her room, let alone in her bed. But mostly, a contentment so rich and deep she couldn't quite give it a name rolled over her so thoroughly that she let her head fall back on the pillow with a soft thud.

The three of them in a bed was pure magic.

On the other pillow, a honey-blond head moved, and then two beautiful blue eyes opened and pinned her with a look.

"We have company," she said.

"I let him in," he admitted. "He was crying."

"You're a pushover."

He slid a hand over Ruff's head and threaded his fingers in her tangled hair. "You were sound asleep, or you'd have done the same thing."

"Someone tired me out."

He smiled. "I need to hold you." He rubbed Ruff's belly, which woke him and made him automatically roll over. Then, Aidan gave him a gentle nudge toward the bottom of the bed. "Out of the way, Beasto. I want my woman."

Something stretched in her chest, a dangerous, delicious pull of pure pleasure at the very idea of being *his woman*. No such stretching for Ruff, though. He repositioned, claiming his space with a yawn that put every inch of a five-inch tongue on display, then let his head plop right back down again.

"Maybe this was Charlie's plan," Aidan muttered. "He didn't care who got the dog, only that he did the job of getting between us."

"Almost worked," Beck said on a laugh.

Aidan sat up, got both arms around Ruff, and gently shoved his big body downward, instantly taking his place and wrapping himself around Beck. "That's better."

Ruff jumped off the bed and gave a shake, ambling out of the room, no doubt searching for food.

"I have to take him out," she said, but even as she spoke, she knew that would be impossible. Because right this minute, a strong man with talented hands and a sexy body was holding her so securely, she knew poor Ruff would have to wait at least a few more minutes.

Aidan kissed her head and slid his bare leg around hers. "Tell me what changed, Beck. What pushed you over the edge?"

She blinked in surprise at the question, then smiled. "Honestly? I think I knew I wanted to sleep with you the minute I laid eyes on you," she admitted. "First, I wanted to kiss you, and I thought that would be enough." She touched his lips. "But of course, it wasn't. Then I got to know you and watch you work and see you with Ruff. And then, last night, with your family around, I saw a man I like a lot. And you're sexy. So sexy." She laughed. "Maybe I should have led with that. What about you?"

He stifled a laugh. "I meant what made you finally eat pizza."

"Oh!" Her jaw dropped, and she playfully punched his arm. "And you let me do that whole speech?"

"It was too good to interrupt." He kissed her nose.

"It was Gramma," she said, thinking about the real question. "She made me feel secure enough to try it."

"So I can't take any credit?"

She stroked his arm and shoulder, loving the cuts of each muscle and the warmth of his skin. "You get credit for taking me into your family and letting me feel things I forgot and...long for."

He squeezed her lightly. "You make me feel things I forgot and long for, too."

"Then we're good for each other." She pressed a kiss on that shoulder, because it was so strong and felt so good. Then she looked up at him. "What put you over the edge?"

"I can pinpoint the moment when I started to...think about you as more than a rival for Ruff. It was when you didn't freak out about the paint. Hated that you were taking him, but admired your attitude."

"Moments after you called me weak," she reminded him.

"Man, I got that all wrong." He cuddled her closer, not forcing anything, letting a slow morning heat build. "You're strong and sexy and sweet, all in one." He rocked her against him, taking her breath away. "Let's go see Mike today."

She choked a soft laugh at that. "You press your whole hard body against me and suggest we see Mike? So romantic."

Inching back, he looked at her. "If I were romantic, I would not have suggested that."

"Not sure I'm following your logic."

"If I were romantic, I would never want you to leave Bitter Bark. Helping Mike win that contest and get on

TV will catapult sales, then Slice will be back on its feet and so will its original owner, then you will fly back to your life in Chicago to take pictures of babies and have brunch with friends and..." He narrowed his eyes. "Oh, please tell me you don't have a boyfriend."

"Little late to ask, hon. No, I don't."

"But you will, especially now that you've come to terms with your past."

Had she? Silent, thinking about that, she closed her eyes as he stroked a few strands of hair off her face. "You're a catch, Rebecca Spencer."

"Not if I don't want to be caught."

Searching her face, he slid his hand over her shoulder and under the comforter to caress her waist and hip. "Do you?" he finally asked.

She'd have to be honest. As difficult as it was, he deserved total candor. "Aidan, I've lost enough people in my life not to want to take that risk. I'm not planning to dig in my heels and stay single forever, but I'm petrified of getting so close to someone, and having to endure the pain of losing them, whatever that loss might entail."

Still touching her, his hands searing her skin but soothing at the same time, he stayed quiet for a while. A long while. Long enough that she had to break the silence.

"What about you? I mean, obviously you're single now, but will you stay that way?"

She expected a joke about his dad, or an easy answer, but there was nothing light about the way he looked at her. "I don't do anything casually," he said, the intensity of his words as powerful as his touch.

"So this was not casual sex?"

He was quiet for so long, a tendril of fear started to worm up her chest.

"Then what was it?" she asked.

"Amazing. Healing. Hot. Critical for my survival. Pick a description."

"But not casual."

He gave a dry laugh. "Casual is a way you dress, Beck, not the way I make love. Not to you."

She tried to swallow, but that wasn't happening. Her chest was getting tighter, too.

"You're scared to death of that," he said, scanning her face like he could read every emotion swirling in her.

"I told you, getting close to someone terrifies me. I've lost the three people I've loved the most."

"I'm not gonna die."

"You don't have to. There are other ways to lose people, but that's the worst."

He blew out a long, slow breath. "Then let's call it casual," he said, and she could tell from his tone that was a huge concession and maybe a way to end a conversation he didn't like. "Or fun. Or wonderful. Or temporary. Call it a freaking taste test, if you want."

"In other words, you don't care what we call it."

"Bingo." He kissed her on the nose. "As long as it's not rare, occasional, or over."

"So you want to sleep with me again?"

"Tonight," he said, not a nanosecond of hesitation. "If I can wait that long." His hand coasted over her again, turning her to the side, sliding his leg between hers. "Nope. Can't wait that long," he muttered as he leaned over to press his lips to the slope of her breast.

Like last night, she shuddered under his touch and instantly melted.

Poor Ruff wasn't going outside anytime soon.

Chapter Twenty

That afternoon, Aidan and Beck took off with Ruff and headed to Mike's house with their whole speech planned, along with a Jeep full of pizza slices they hoped were from heaven. They'd certainly worked hard enough on them, which hadn't been easy since the Monday lunch had been the busiest yet, and neither one of them could wipe the silly-ass grins off their faces.

They'd worked side by side all morning, with Sarah buzzing around and chirping about a new table or another rush, both of them working on autopilot and thinking about last night. When they were alone, he'd steal a kiss or brush his fingers over her cheek, their silent look saying what they both were thinking.

More. Tonight. Again.

It was certainly the only cohesive thought in Aidan's brain that morning.

But once the lunch rush ended and they selected their samples, he tried to focus on their plan for Mike to win the twenty-fifth Best of Bitter Bark award in the pizza category. He had to get Mike to think like a

Night Stalker and not quit until the mission was a success.

Ruff greeted them at the door with a few friendly barks, but he backed off when Mike called him from the living room.

"That's a good boy." Since Aidan held the pizza boxes, he let Beck open the screen door that not so long ago Ruff had nearly annihilated. But he was a different dog now, content in his new situation, and happy when he went to work in this house.

"Hello, my precious." Beck bent over to greet him, snuggling her face over his. "Did you have a good time with Uncle Mike?"

He barked twice, turned in a circle, then trotted to the living room where Mike sat, showered, shaved, and dressed in a clean shirt and fresh khaki slacks. *He* was a different dog now, too, Aidan noted.

Beck greeted him with a big kiss and hug, that he returned. His left arm lifted—slowly and with effort—to complete the embrace, making him add a proud grin. "You feel that, Beckie?" he asked, patting her back. "That Janet is a mean one, but she knows what she's doing."

They'd met the physical therapist the last time they were here, and the petite twentysomething with a few tattoos and a nose ring was hardly mean, but she was a damn good therapist.

"Somethin' smells good," Mike said, turning his attention to Aidan and the boxes. "More secret-recipe attempts?"

"Not attempts." Aidan set them on the coffee table. "This is the stuff right here, Michael Leone. Somewhere in this batch is the pizza worthy to be called a 'slice of heaven.' Dig in, my man. Eat it and weep."

As Mike chuckled at that, Beck got right in his face with a big grin. "And guess who you're looking at?"

"My favorite niece?"

"And a girl who ate pizza last night."

His jaw dropped, and he inched back, looking at Aidan in shock. "What did you do?"

A slow burn started in his chest because, well, he didn't do anything before the pizza. But he did plenty after. "Not a thing," he said quickly. "Beck finally...let her guard down."

They shared a quick glance, and Aidan added a wink. She let her guard down, all right. All the way down. To the floor, along with her clothes.

"Well, that's music to my ears," Mike said. "Now lemme taste your offerings. And, uh, Beckie, can you get me some water?"

"Sure." She snagged his glass from the table and snapped her fingers for Ruff to follow. As they left the room, Mike's gaze followed her, then his attention shifted right back to Aidan, no smile, not even one of his half smiles. Nothing.

"You hurt her and I'll kill you even if I only have one strong arm."

Oh boy. Was it that obvious? "I won't hurt her, Mike. You have my word."

His gaze flickered, making Aidan sure Mike and Charlie had the same promise that he and Charlie had. Your word was your word. Maybe Mike had been the one to teach that to Charlie.

"Because she's a gem." Mike's words were much clearer now, along with his intent to protect his niece.

"Yes, sir. She's amazing. I've never met a girl like her." The admission slipped out, surprising Aidan a bit, but not Mike.

"And you never will," the other man assured him.

Aidan swallowed and leaned closer. "I know that," he said softly. "And I have no intention of hurting her, sir."

Mike's brow twitched, and that wasn't an involuntary muscle movement. It was *doubt*. And warning. And the abiding love of a man who considered himself her father.

"She's been through hell," Mike said, fighting to make every word crystal clear. "The only thing she needs is a solid, steady, stable man who keeps his word and protects her."

He doubted that Beck would agree that was the *only* thing she needed, but Aidan certainly knew she deserved exactly that. And one who'd make love to her like he had last night and would again tonight. And for many, many nights, he hoped.

"And no more pain," the older man added. "No more loss."

"No more." He heard Ruff's approaching steps, and by silent agreement, they ended there. But Mike's arm wasn't the only thing working better. His gaze was direct, and the message in it was clear. He meant business.

"So, Uncle Mike. We want you to try three slices today." Beck set the glass down and opened the first box. "And while you eat, we want to tell you some very big and exciting news."

He took the first slice. "Even bigger and more exciting than you eating pizza?"

She threw a look at Aidan and smiled. "So big. So exciting. Now, taste this one first. It's mine. Did we find the secret ingredient?"

He bit down on the slice she gave him, carefully and slowly, the way he did everything. When he swallowed, he slowly shook his head. "My secret ingredient would never be that crunchy salt."

"It's sea salt. Finishing salt. Don't you like it?"

"Feels fake. They don't use it in Italy."

Beck's shoulders slumped, and Aidan reached over to give her hand a reassuring squeeze. "Good try, Beck."

"This one's good, though." He nibbled on the edge of Aidan's experiment with saffron. "Sweet. Maybe a tad too exotic. Not my recipe, but this one isn't bad."

The last one was a hard pass. He ate it, but made it clear there was no secret recipe. "What's this big news?" he asked, wiping his own mouth now, which was a pretty major step forward from where they'd started on this journey.

Beck leaned closer. "Did you know the Best of Bitter Bark contest is coming up in three weeks?"

His eyes flickered, then faded. "I forgot."

But something told Aidan he hadn't forgotten at all. "You need to make it twenty-five consecutive wins, big guy."

Silent, Mike looked down at Ruff, who was curled at his feet.

"Uncle Mike, this year is different. Food Network is coming to town to film a segment of *Best Kept Secrets*, and they're going to go into the kitchens of two winners. We have an inside track since Aidan's sister-in-law is the tourism director who set it up. You have to win, and if you do, they'll do a segment at Slice of Heaven." Her voice rose as she tried to get him to react to this news.

"I can't win without the secret ingredient," Mike replied, his voice low and harsh, but his words were no longer slurred, though halting in delivery. "I don't remember it, and you haven't found it. And you never will."

"Well, that's a positive attitude." Beck let her shoulders sink in defeat.

"Come on, Mike," Aidan urged. "Dig through that brain. Try to remember. Don't give up so easily."

"All I can remember is Sarah. She must be the secret ingredient." He attempted a playful grin. "It must be love."

Aidan glanced at Beck to see her reaction to that, but she shook her head. "Sarah doesn't remember what it is," she said. "And she's been in and out of that kitchen for every pie we've made you. And every pie you ever made. How can she not know?"

"I think you're the secret ingredient, Mike." Aidan fought a burn of frustration about the damn secret stupid ingredient. All this pizza was prize-worthy, in his opinion. "Your hands, your work, your signature." He inched closer to make his point. "You have to try, Mike. You have to get in that kitchen and not give up."

Mike sighed, but at least didn't argue.

"Aidan's right," Beck said. "You need to try. Your muscle memory will kick in. You'll make that sauce like nothing ever happened, and it won't matter what you remember or forget sitting in this room."

He lifted his gaze to look hard at her. "I don't have

muscle memory in my brain, and something did happen."

She slipped off her chair to kneel next to his. "Couldn't you try? This publicity could save Slice of Heaven. And once you go back in, I know you won't want to leave."

He studied her for a long time, then lifted the very hand that no longer hung useless to touch her face. "I should have told you and not Charlie."

She patted his hand in forgiveness. "I was never the one who was going to take over your business, Uncle Mike. It's okay."

"And every time I go to look, Sarah scolds me for going into his room."

She drew back, throwing a look at Aidan to see if he was also confused by that statement. He sure was. "What are you talking about?"

"He wrote it down."

"Charlie wrote down the secret recipe?" Beck and Aidan asked the question in perfect unison.

Mike nodded. "I remember that, clear as if it was yesterday. We were in the kitchen, and I was giving him a list of instructions."

"When?" Beck demanded.

"Oh, he was still in high school, working for me in the summer."

"Between our junior and senior years," Aidan chimed in. "I worked for my dad, too, at the vet office that year."

Beck was already up. "Why didn't you tell us that? I know my way around his room. I'll go look now."

"Beckie, you haven't seen that room for a while. Sarah tried to clean it out, but..." He added a warning look. "She couldn't finish. And I haven't had any luck looking. I tried once when Ruff was here, and he 'bout lost his mind diggin' around and sniffing under all the furniture."

Sniffing for Charlie, Aidan thought, reaching down to give Ruff a loving pet. That couldn't have been easy for him. And it wouldn't be easy for Beck. "I'll go look with you," Aidan said.

"Okay. You keep Ruff down here, Uncle Mike. Aidan and I will go look."

Mike didn't argue as they headed up the stairs, but Beck paused halfway up, turning to Aidan. "I tried going in there after his funeral," she said. "I couldn't."

"I can do it," he told her. "You don't have to go."

"But I know where he kept stuff. I...need to." She slipped her hand in his and gave a squeeze. "I didn't have you with me last time."

He lifted her hand to his lips. "We'll go together."

The room wasn't locked or, surprisingly, dark. The drapes were wide open, and sunshine poured in. Aidan expected a pang of misery when he went inside the room he'd hung out in plenty in high school, but sometime in the fourteen years since then, it had changed enough that it wasn't like walking right into the past.

The bedding was different, just a simple beige with some geometric designs. Not the navy blue comforter with a UNC throw blanket. Of course not. Aidan had made Charlie get rid of that blanket when they got into Wake Forest. There were no Army posters on the walls, either, but innocuous art, as though Sarah had attempted to decorate a guest room and, in the process, had taken out all the personality.

The dresser was there, still. And a chest of drawers. And a sizeable closet along one wall. And all over the floor was...stuff. Open plastic bins, some cardboard boxes, piles of books, magazines, and music CDs. An older-model computer was on a desk under the window, all of it covered with a thin layer of dust.

"Beck, this could take hours," he said, checking his watch. "Do you want to pick a day and spend it here, rather than squeeze it in between lunch and dinner rushes?"

"It won't take hours." She closed the door and headed directly to the dresser, gingerly passing some bins. "Unless Sarah cleaned out these drawers." She pulled the top one open, far too easily for it to have anything in it. "Shoot. Okay. Next?"

The second and third were empty, too.

"Should I start looking through bins?"

"You can, but..." The fourth drawer was stuck, making her grunt.

"Here, I can get it." He climbed over in a flash, dropping down and pulling the drawer out easily. It was stuffed with crap.

"His high school drawer," she said. "After he went to college, Sarah demanded he clean all the stuff out of his room one break when he was home. He wanted me to help, but wouldn't pay me—"

"Brat."

"Seriously. But I watched him from the hall, and he literally dumped everything into these drawers. So if he wrote down the recipe in high school, my guess is it's in here."

Aidan scanned the contents. Papers, trophies, tin boxes with *Star Wars* images on the top. Fat files, filled notebooks, and three baseballs Charlie had signed himself.

"Home-run balls," Aidan said, reaching for one. "This was from the championship tournament against Holly Hills our junior year. Number nine hit a killer over the center-field wall."

She smiled, but it faltered. "I should have been there."

"Why weren't you?"

She lifted a shoulder. "Too busy wallowing in my own sadness."

Well, from the looks of this drawer, they might be wallowing in more of that today. Aidan thumbed the seams of the ball. It felt as familiar to him as the scent in this room and the handwriting on the front of a blue spiral notebook with *World History* in one corner and a lousy interpretation of the Call of Duty logo in the other.

Man, they'd played hours of that game. Then did it in real life.

There was the punch of pain he was expecting, low and right in the solar plexus.

"You okay?" Beck looked up at him, her eyes clear.

"I'm good."

"Then let's divide and conquer. We're looking for a recipe, not a trip down memory lane."

"A recipe." He snorted. "Not what I'd ever expect to be hunting for in Charlie Spencer's high school memory drawer."

"You look in his memory drawer," he said, going to the bed. "I know where the good stuff was."

She glanced over her shoulder. "If you mean those

well-worn copies of Maxim and that joint he had since you guys went to that Good Charlotte concert in Raleigh, they're gone. I found them on my one visit to this room and got rid of them."

He laughed softly. "We wanted to smoke it but chickened out at the last minute. Fear of not getting into ROTC." The stash in the mattress gone, he sat next to Beck to help her look in the drawers, bracing for more emotional explosives as he perused the *Star Wars* box and fluttered a few notebooks. After about twenty minutes, they'd finished going through the drawer and come up with nothing.

Below it was another much like it, only this one had less school and sports stuff and things that were more personal. A few yearbooks, a handwritten notebook that contained something that might have been poetry, but no recipe. While he flipped through those pages, he smiled at the mention of a girl named Dana DeWitt. God, she was hot, and they'd fought over who had a chance with her.

Neither one, if he recalled correctly.

He and Beck dug through that drawer, came up with nothing, then moved to the bins, picking through the remnants of Charlie's life. Each fragment kicked Aidan's gut, mining fresh grief, but no recipe. As he looked up to meet Beck's gaze and confirm the exercise was doing the same thing to her, they heard a low growl outside the door.

"Someone doesn't like that we're in here and he's not," Aidan said.

"Can we let him in?" Beck asked. "He's not barking and acting wild."

Aidan pushed up to get the door for Ruff. "Sure.

I'm not sure how much more of this I can take, though."

She closed her eyes and nodded. "Yeah. This is tough."

When Aidan let him in, Ruff gave one short bark of gratitude and marched inside, sniffing noisily before he was all the way in.

"Brace yourself, buddy," Aidan said, giving his head a rub. "Nothing but heartache in here."

Beck looked up, her eyes misty. "I know. This is a fool's errand, and this fool is about to burst into tears."

Instantly, he reached down and brought her up to hug her. "We don't need to do this, Beck. Let's keep working on the pizzas. We'll find it on our own secret."

She laid her head on his chest and sighed. "I feel like I've lost him all over again." Her voice cracked, and so did Aidan's heart.

"I know." He pulled her closer, adding a kiss to her hair. "And I don't know why we're putting ourselves through this to make this happen."

She inched back, eyes wide. "What? You don't know why? To save Slice of Heaven, remember?"

Why not state the obvious? Maybe because it wasn't obvious to her, only to him. "The sooner we succeed, Beck, the sooner you leave."

"Aidan." She sank in his arms. "What happened to casual?"

"I hate that word. It's the antithesis of everything I am." He lowered his face and kissed her lips lightly. "Let's go back to your apartment and use this afternoon for good instead of sadness."

"Don't complicate this," she whispered.

"Too late. Complicated." He kissed her again, but she drew farther away, and he could practically count the bricks as she built her wall. And he didn't want to have to start all over tearing them down. He'd take what he could, casual or otherwise. "But, you're right, we can just—"

A loud, frantic bark interrupted him. Ruff was bent over, his nose shoved under the space at the bottom of the dresser, sniffing noisily, barking madly, then growling at whatever was down there.

"Probably a twenty-year-old bag of M&M's, if I know Charlie," Beck said, pulling away to get down next to him and look.

Aidan snorted. "More like a dirty sock."

"We're both wrong," she said, her face as deep in the crevice as Ruff's, but with a much better backside in the air. "It's a baseball mitt. But I can't get my hand in there."

"Really?" He joined them on the ground. "Well, I'll be damned. It's his glove. And even *I* can smell Charlie on it. No wonder Ruff's going crazy."

"Let's get it for him," Beck said. "He'll sleep with it. It'll make him happy to smell Charlie on that."

Still on the ground, he turned to her. "I'd have never thought of that," he said.

"That's why Charlie left his dog to me," she teased. But the reminder gave Aidan a kick in the stomach.

He'd never told her about that DD93. Did it matter anymore?

"Can you lift the dresser?" Beck asked from the floor. "I can get it out then."

He did, easily, and Beck slid out a tan mitt he instantly recognized. Before he could get down there to look at it, Ruff had his face deep in the pocket, his tail *thwomping* back and forth with pure joy.

Aidan got on his knees to take the mitt, but Ruff growled protectively, getting his teeth around the webbing and turning to make a getaway from anyone who threatened to take his treasure.

Watching him go, Aidan slipped his arm around Beck. "He's happy," he said. "And that's all Charlie ever wanted, right?"

"Yeah."

That eased his guilt…a little.

Chapter Twenty-One

Aidan knew when he pulled into the driveway of Waterford Farm that something was amiss. No, he didn't expect the drive to be full of cars or the pen to be full of dogs. It was after eight, and the last of the early June day was fading over the mountains in the distance.

But he couldn't ever remember seeing the place so deserted. He should have texted Dad and told him he was coming over after they finished dinner at Slice. But he was afraid Dad would have turned it into a thing—a late dinner, a couple of drinks, an invitation to crash here.

And the only place Aidan was crashing tonight was at an apartment upstairs from a pizza parlor.

He couldn't wait to get back to Beck, hopefully with the news that Dad was all over the idea of a Waterford plane to transport rescues. He glanced again at the empty drive, wishing Garrett had hung around, because his support for this project would be massive.

But even the house looked dark, without a light on. Very weird.

Well, if no one was home, he'd get back to Beck sooner and set up something definite tomorrow. Or at Wednesday night dinner, because Liam and Andi were coming with the newborn, or at least stopping by. Maybe he and Beck could get Carly to cover the restaurant and be here instead. He didn't want to miss...

He gave a dry laugh as he climbed out of the Jeep. Since when were Wednesday night dinners a priority?

Since Beck.

He walked up to the porch, squinting into the kitchen, which was freakishly dark. Not a light over the stove, not one in the distant family room, either. He lifted his hand to knock, then stopped, realizing how wrong that was.

This was his home, but he didn't have a key.

Still, he reached for the knob, and it turned easily, wide open.

Again, it felt strange to B&E his own home, but he did anyway, stepping inside and opening his mouth to call out and at least warn a sleeping dog that he was here, when he heard a soft chuckle. Then a low, male voice he instantly recognized as the baritone of his father.

But normally that voice boomed. It owned this house and echoed in every corner.

But nothing echoed tonight. Dad's voice was soft, as if in prayer, and coming from the formal living room where few Kilcannons stepped if it wasn't Christmas. Aidan headed toward the wide center hall to the front of the house, moving stealthily on instinct.

He didn't want to startle him, or freak out Rusty, but something deep inside told him he shouldn't interrupt whatever private moment this was. He paused outside the living room, standing at the bottom of a large staircase wrapped with a bannister he and Garrett used to slide down when no one was looking.

In the living room, still out of his sightline, he heard Dad laugh softly again. Who the hell was he talking to?

"You'd have laughed at Liam if you'd seen him, though. More nervous than I was when you were having him."

Aidan blinked at that. *You?* He was talking to...*Mom*?

"But I was nervous with every one of 'em," Dad added. After a long pause, Aidan heard the distinct sound of a glass being placed on a wooden end table. The whole scene became as clear in his mind as if he'd taken the last three steps and stood in the arched opening.

Dad, sitting in his favorite chair next to the fireplace, a whiskey, neat, at his side. Mom used to sit in the other chair sometimes, but now only her face was in the room, one of many portraits and family photos that hung on the wall above the fireplace.

And Dad was having a moment with her.

"No, babe, Liam's certainly not your unhappiest right now. So you can stop worrying about him. Molly, too. You wouldn't believe how she glows with love." Another chuckle. "Good thing you whispered Trace Bancroft's name to me all those years ago. He could have come and gone from Bitter Bark without me knowing and doing my usual wrangling to get those two together."

At least he openly admitted his matchmaking meddling, Aidan thought with a smile.

"Garrett and Shane are all settled, too, as you know. I'll be expecting another trip to that hospital for one of those two in a year or so." He let out a heavy sigh. "You always wanted this place filled with grands, Annie girl. I'm telling you, I'm doing my best. Listening to all your advice."

Aidan leaned silently against the wall, closing his burning eyes. How had he dared think any of them—especially Dad—had sailed on without the agony of grief? He just hid it well. He was classy and cool and kept his pain secret. At least, until someone walked in on him.

Without moving, he glanced left and right, wondering if he should clear his throat, make a footstep, or slip out as silently as he'd come in.

"Now, Aidan? There's a problem, babe."

Or he could stand here and be analyzed by his father and his mother's ghost.

"Restless as a newborn terrier, looking for something to sink his teeth into, digging in his own emotional dirt."

Was *that* what he was doing?

"Suffering from some sort of PTSD, though he'd never admit it."

Like hell he—

"But I worked some magic. Got some help from someone I suspect you've run into up there, but things look good. So you tell Charlie Spencer thanks for me when you see him. I think this girl's good for Aidan. He's ready."

Aidan swallowed, kind of stunned that he'd forgotten how well his father and, when she was alive, his mother, understood their children. It was uncanny, really. And something he should never take for granted.

"Here's the thing, though, Annie. He's got one foot out the door. I can't think of a way to get him to stay, if she doesn't. And she doesn't even live here. I know, I know. They don't all have to be in Bitter Bark. Big family, all adults, it's crazy to try and leash them up and keep them in our pen." Another pause, followed by the whiskey thud. "But I need them all," he said, his voice thick with emotion. "It's the only way to bear it without you. The only way."

When his father's voice cracked, Aidan looked side to side again, planning his escape. He couldn't intrude on this. It would embarrass his dad.

As he took a step, his foot made the softest scuff on the wood, and he froze, praying Dad hadn't heard. But instantly the *tap-tap-tap* of four paws crossed the living room floor, followed by a quick bark.

Damn. Dad might not have heard, but Rusty had.

He backed up, letting his boot hit the floor with a purposeful thud. "Dad? Gramma? Anyone home?"

Rusty vaulted through the doorway, barking noisily.

"Hey, dude. Where's your master? This place is like a morgue." Whoa, that was some bad choice of words, he thought as he got down to rub Rusty's head and press his face into the fur, composing his emotions.

"Aidan." Dad came right out behind his dog. "I didn't hear you come in."

"Where is everyone?" He stood slowly, almost afraid to look at his father, half expecting tear-stained cheeks and the red eyes of a drunk on a bender. But he couldn't have been further from the truth.

His father's face was its usual color, maybe a tad tanned as the days inched closer to summer. His blue eyes were clear, his smile as real and wide as the day Aidan had come home from the Army. And the hug he got in greeting was as warm as always.

"What are you doing in there?" Aidan asked.

"Finishing up some paperwork. I get bored with the office and need a change of scenery occasionally."

Right. "Where is everyone? Darcy? Gramma?"

"All at Vestal Valley General with Liam and Andi and baby Fiona."

"Fiona?" He grinned. "Good Irish name."

"Fiona Harper Kilcannon," he said proudly.

"Mom's maiden name for the middle? Love it."

Dad beamed. "Isn't it perfect? I was with her all day, and I can tell you she's got Andi's spirit, Liam's heart, and a heaping dose of that Harper beauty."

"You could tell this by holding a one-day-old newborn who probably didn't open her eyes?"

Dad laughed. "No, Liam told me, and anyone in earshot, for that matter. I only held a precious baby. But that was enough, and they all wanted to go to the hospital and have the first family gathering to indoctrinate the child."

"And no one thought to call me?"

"Pretty sure every one of them called you."

He'd never looked at his phone. He'd been making pizza and stealing kisses and planning to come over here to talk to Dad without even looking to see if anyone in his family needed or wanted him. The only call he'd cared about was Beck's, and she had been with him.

"You can probably catch the tail end of the festivities if you leave now."

For a split second, he considered it. That was how much he didn't want to miss out on this latest family fun. That was how much he...belonged.

"I would, Dad, but I want to talk to you about something."

His brows lifted. "Of course."

Aidan nodded toward the living room. "In there?"

He started to frown, making Aidan think maybe he didn't want to go in there and have to admit there was no "paperwork" unless it was the label on the whiskey bottle. But then Dad gestured him in. "Sure. I could use the company and a break."

There was a glass on the table, but it was water. And files were spread out over the coffee table. A pang of guilt threatened, but Aidan tamped it down. He had been talking to Mom—that much wasn't debatable.

Dad took his seat and gestured for Aidan to sit in that opposite chair. Mom's chair.

"I'll sit over here," he said, choosing the end of the sofa near to Dad's chair.

His father chuckled softly. "Not one kid will sit there," he noted. "She wouldn't mind, you know. But what's on your mind, Son?"

He took a breath and considered a long-winded build-up and rationale, but knew in his gut it was never wise to beat around the bush with Dad. "I want to do something new and different for Waterford Farm."

His father's gaze was steady, but even in the evening light, he could see the twinkle in his eyes. "Go ahead."

"I think we need a plane. A small, private plane that I could use to take rescues to new homes, to pick up dogs from around the country, and maybe even start an animal air transport service for customers. The K-9 training op would grow if we could reach out to law enforcement beyond North Carolina and we could even fly in private trainees. Liam sometimes has to drive for days to deliver a new *schutzhund* once he's trained one, and Trace's service dog business could really expand."

The twinkle flashed to a full blown spark. "That's brilliant. It makes us national, not statewide."

"You'd have to fund the plane, and take money from the profits to pay off the loan."

"We can do that." There was zero hesitation in that response.

Aidan nodded, encouraged by the response. "Then I'll run the operation, fly the plane, and take a salary commensurate with the work."

Dad leaned back, exhaling. "And you'll stay here in Bitter Bark?"

"Unless I'm flying."

With a quick laugh, his father picked up the water glass and held it toward the pictures over the fireplace. "Annie girl, you do work fast."

Aidan had to smile at that. "With all due respect to Mom's powers, I had the idea yesterday. Well, to be honest, Beck did."

"I knew I liked that girl. And I like this idea, Aidan."

Aidan grinned. "I kind of hoped you would. So did Beck."

"Then she wasn't upset about the DD93?"

Aidan's smile faltered. "I haven't told her." At his

263

father's questioning look, he added, "Not sure I can, Dad. Ruff's settling in with her, and she's happy, and...and I care about her."

"I can tell," he said.

"A lot," he added, suddenly wanting the very advice he'd been running from for several weeks.

"I'm glad to hear that, Son."

"So, could you and, uh..." He glanced at the wall. "Mom work some of that black magic to keep her here?"

He laughed. "No black magic, Aidan. Just love. And my advice would be to show her how you feel, and be honest. Including about that DD93."

"You don't think I'd lose her if I took a hard line about Ruff?"

"You'd lose her if you aren't truthful. You both agreed that Ruff should go where Charlie wanted, not where you wanted."

He nodded, considering that.

"If you care about her, you'll be honest."

"I do care about her. A lot. A hell of a lot." He gave a quiet laugh. "Feels so good to admit it."

"I know the feeling," Dad said. "Remember it well."

"Do you?" Aidan leaned forward. "How'd you know? Why was one woman so different than any other?"

Dad thought about that for a moment, dropping his elbows on his knees to let his chin rest on his knuckles, his inward gaze somewhere in the distant past. "I'd never met anyone so strong," he finally said. "Fierce, you know? Nothing threw her. Nothing made her doubt or second-guess."

Aidan nodded, thinking about Beck's strength, too. The thing he'd totally missed about her the minute they'd met. "Did you see that instantly?"

"God, no." He laughed. "I'm sure you've heard about our conspicuous blind-date meeting."

At every anniversary, they'd insisted on sharing that with their kids. "You were dating Mom's friend, right?"

"Katie Rogers," he said. "Nice girl who made a strategic mistake trying to do a favor for a friend."

"Setting Mom up with your friend?" Even though he knew the story, it never really got old.

Dad chuckled. "I remember walking into that bar where the four of us were supposed to meet and seeing Katie's friend, Anne Harper, sipping on a white wine, wearing jeans, a T-shirt, and the godawfulest shit-kicking boots I'd ever seen. Katie was all dolled up in a dress, and all Mom could do was joke that she'd been working at a dog kennel all day and didn't need to impress some guy she'd never met." He grinned and pointed playfully at the picture. "She impressed the hell out of me, though. By the end of the night, I knew I had to end things with Katie and pursue the woman of my dreams."

"You knew that from one night when she was out with another guy?" Maybe the story had gotten romanticized over the years.

"I knew I wanted to sleep with her."

Aidan choked. "Did I need to know that? She's my mother."

He tipped his head. "Be real, Aidan. We're human. You think we had six kids by praying for them?"

"Uh...TMI."

"You asked how I knew. It starts with a pretty basic instinct that is, one hopes, mutual and all-consuming."

Perfect description, which reminded him that his basic instinct was at her apartment, waiting for him. "And then what?"

"And then…well, I broke up with Katie ASAP. It took one call to your mother to know the attraction went both ways, and then…" Dad took a deep drink of his water, as if talking about those days parched his throat. "Then I realized I'd found a woman who made me the best possible version of me. When you find that, you keep that. No matter what it takes."

"But Beck's leaving."

"Well"—Dad shifted on the sofa—"I suppose you could follow her. Or visit her in the Waterford private plane."

He waited a beat, then looked right into his father's eyes. "I don't want to leave, Dad. That's the irony of what she's done. She's helped me to see that this is where I want to be, with my family and with my own place here. But…" He didn't want to do that without her.

Dad shook his head. "That's advice I can't give you, Son. You'll have to figure it out. Or…" He shrugged and angled his head toward the fireplace. "Ask your mother."

Aidan laughed nervously. "I don't generally talk to her."

"I do."

"You talk to Mom." He did his level best to sound surprised.

"All the time, Son. When I wake up, when I go to sleep, when I'm driving, when I'm alone in this big old house, which is rare, but does occasionally happen."

"Do you think that's...healthy?"

Dad raised both brows in question. "I thought you were the one who said we didn't talk *enough* about her."

"I never said—"

"You didn't have to. I know my kids the same way, someday, you'll know yours."

Aidan averted his gaze for a moment, feeling a quick splash of shame. "I guess we all grieve in our own ways," he admitted.

Dad leaned forward. "I'm glad you finally realize that. I know you think we've moved on, but—"

"I don't—"

His father lifted a hand to stop the argument. "There's something you should know about grief. It could help you, with your mother and Charlie." He took a moment, sipped his water, and Aidan waited for the pearl of wisdom he knew from experience would probably be exactly what he needed. "It's okay to grieve as long as you have hope."

"Hope?" What hope did Dad have? "Do you mean all this joking about you dating again? Is that what gives you hope?"

With a dry snort, Dad looked skyward. "God, no. I would no sooner get involved with a woman than I'd...I'd..." He flicked his hands, as if he couldn't even think of anything further from reality. "That's not what gives me hope."

"Then what does?"

He looked at Aidan a long time, then nodded slowly. "You already know."

But he didn't, unless Dad meant Beck.

"Waterford," his father said simply. "Hope is this place. It's the business. This isn't a distraction from grief, Aidan. And it's more than honoring a woman's legacy or building her dream facility posthumously. Waterford Farm, the dogs, the rescues, the purpose, and the fact that we do it as a family...this is the source of all our hope. All our peace. All our understanding of why the good Lord only gave Annie to us for a short time."

Aidan tried to get his arms around that idea, ignoring the sting in his eyes. "What you're saying is Waterford Farm is how Annie Kilcannon lives on, every day. You haven't moved on. You've kept her alive."

He smiled slowly and nodded. "And that's why I can talk to her. And you can, too."

Aidan inched forward, reaching out over the space that separated them to put his hand over his father's. "I don't have to, Dad. Because I have you."

From the look on his face, nothing could have made his father happier.

Chapter Twenty-Two

"Everything is amazing. Perfect. Like, crazy good." Beck put her feet up on the coffee table and tapped the speaker button so she could talk to Jackie with her hands free. "And I finally made it to the post office to get this package. Thanks for sending it."

"No worries, it was easy. Just be warned, hon. The letter was right on top, but there was more in the file and some of it looked super personal, so I stuck the whole Charlie folder in there. Sorry if you hit a few emotional land mines."

Beck sighed and fingered the thick envelope. "I can handle them. Heck, if I can go through Charlie's bedroom with Aidan, I can do anything."

"You sound good, Beck."

She stretched, sore from a long day downstairs, but it was a good sore. She stroked Ruff's head, who lay next to her, taking up way more than his share of the sofa. "I feel good," she admitted.

"Pizza wars progressing?" Jackie asked with enough tease in her voice that Beck figured she knew it was more than pizza putting a smile on her face.

"We've come to the conclusion that there is no secret ingredient, only Uncle Mike's magic touch."

"Seriously?" Jackie laughed. "But he still won't go in and make it?"

"We have another week until the big contest. I'm hoping he rallies."

"And Aidan?"

"Oh, Aidan." She dropped her head back and let out a gushy, girlie sigh of pure delight. "Where do I start?"

"The good stuff."

Relief washed through Beck. She was so ready to spill everything to her best friend. And maybe get clarity on the situation. She'd been with Aidan practically twenty-four seven for weeks now, which explained the delay in picking up Jackie's package, which she'd kindly sent Priority, or why she'd forgotten to call until this evening. It was like Beck had lost focus on anything but Aidan.

"Well, it's *all* pretty good," she said on a laugh, the understatement of *pretty good* being what was funny. "Actually, it's ridiculous."

"Oh boy. Didn't see that coming or anything."

"What do you mean? We met fighting over the dog."

"But he let you keep Ruff, so obviously he has a soft spot. Or maybe 'soft' isn't the best way to describe it."

"Definitely not," Beck agreed. "But he didn't really have a choice. I have the letter." She tapped the envelope Jackie had sent. "Happy to say I don't need to wave it in his face now. We've all reached an understanding, right, Ruff?" The dog looked up, and his sweet eyes made her heart roll around with love. "Ruff actually likes me now, or at least he's protective of me. Maybe he likes Uncle Mike better than both Aidan and me, but it's all worked out."

"That's good, because I don't know much about the Army, but my guess is that form Charlie filled out would supersede the letter."

Beck frowned. "What form?"

"The DD something? It's in the file. I figured you'd seen it since it was with all his papers."

"Oh, I know what you mean," she said. "I did request that as next of kin, but I forgot they were sending it. I got it right before I left and never really looked at it."

"Good thing, since you might not have fought for the dog as hard."

Beck sat up, lifting the envelope. "What are you talking about?"

"Charlie's instructions. About Ruff."

What? She instantly tore at the back of the thick cardboard envelope, peering inside. She recognized the file, and Jackie was right—it was stuffed with emotional land mines.

"I don't know about any instructions," she said, spying Charlie's infamous letter, but setting it aside to leaf through papers. She remembered getting the official looking form, but not reading it very closely. "What does it say?"

"He wanted Aidan to have Ruff."

What? She found the form, and her gaze dropped to the section where there was a typed addendum. "In the event of my demise," she started to read, but her voice faded out as she silently skimmed the words.

...my dog, Ruff, is to be officially transported to Waterford Farm in Bitter Bark, North Carolina, by contacting the owner, Daniel Kilcannon, who will arrange transport. The dog is to be kept there until which time Major Aidan Kilcannon returns home, when he will become Ruff's rightful owner.

"Oh my God," she murmured. "Charlie really did want him to have Ruff."

"What are you going to do?" Jackie asked.

"I don't know." She pressed her hand on the paper, a signed original. Charlie had touched this very paper. He'd made this decision. And it was dated... She grabbed the letter she'd set aside. "Two days after he wrote to me?" Her voice rose in shock. "What the hell, Charlie?"

"Aidan's is more recent."

But Beck shook her head at Jackie's logic this time. "Two days apart? He had to know what he was doing."

Jackie laughed softly. "Maybe *he's* the matchmaker of this latest romance."

"No, he would never guess this could happen. He wanted to cover his bases, I think. Maybe the more people in the States who had a claim on the dog, the better chances of getting him shipped here. That's the only possible explanation."

"Where's Aidan? Are you going to tell him?"

"He's home tonight. He spent the whole day away on a plane-hunting trip with his brother and dad. He's going to start a rescue dog transport program for them, and he's so happy about it, but..." She ran her fingers over Charlie's signature again. "I don't know how he's going to react to this. Hell, for all I know, he'll take Ruff back."

"Which would make him kind of an asshole. Just sayin'."

"But we agreed from day one that all we wanted to do with Ruff is honor Charlie's requests. Who knew my brother sent two of them? Although, this one is awfully official." She glanced at the clock and made a quick decision. "I'm going to go talk to him about this. Show this to him in person. I don't want to wait until tomorrow."

"Okay, but Beck, I'm not done with news. I have some."

Something in Jackie's voice told her it wasn't good news. "What's wrong? Problems with the business? I know we're not making any money right now, but..."

"We're not," she said. "And that's why I accepted a showcase opportunity in Seattle."

"Seattle?" Beck sat straight up, a mix of elation and dejection punching her on both sides. "A showcase? What is that? Other than temporary, I hope."

"It's actually a permanent place in a studio-slash-exhibit-house," she said. "It would put my work on display and for sale to a very wealthy, very artsy community. And I'd get huge private commissions."

"Oh my God, that's amazing, Jackie. That's what you've always wanted. That's...so far away." She grunted in physical pain. "I'll miss you so much, but I'm so incredibly happy for you."

"Thanks. I'm stoked." She could hear the joy in her friend's voice. "But who knows if you're even coming back? You can move Baby Face to North Carolina, you know."

Beck sighed, mostly because it wasn't the first time in the last few weeks that the thought had crossed her mind. "You do remember that I spent every dime and ounce of energy and drop of talent I had trying to get out of here, right?"

"Different life, Beck. Different time. Different landscape."

Oh, that voice of reason. It could be so…reasonable. "But what if I take that risk and something changes? I mean, we're basking in the glow of toe-curling, sheet-soaking, mind-blowing—"

"I get the point, Beck. It's good sex."

She laughed. "But that might be all it is. That's kind of what I asked for—to keep it casual. And then these…these visions of 'more' dance in my head. And I…" She swallowed and closed her eyes. "I don't want to lose again. And don't tell me that's the risk you take when you love another human being, because it could be me, you know. I could be this…this curse on people."

"I'm not even going to dignify that with a response. You know what you should do? Get over to Aidan's house, show him that form, and see what he's made of. If he wants you to keep the dog, and only if he does, tell him your only business associate is leaving and your business is portable. And then ask him, 'Do you want me to stay?' You'll be able to tell by the look in his eyes if he's forever or not."

"After a month? That doesn't sound very reasonable."

"Who says love is reasonable? Why do you think it avoids me like the plague?"

Beck laughed. "You are a walking contradiction, Jacqueline Saunders. Logical and artistic. How does that happen?"

"I don't know, but this isn't about me. Are you going to follow my advice?"

She dropped her head back and tunneled her fingers into Ruff's neck, scratching him. "Yeah. I am."

And because of that, Beck knew this wouldn't be a casual visit. Even as she said goodbye to Jackie and folded up the form to slide it into her purse, her whole body braced for the fact that this wasn't merely a trip to Aidan's house to share this new twist in their lives.

It was do-or-die time. As much as she wanted them to be, she and Aidan weren't casual. Now she had to find out exactly what they were.

Aidan looked up from the laptop on the kitchen counter when a car pulled into the driveway. Leaning over, he peered out the window and muttered a soft, "Yes," at the sight of Beck's car.

He'd been debating whether to break their pact not to get together tonight so they could focus on something other than each other.

He'd focused on planes all day. That was enough attention on anything that wasn't her.

Opening the door before she even reached it, he realized they'd never spent the night at this house yet. They always stayed in her apartment, which made it easy to walk Ruff in the square and roll into the kitchen in the morning.

Stepping outside into a warm, dry evening, he walked barefoot to the car and opened the door when she turned off the ignition.

"And here I thought finding that 172 Skyhawk for a bargain-basement price was the highlight of my day." He leaned over before she could get out, kissing her right on the mouth. "Then my girl shows up with…" He frowned into the backseat. "Where's Ruff?"

She inched back with a sigh. "I left him at home for a few hours. He was dead tired after a long walk and…" She reached for her bag as if stalling for time. "Can I come in?"

"Dumb question. Of course. I was about to make something to eat. You hungry?"

Stepping out of the car, she shook her head. "No, I'm not. I want to talk to you."

He made a face. "Why don't I like the sound of that?"

"You might like it very much," she said, using her hopeful voice that he liked so much. "I have some exciting and wonderful news for you."

"You found the secret ingredient?"

She laughed. "You're convinced there isn't one."

"You got him to come in and make a pizza?"

She looked up. "Not unless the sky fell today."

"You decided to ditch that life in Chicago and stay right here in Bitter Bark?"

She froze in midstep. "I guess…that depends on this conversation."

Something in Aidan's chest slipped, rolled around, and threatened to crack. "You think that last one is a serious possibility?"

She didn't answer, but sort of tugged her bag closer as they went in. "Let's talk."

Okay. He ushered her toward the living area and

gestured to the open kitchen next to it. "Want something to drink? Water? Beer? I think I have some soda, too." Although he'd spent so little time here in the past two weeks, he couldn't be sure.

"No, no, I'm fine." She headed to the couch, opening her bag. "I want to show you something."

"What is it?" He sat next to her as she pulled out papers. And his heart dropped when he saw the words Record of Emergency Data. The DD93. "Shit," he mumbled.

She drew back with a soft gasp. "You knew?"

Swallowing, he took the papers and set them down, not needing to see Charlie's words again. "Yes. I knew."

"When?"

"Several weeks ago."

Another gasp. "Why didn't you tell me?"

Wasn't it obvious? "I knew what you'd do. You'd try to give me Ruff, claim it was Charlie's real wish, and break your own heart. And then you'd leave." He closed his eyes. "I'm dreading that day, Beck."

"If we hadn't succeeded with bringing the restaurant back, why would I leave?"

"Because you would. You will. As soon as you can, because you're not…"

"I'm not what?" she asked when he didn't finish.

"As deep into this as I am."

"Oh." She breathed the word, reaching up to touch his cheek. "So much for casual."

He put his hand over hers, pressing his lips against her palm. "Casual is for idiots," he said. "For people who are scared and quit. Night Stalkers—"

"Don't quit."

"Unless they have to," he added. "Unless they stupidly put everything on the narrow shoulders of one woman who lives in another state even after he was warned not to."

She turned completely, folding her legs under her to face him on the sofa. "What do you mean you put everything on my shoulders?"

He huffed a breath, trying to figure out where to start. "I went plane shopping today," he said.

"I know. How'd that go? I thought you'd text me if you found something."

"I did find something, and it was too much to text." He took the strand of hair that fell from her ponytail and twirled it around his finger. "Because the plane took on this monumental meaning. This…*fantasy*."

She arched a brow. "I won't do it in a plane you're flying, if that's the fantasy."

He didn't smile. "I wish it were that simple."

"Aidan." She closed her hand over his, pressing it to her cheek. "Tell me the whole fantasy, then."

He waited a beat, considering how that would play out. It might scare her. Hell, it scared him. They'd known each other for years, but their romance was young, far too fresh for fantasies of forever. But what the hell? That was what he was having, all day long.

"I went to the airfield with Dad and Garrett, and it was…it was perfect, Beck. We talked, we laughed, we strategized this new business. Garrett is one hundred percent down for air rescue transport, and Dad already has the bank on board to finance the plane."

She searched his face. "That's the fantasy? You found your place at Waterford?"

"That's a fact, and I have you to thank."

"You'd have done it without me, Aidan. This direction, this life? It was right there waiting for you to discover it."

"Maybe," he agreed. "Maybe I could have done it without you, but the point is..." He turned his hand and threaded their fingers together. "I don't want to do it without you. I don't want..." He took a breath, vaguely aware of how his pulse thumped. "A life without you."

Silent, she stared at him, the golden flecks in her eyes giving away nothing. Not shock, fear, disappointment, or, sadly, the same emotion that hammered in his chest.

"It's a good life," he said softly. "It's a fine life, I guess. But with you, Beck? It's better, brighter, safer, and smoother. I'm like Ruff," he added with a laugh. "I got here all unsettled and restless and pawing at the world. But then I found you, and now I want to curl up and stay put. With you. And when you leave, I'll go pacing from the window to the door, looking for you to come back."

Finally, he saw the emotion. Her eyes misted, and she swallowed, taking a breath he hadn't realized she'd been holding. "And the fantasy?"

He shrugged. "Fill in the blanks. You, me, Ruff, a house, a yard, a date with a bunch of Kilcannons every Sunday. Does that sound awful?"

She bit her lip, gave the softest laugh. "Oh yeah. Wretched." When she blinked, the dampness in her eyes trickled over her lashes. "I can't lose another person, Aidan. If I let myself fall in love with you, I'm putting it all out there and taking a risk that absolutely terrifies me."

"You won't lose another person," he insisted. "Not this person." He sealed that promise with a kiss on her lips, feeling her sigh into him, and then she eased back.

"Can I ask you a question?"

When he nodded, she looked down, grazing his knuckles with her fingertip. "When you got into the cockpit of a helicopter and turned it on, or whatever you do before you actually fly, did you have any trepidation? Was there anything deep inside of you that said, 'This could be it. I might not get back alive. I might die'? Did you ever think that?"

"Every single time, even after intense training. That's what keeps you on your toes, that knowledge that you're one mistake away from eating it."

"That's how I feel every time I inch close to a person. Like I'm one instant away from devastation. I always felt that way because of my parents dying so young, but then when Charlie died, it all came back. The fragility of life."

"Life is fragile," he agreed. "It's also meant to be lived and conquered and enjoyed." He pulled her closer. "Just tell me if I have a chance. If you'd consider staying here. If you could be with me, love me."

"Aidan, I—"

He put his hand over her mouth. "Wait. Don't say no. Not yet. Let me dream."

She didn't finish her sentence, but leaned into him to kiss him, sliding right onto his lap. There, she braced her arms on his shoulders and wrapped his head in her hands. Without breaking the kiss, she angled her head, opened her mouth, and bowed her back in invitation.

As always, blood surged and brain cells fried, and his hands went to every inch of her he could touch. Everything was smooth and warm and sweet and…Beck.

She kept kissing and kissing, rolling her hips over his as they moved in a way that was second nature now, the heat building, the need growing, the clothes…had to come off.

For *casual sex*. The words punched, and he somehow managed to break the kiss and still his hands in the act of getting her T-shirt over her head. Casual sex didn't work anymore. He wouldn't do it.

"What?" she asked, breathless.

"I can't—"

"I'm *showing* you how I feel, Aidan," she said in a husky whisper. "I'm scared to say the words. I'm terrified to get in that…that imaginary plane or helicopter and fly. And I'm petrified to lose someone again, because the ache is consuming and horrible."

"Please tell me there's a 'but' at the end of that sentence."

She exhaled. "But I want to try with you."

"Beck. Beck." He pulled her into him. "Rebecca Spencer, I love you."

When she inched back, tears filled her eyes. "Let me show you, Aidan. I can't say it yet, but let me show you."

He'd take it. Pulling her back to him, he kissed her again, but she jerked away. "Should I answer it?"

Only then did he realize her purse on the floor was humming. "You're kidding, right?"

"But that's the third call." She twisted and reached down. "Let me see who it is." With a glance, she closed her eyes with a kick of defeat. "Aunt Sarah. I have to get it."

"Pizza business can wait." He continued his exploration under her shirt. "Call her back."

"Mmm." She seriously thought about it, he could tell, but then she tapped the phone and put it to her ear. "Hi, Aunt Sarah."

He could hear the high-pitched voice through the phone and knew her aunt well enough to know that wasn't normal. Immediately, Beck drew away.

"What do you mean, gone?" She flashed a horrified look at Aidan, moving off him back to the sofa. "He left? How? Where'd he go?"

"Ruff?" he asked, leaning forward.

"Uncle Mike!"

"What the hell?" Then he stood and took her hand. "He's making pizza. I'd bet my life on it."

"Sarah, we're going to Slice. No, no. I'm not there. I'm at Aidan's house. But we'll run over now, and if that's where he is, we'll find him. Don't worry. I can't believe he drove, though. He must have been determined to get there." She listened for a moment, gathering up her stuff and walking to the door with Aidan. "This is good news, Aunt Sarah. Great news. He's cooking again." As she hung up, she glanced up at Aidan. "I hope."

"He is. We got through to him, Beck. I know it." As they walked outside, Aidan pointed to his Jeep, parked next to her car. "But let's go make sure. I'll drive."

"I'm sorry," she said. "That was about to get good."

He smiled. "Life's about to get good, sweetheart. I know all I need to know."

"Except, about the DD93. It was dated two days after the letter to me, Aidan."

"What DD93?" he joked. "Army doesn't send them all the time, so I never saw it. Don't remember it. Plan on tearing it up." He held the door for her. "You?"

"I want to do what Charlie wants," she said.

"Two days apart?" He laughed as he jogged around the Jeep to the driver's side. "Dude never did anything without a good reason." He turned the ignition and rumbled out of the drive. "Let's go find your uncle."

"Who just interrupted the best—"

He held up a hand. "It's what families do, Beck."

The gleam in her eyes when she smiled was all he needed. They'd get to *I love you* and forever and fantasy lives. But for now, he couldn't remember the last time he'd felt so good and drowning in hope.

"Plus," he added, giving her hand a squeeze, "Uncle Mike's not going to lose that contest. He's an honorary Night Stalker and, as you know—"

"Night Stalkers don't quit," she finished. "And maybe he'll even share the secret sauce with us."

Aidan put a hand on her shoulder and eased her closer for a kiss. "He told us the secret, Beck. It's love."

Beck's body hummed like the engine of the beat-up old Jeep as it ate up the roads into town, the wind whipping through their hair, their hands locked except when he needed to shift gears. Even then, Aidan barely let go, occasionally glancing at her with a knowing smile.

Of all the times for Uncle Mike to decide to go back to work. And to leave without telling Sarah, just climbing into his car while she was out grocery shopping.

"Didn't he know Sarah'd freak when she got home?" she asked, voicing her thoughts over the noisy Jeep. "She was so upset, I didn't want her to drive."

"Then I'm glad we can go."

"What would she do if I wasn't here?"

He tipped his head and lifted both brows. "Exactly."

She couldn't help laughing at his low-key determination. Night Stalkers didn't quit, she knew, and something told her Aidan wouldn't take no for an answer. And she'd been so close to giving him the answer he wanted. So close to whispering the three words that suddenly felt more natural than terrifying.

She *did* love him.

"Someone's parked in your spot," he said, pulling her attention to the alley.

"Oh, that's his Buick. Hallelujah. He's making pizza."

Aidan whipped into a spot Sarah used, next to Uncle Mike's car, not far from the back door and the bank of kitchen windows. With the thick curtains drawn, they couldn't see if the kitchen light was on. "Got the keys? We can surprise the maestro at work."

"Don't need them. Uncle Mike never locked that door in his life when he was at work."

He turned her face to his. "Then let him work. We can sit in this dark alley, finish our conversation, make out like teenagers, then go in and eat all the pizza."

She laughed and leaned in. "You had me at 'make out.'"

"Then you'd skip 'finish our conversation'?" He kissed her, holding her face. "Would you mind if I tell you I love you again? Because I really enjoyed saying it before."

"I wouldn't get mad."

"I…" He kissed her forehead. "Love…" And her nose. "You." Finally, her mouth, making her kiss back. "And you know what else I'd love? To hear you say it right back to me."

Her heart tripped and danced and did a few other crazy things that took her breath away. "You would, huh?"

"I would." His blue eyes cut through her, warm and direct. "But I'll wait until you're ready. I'm telling you, Beck Spencer, I'd wait for—"

A sudden shattering noise crashed through the night, deafening and sharp, raining glass into the alley and making Beck shriek.

Turning, she looked in horror as the back windows of the pizza place vomited giant clouds of black smoke, and flames devoured the drapes with a menacing, crackling sound.

Beck screamed again, shock slapping her in the face, along with a wave of heat and smoke that nearly knocked her over.

Aidan threw himself out of the Jeep without even opening the door. "Call 911!" That order was the last thing she heard him say before he ran to the back door, yanked it open, and disappeared inside a burning building.

Chapter Twenty-Three

Help me out, Spence. Help me find him. Help me.

If Charlie had an answer from the great beyond, Aidan couldn't hear it over the roar of a fire consuming the front half of the pizza kitchen. He ducked down, then crawled across a floor he'd learned every inch of in the past few weeks. Good thing, because he couldn't see a thing through the smoke.

"Mike!" He hollered once, but had to pull his shirt up to cover his mouth and nose, feeling his whole body slide into combat mode. He'd been in worse. He'd survived worse. And so had most soldiers he knew.

But Mike was no soldier. He was a sick old man who was nowhere to be found.

He rounded the counter, noticing fresh semolina on the floor. He had to be here. He had to be close. He called out one more time, crawling around to the oven where—whoa!

Flames danced and ate up the whole front and left side of the restaurant, devouring the shelves and counters around it.

The oven. The damn fifty-year-old beast that couldn't go over 647. Maybe it shut off...or maybe it *sparked*. They'd never tested it. Had Mike's faulty memory failed him? Had he turned the dial and forgotten his own rule?

Smoke stung his lungs with every labored breath as he powered through to the other side of the kitchen. Could Mike have gotten out through the dining room? Flames engulfed that door, and the smoke blinded him so he couldn't see through the small broken window.

"Mike!" Where the hell was he? There wasn't much real estate left in this kitchen. The prep area. The fridge. The—

The *apartment*.

Of course, he went upstairs to save Ruff. Where they would both die if Aidan didn't get to them. And Beck would be the next victim, dying of a broken heart at the very moment she was about to heal. He would not let any of that happen. He wouldn't quit. He wouldn't.

Come on, Spence. I know you're up there. Help me out, buddy.

Crouched in a half crawl, Aidan took a shaky breath, refusing to cough it out or let his stinging eyes close. Instead, he made his way to the stairwell door. Flames danced around it, and he knew the glass window in the middle could shatter at any second, which would send the smoke up the stairs and let in enough oxygen that the fire would follow.

A few feet away, a hundred dishes crashed to the floor when the shelves burned, and a stack of pizza boxes combusted with a whoosh. Heat slammed him, but he stayed steady and used his shirt to cover his hand so he could turn the searing-hot knob. The stairwell was smoky, but totally passable if he could get up and down with both of them in a minute.

Of course he could. He *had* to.

Making sure the door behind him was latched, he started up the stairs, but didn't make it two feet before the glass in that door shattered, too, letting the smoke roll in. The flames wouldn't be far behind, and they'd eat up these old wooden stairs in seconds.

Which would trap Mike and Ruff—and Aidan—upstairs.

"Mike!" He bellowed the name, hearing the amplified echo in the dense air. "Ruff!"

In the distance, he heard a siren scream and...a dog bark. Muffled. Low. Terrified and frantic.

Taking one more look at the flames on the other side of the broken glass, he made a calculated guess. The stairwell would be completely impassible by the time the firefighters got here. Could they get Mike and Ruff out through the apartment windows? Maybe.

But they'd have a better chance if Aidan was up there and told them where to go. He stood stone-still for a split second. Run up there and save them himself, or find a way back outside and let a firefighter go up there?

He couldn't leave. He couldn't. It went against his training, his gut, and his knowledge of right and wrong. He charged up the stairs, grabbing the still cool doorknob and swearing mightily that apparently Mike *did* lock some doors.

He pounded with full force, thanking God that whoever added this apartment hadn't followed code. This was a hollow door, and he could kick it open if

Mike didn't unlock it in the next five seconds. "Mike! Lemme in! I can get you out!"

The only reply was Ruff's insistent, out-of-control barking.

Maybe Mike was unconscious. Maybe shock or fear had knocked him out. Oh hell, maybe he'd had another stroke.

Without giving it another moment's thought, he backed up, braced against the opposite wall, and lifted a booted foot to slam against the door near the lock. It broke enough for him to finish the job with one more kick and use his shoulders to muscle all the way through. Instantly, Ruff lunged at him, throwing his full weight on Aidan in a panic.

"Down! Down!" He roared the command, blinking into the red lights that flashed through the windows. Up here, the sirens were easy to hear, but he didn't take a second to look outside.

"Mike, where are you?" he ground out, circling, then running toward the galley kitchen. And there he was, on the floor, lurched against a cabinet, his cell phone still in his hand. He'd come up here to save Ruff and passed out. Or worse.

Aidan vaulted toward him, checking his pulse, saying a silent prayer when the vein tapped his thumb.

"Move, Ruff!" He scooped up Mike's limp body, hoisted him over his shoulder, and turned to the windows, ready to kick one out if he had to. He went to the middle pane and managed to shove the frame up, swearing under his breath when the paint stuck.

"Up there! He's up there!" A chorus of voices from the small crowd that had gathered floated up, and instantly he saw the jacket-clad firefighters swarm and get the ladder in position.

"We got this, Ruff," he said over his shoulder. "We got this!"

Next to him, Ruff barked and spun and essentially lost his mind over the chaos. In seconds, the ladder landed, and he could see the helmet of the man climbing up.

"Mmmm." Mike moaned over Aidan's shoulder, coming to. "Help me."

"I got you, buddy. We're getting you out of here."

Smoke started to fill the room. The clock was ticking. The fire was on its way. He had to move *fast*.

In the next second, his cousin Connor's familiar face popped into the view.

"Out of the way, Aidan. I'll get the screen and take him," Connor ordered.

Aidan didn't argue, doing exactly what he was told, then easing Mike's body out onto Connor's sizable shoulder. He stole a glance below to see four more men, in position to catch anyone who fell, including his cousin, Declan, shouting orders to his crew.

But where was Beck?

He scanned the crowd being held back across the street along Bushrod Square, his gaze finally landing on Beck, who stood at the side, her arm around a wailing Sarah. She must have driven here, after all. Damn shame to witness this.

Beck looked up as Connor started down with Mike slumped over his shoulder and instantly turned her aunt around so she couldn't see.

Aidan stuck his head out the window so she'd know he was okay. "One more!" he called. "A dog!"

"Then you!" Connor hollered from down the ladder, the insistence in his cousin's voice easy to hear even over the noise of sirens and the fire behind him. He stole one more look at Beck, able to see the relief on her face. Horror, anxiety, and all those ancient fears were bubbling up inside her, no doubt. But everyone was alive.

Time to prove that to her.

"Let's go, Ru—" He spun around, only then realizing that Ruff was gone. And then he heard a single bark from the staircase.

"He's okay, Aunt Sarah. He's down. They have him. The medics have him." Beck kept repeating the same things over and over to her aunt, who thought she'd surprise them all by driving over to restaurant to celebrate Mike's return.

Bitter smoke burned the lump in Beck's throat as she fought back tears and tried to stay strong for her aunt.

Despite her body's own quivering, Beck wrapped Sarah in her arms, keeping her aunt's face pressed against her shoulder so the poor woman didn't have to witness her livelihood going up in smoke and fire.

But Sarah lifted a tear-stained face, stealing a glance in time to see the firefighter reach the bottom rungs of the ladder with Uncle Mike's limp body. "There he is."

Please let him be alive, dear God. Please.

"Is he—" Sarah started to pull away, but Beck wouldn't let her move.

"Let them take care of him. Let them give him oxygen or whatever he needs." *And please let someone get to Aidan and Ruff.*

A team of fire engines, a squadron of firefighters, and at least four smaller utility trucks had arrived less than five minutes after her call, with the captain showing up first in a separate vehicle and Sarah shortly after that. Somehow, Beck had stayed calm enough to tell him who was in there, stunned when he nodded and said, "Aidan's my cousin, ma'am. We'll get him."

She'd totally forgotten Declan Mahoney was Aidan's cousin. He seemed to know the building well as she heard him holler commands to the dozens of men and women in heavy jackets and helmets dragging huge hoses, as choreographed as a dance.

All along, Captain Mahoney directed every move, shouting orders, on a phone, pointing men to doors, sending a team into the dining room through the shattered glass door. It was the only place not on fire in the whole building.

A flash of twenty-four medallions on a seafoam-green wall appeared in Beck's head, but she shoved it away. One loss at a time. People mattered, not awards.

But if she hadn't been hell-bent on winning one, would this have even happened?

She grunted at the thought, forcing her gaze to join everyone else's—at the window where Aidan had been.

Except...where was he now?

Another firefighter was almost at the top of the ladder now, moving with remarkable speed, considering the weight of equipment on his back.

She couldn't see flames in the apartment windows...yet. Plenty of smoke, though. But that was where Aidan and Ruff must have found Mike. She re-created the scene in her mind, trying to imagine how Mike had ended up there—to get Ruff when the fire started, no doubt. And then Aidan had gone in, scoured the burning kitchen, and bravely marched up to save two souls she loved with her whole heart.

But what about his soul? She loved that one, too.

Why wasn't Ruff coming out of that window and Aidan following right now? Frustration burned inside her like the fire, as harsh as the smoke scorching her throat, making her want to scream out.

What's happening up there? Where are they?

"Why doesn't he come down?" she ground out the question, still squeezing Sarah, only vaguely aware that the crowd had grown. Every cell in her body was focused on the window, willing Aidan and Ruff to appear.

The firefighter turned and looked below, hollering something to the captain. Declan Mahoney didn't even hesitate, but raised his hand and pointed. "Get him!"

Yes, please, God. Get him.

"Why did he go?" Sarah wailed, twisting in Beck's arms to see what was going on. "Why did Mike leave tonight? *Why?*"

Because Beck had begged him to go into the kitchen and cook. And something had gone very, very wrong. She had no idea what, but it had.

She blinked at the tears blurring her vision as she stared up at that window, where all she could see was clouds of smoke. Where could Aidan have gone?

Ruff had run away. There was no other explanation. Aidan would die to save that dog, and she knew it.

"Please, can we see Mike?" Sarah pleaded. "Please."

"Of course, of course." Still watching the window, Beck wove through the crowd to get closer to where the ambulances were lined up on Ambrose Avenue. A group of medics surrounded Uncle Mike, who appeared to be on a gurney. She stood on her tiptoes to see if Mike was hurt, burned, or worse, before she let Sarah go closer.

But she couldn't see over the crowd, adding a new frustration.

"Let's give them a minute," she said. A minute of chaos. Heat pressed on her face, the fire crackled and whooshed with the occasional deafening pop, sheriff's deputies hauled out barriers and moved the crowd back, the bitter, deadly smell of smoke seeping into her every pore.

And still no sign of Aidan.

It all blurred in her teary vision and screamed in her pounding head. Again. Again. *Again.*

This time a fire. Last time a bullet. The time before that, a car accident. How many people would Beck Spencer lose?

"Mrs. Leone." One of the paramedics came rushing over, a woman Beck recognized as one of the few regulars who stopped in at Slice of Heaven a few times a week. "Your husband's asking for you."

"Thank God," Beck muttered as relief swamped her. She wouldn't lose Uncle Mike. Not tonight.

"He's had a stroke, you know," Sarah said, stumbling toward the woman. "He's not healthy. Do they know that? Do they—"

"He's fine," the paramedic assured them both as they came closer to the group around the gurney. "But we're going to take him over to Vestal Valley General to be sure."

As the crowd spread for them, Beck could see more professionals in action around a gurney, taking Mike's blood pressure, checking his lungs and heart with a stethoscope, giving him oxygen through a mask. Just as Sarah and Beck reached him, two more paramedics lifted the stretcher into the back of the ambulance.

"Can I go with him?" Sarah asked.

The woman who'd brought them over didn't hesitate. "In the front, with the driver." Then she looked at Beck. "Will you follow?"

"I can't leave," Beck said to both of them, giving Sarah a reassuring hug. "I'm waiting for Aidan." *Who will come out of that building alive, damn it.*

"And Ruff," Sarah added on a soft sob, ripping Beck's heart out.

"Oh, Aunt Sarah. We'll survive this," she promised with another hug. "We've been through worse."

Sarah looked up at her, green eyes filled with pain and fear. "Thank you, Beck. Please thank Aidan. He saved Mike's life."

"I will. I promise." And she added a silent prayer that she could keep that promise.

At the sound of a loud noise, she whipped around, seeing a massive cloud of smoke erupt into the night air.

"Stairwell collapsed!" She heard one of the firefighters holler the announcement to the team, and her heart did exactly the same thing.

Collapsed? What if he was on it?

Beck pressed her knuckles to her mouth and stepped back into the crowd, aching for the nightmare to end.

"Beck! Beck, we're here." At the sound of a man's voice, she spun around to see Daniel Kilcannon running toward her, with Garrett, Jessie, Shane, Chloe, and Darcy right behind him.

"He's inside," she managed to say through a sob. "He's in there."

She saw Daniel's step falter at the news, but he continued toward her, folding her into strong arms. She nearly buckled against him, falling into the comfort she so desperately needed.

"I'm going to talk to Dec," Garrett said, heading straight to the captain, Shane right behind him. Jessie and Chloe wrapped their arms around Beck, too, forming a tight little circle of support.

"Is Aidan in there?" The high-pitched question came from Molly, running toward them with Pru and Trace on either side of her.

"He is," Daniel said, refusing to let go of Beck. "But they'll get him. I know they'll get him."

"It's Ruff," Beck said, tears streaming down her face. "He got Uncle Mike out, but then he didn't come out because...Ruff..." She choked as Daniel stroked her hair and Pru patted her back.

Another shattering of glass and a small pop of an explosion made her cry out and pull away from Daniel to see what had happened. The dining room was on fire now, but the flames were sputtering under roaring hoses that doused the entire building with water. The façade above her apartment was hanging down, drenched by the hoses, with only the occasional flame up there.

How long had it been? How could he—

"Look! Look!"

As though they were one, the entire family turned in the direction Molly pointed, as a man emerged from the smoke of the dining room and stepped through the debris and broken glass of the front door.

Covered in soot, coughing, but alive and walking with Ruff draped over his shoulders, Aidan emerged from the smoke. He stumbled under the dog's weight but was caught by the firefighter next to him.

"Thank you, Annie," Daniel whispered, so softly that no one else but Beck could have heard it.

But the words to his deceased wife gave Beck a wave of chills as powerful as the tears that streamed down her cheeks.

"He's fine!"

"They're alive!"

"Thank God!"

The chorus of exclamations and gratitude was drowned out by Beck's heart thumping at a rate she didn't ever remember feeling before. The group broke up, Daniel let go, and they all sort of moved like one single unit toward Aidan, drawn like moths to their flame. But Beck stayed rooted in one spot and stared at Aidan as he marched toward the ambulance and finally eased Ruff to the ground.

She saw a medic bend over with an oxygen mask for Ruff, which folded her heart in half. But then her view was blocked by the paramedics and Kilcannons who circled Aidan. Immediately, someone wrapped him in a blanket, and someone else tried to put an oxygen mask on him.

But he shook his head, throwing off the blanket as he searched the crowd with a desperate, wild expression.

"Where's Beck?" His voice was raspy but determined. "Where the hell is Beck?" he demanded, shaking off the hand of someone who tried to get him to lie down.

Finally, his gaze landed on her, making her realize she hadn't taken one step closer to him.

Because she couldn't. Couldn't run to him and throw her arms around him. Couldn't surrender and take the risk of losing a man she loved.

Love meant loss. Didn't this prove it to her? She couldn't take this chance again, couldn't fall into that dark place again, couldn't wake up and go to sleep mired in grief. Love wasn't worth that pain to her. Hadn't life made that clear enough to Rebecca Spencer?

Aidan muscled past everyone in his way, zeroing in on her. As he got closer, she could see the streaks of soot on his face and how dark his hair was. His chest heaved with every ragged, compromised breath. But nothing stopped him.

"Beck!" He yelled her name, snapping her out of her shock-induced trance.

"Aidan." She tried to lift her arms to reach for him, but they were so heavy that she stood there until he got to her and circled his around her.

"I found Ruff. In the kitchen. I had to..." He struggled for a breath. "He's going to be okay," he said huskily, choking softly. "And so are we."

But deep inside, she knew that wasn't true.

Chapter Twenty-Four

"You have a visitor."

Aidan looked up from the agility jumper he was disassembling after the training session had ended, hating that his heart kicked up at his father's announcement.

Please, God, let it be Beck.

He stood slowly, wiping dirt from his hands, refusing to let his gaze go past Dad and up toward the house, which was quite a distance from this field.

"Two, actually," Dad added as he came closer. "And only one has four legs."

She'd brought Ruff. He couldn't help blowing out the breath he'd been holding since, well, since the fire four days ago. He'd seen Beck twice in that time—the next day, after Mike was released from the hospital and sent home to recover, and another time, when they met with fire investigators and the insurance adjuster.

As he'd suspected, the oven had been the culprit, with aging wiring that had sparked. After that meeting, Beck had asked for some space to take care of Sarah and Mike, promising to call. But she hadn't. Not once.

And every hour that had gone by, Aidan had slipped more into the certainty that the timing of this tragedy could not have been worse.

"Did you talk to her?" Aidan asked.

"Briefly." Dad glanced over his shoulder in the general direction of the barking that came from the main training pen in the distance. "She said Mike's doing well. And Ruff seems...well, like Ruff." He gave a dry laugh. "But that's not what you want to know, is it?"

Aidan cringed. "I lost her, Dad. I know it. She's retreated to that place where she goes when she loses someone, even though no one died this time."

"Something died," Dad said. "That building'll be leveled. And she told me Mike and Sarah are moving to Florida with the insurance money."

He grunted as the news gutted him. "So she has no reason to stay." Because he would be the only reason, and he wasn't enough.

Dad put a hand on Aidan's shoulder. "I thought you never quit."

"There comes a time when the decision to keep going isn't yours anymore, Dad. This one's in her court."

His gaze drifted behind his father's sizable shoulder to Beck on her way toward him, wearing jeans and a black tank top he'd never seen before. Of course not—her clothes had all burned. Beside her, Ruff trotted at his usual clip, but then he caught sight of Aidan and nearly yanked Beck over. She let go of his leash, and Ruff tore at full speed, barking in frustration when he reached a fence.

"Whatever you want to do, Son," Dad said right

before he walked away, "I'll respect and honor any decision. Even if that decision is to leave to be with her."

That wouldn't be his first choice, but if it were his only choice? He'd move to Chicago in a heartbeat. It was Beck he wanted, anywhere, anytime. But he doubted she'd ask that. It wasn't geography standing in their way. It was history.

He narrowed his eyes to watch her come closer, taking a moment to feel how the sight of her hit his heart. Hard.

When Dad left the training field, opening the gate, Ruff came barreling over to Aidan, running with the fury, love, and determination Aidan ached for Beck to show. But her steps were slow and tentative, as if she dreaded this reunion.

He tried to swallow, tried to accept that, but there was a big fist in his throat that only threatened to make things worse.

"Hey, Ruffer!" He reached for the dog, who leaped into the air and smacked his paws on Aidan's chest. Together, they rolled to the grass and wrestled for a minute, an old and familiar contentment rolling through Aidan.

Then he looked up and saw Beck, and every emotion he'd battled for days and weeks came screaming to the surface. He loved her. God, he *loved* her. He didn't have a doubt, not one single one.

But that expression on her face, visible as she got closer and closer? The pull of her brows, the set of her chin? Beck was mired in doubts.

Oh man. Here we go. Crash-and-burn time.

As he got up, he grabbed a tennis ball they'd been

using during training and whipped it across the field, sending Ruff on a tear and giving them some time alone.

"Thrown like a baseball player," she said as she reached him.

He acknowledged the compliment with a silent nod, not entirely sure what would happen to his voice if he said her name.

"Bet you could teach Ruff to catch with his mitt, too," she added. "He rarely puts it down."

He started to answer, then let her words hit him. He could teach Ruff? Like, in the future? Did that mean…

"You're not leaving?" He could have kicked himself the second the question came out. What the hell kind of greeting was that, other than desperate?

She slowed midstep, silent for a beat. A beat too long.

"That would be a yes," Aidan concluded quietly.

On a sigh, she gathered up her hair in one hand, pulling it off her shoulders and letting it drape down her back in a nervous gesture he knew often preceded talking about something she didn't enjoy.

"Mike and Sarah are moving to Florida," she finally said. "When the insurance money comes through and the house is sold."

"My dad said Mike's doing okay." Aidan took a step closer because, well, he needed to. Needed to touch her, too. "Lungs are clear? No aftermath?"

"You saved him from anything serious, Aidan," she said, not for the first time since the fire. He couldn't question her gratitude, that was for sure. "You got him out of there so fast, so safely. It could have been..." She let out a rough exhale. "I can't think about what might have happened."

"Then don't."

She squished up her face. "I can't help it. It's all I think about."

"Then you need to get out more often." One more step, and now she was within reach of his arms, but he didn't lift them.

She held his gaze, her eyes moving over his face, studying him intently. "I need to get back to...work."

"You can work here." He wasn't going to dance around this. Wasn't going to give up without a fight, damn it. "There are babies in Bitter Bark. Studios. Camera equipment. There's even a guy who doesn't want you to leave so bad, he can't breathe."

"Aidan." She barely whispered his name, but Ruff came back then, not running but carrying the ball. He relinquished it easily, but when Aidan tossed it again, Ruff merely collapsed at his feet, curling around him with one satisfied bark.

"And there's a dog who loves you more than he loves me," she said on a soft laugh.

"He loves Mike more than both of us combined."

"They have a special relationship," she conceded. "And Aunt Sarah's even fallen for him, since Ruff's so calm when he's with Uncle Mike. But there's only one man alive who makes Ruff happy, and that's you."

"I know how he feels," he said, reaching for her hand. "Because there's only one woman who makes me happy, and that's you."

She sighed and barely smiled, letting him hold her hand but not exactly grasping back with any kind of affection. "I can't, Aidan. Not yet. Maybe not ever."

He closed his eyes and let that hit.

"It was so hard that night," she whispered, closing her fingers lightly around his. "It was one of the worst things I've ever been through, and I've been through a few. The feeling of you slipping away, being gone, another—"

"But I'm right here, Beck. Alive and well and in love with you."

She bit her lip, like she had to stop herself from saying what she felt.

"Tell me," he insisted. "Tell me you don't feel exactly the same way, and I will give up right here and now. But you have to be honest, Beck."

She took their joined hands and pressed his knuckles to her lips. "I'm in love with you, too."

"Oh." He tried to pull her closer, but she wouldn't let him, rooted to her spot.

"And that's why I can't stay."

He froze. "No, I'm not going to accept that. It's lame. It's weak. It's not—"

"It's true," she finished. "And you need to respect my fear and understand what I've lived with most of my life. You've lost your mother, Aidan. And you're still mourning her, right?"

"Of course."

"Well, I've lost my mother, my father, and my only sibling." She narrowed her eyes to let that sink in. "And the other night, when I looked up at that window and you didn't come out, my fears strangled me. They *owned* me. They are real, and I can't live with that...that...possibility looming over me."

"So you'd rather not live at all?" His voice rose in frustration. "Beck, every person on earth who loves anyone lives with that possibility. The only way you can avoid it is to never love anyone."

She stared at him…as if to say that was exactly what she was going to do. And nothing would change her mind.

"When are you leaving?" he asked, buying time to plan his next strategic move. He *couldn't* quit.

"I'm helping Sarah and Mike pack up. A week at most."

Oh man. A week.

"And I've decided to leave Ruff with you."

He blinked at her. "What?"

"Ruff belongs to you, Beck."

The words sliced him in half. All he wanted when he met her, and now, that decision couldn't be more wrong.

"That Army form post-dates my letter," she added. "For some reason, Charlie changed his mind, and I think we should respect that. We've always agreed to honor Charlie's wishes."

"Well, it's not *my* wish," he ground out. "I want you. And Ruff. And, hell, I want Mike and Sarah to stay so Ruff has his job. I want…" Everything he couldn't have.

Her eyes shuttered, and a single tear rolled, giving him hope.

"Beck, honey, don't make yourself miserable on purpose. You think that's what Charlie wanted?"

"I don't know what he wanted," she admitted with a sob threatening her voice. "I'm scared and confused and need time and…perspective."

"So you want to go home and get some?"

She nodded, swallowing visibly.

He closed the space between them and slipped his arms around her. If patience was his only strategy, he'd be the most patient human to ever live. "Then take it. Get perspective. When you know that we're right together, Beck, I'll be here, waiting for you."

With one more audible sigh, she backed away, then bent over to pet Ruff. "See ya around, Ruffie."

Her voice broke with a sob, but she turned and headed back to the gate, moving far faster than she had on arrival. As if he understood the battle was over, Ruff didn't run after her. He barked once, then looked up at Aidan as if to say...*you won.*

"But I lost, bud. I lost the girl, the dream, the life, everything."

He watched her go, kept his gaze on her until she disappeared, then scooped up his dog, draped him over his shoulders, and marched down to the creek where no one would see him cry.

Cleaning out Charlie's room wasn't any easier with Sarah than it had been with Aidan, but the job had to be done.

Beck stood in the middle of a room full of big black garbage bags, a dozen plastic bins, and piles of sports uniforms, camos, T-shirts, and jeans.

The two of them had been quiet except for the occasional "donate or toss?" question that helped them divide up the remnants of a life well lived. Twice, Beck had heard Sarah sniff back some tears, but they'd laughed a few times, too. And took one break to look through his high school yearbook. Beck had given up when they hit the K's and she'd seen Aidan's senior portrait.

He'd been a golden boy, indeed. And his hair might have darkened over the years, but his good heart only got...golder.

On a noisy sigh, she climbed over a box and made her way to the nightstand, which was stuffed. "He was such a pack rat," Beck muttered. "I never keep anything for more than a year."

"You keep it in your heart," Sarah said as she snapped the lid off a bin she'd dragged out of the closet. "You carry things around for years, but they don't take up as much space as your brother's...oh, video games." She sighed. "I'll put them in the donation pile."

Sarah was right, Beck thought. She had more baggage than the belly of a 747. But she didn't stuff it into drawers and bins. No, she let it weigh her down, ruin great relationships, and force her to live alone when all she wanted was...

Aidan. And Ruff. And the life she'd started to dream about.

She tried to swallow, but, as always, a sob threatened. In the days that passed since she'd last seen Aidan, she hadn't gone one full minute without missing him.

Was she doing the right thing? It sure didn't feel right.

She pulled out a few magazines, two called *Aviation Week* and another *Maxim* that hadn't been stuffed under the mattress. She tossed it in the trash bag before Sarah could see the six-inch cleavage that graced the cover.

Under those she found… "Oh wow."

"What is it?"

"This was Mama's." She eased out a scrapbook she'd immediately recognized from her mother's worktable in the kitchen. "I totally forgot how obsessed she was with scrapbooking."

"Oh, that's where they went. To Charlie's drawer." Sarah gave a wry laugh. "Who'd have guessed he'd want scrapbooks?"

She flipped open the cover to the first page, where her mother's scripted handwriting was under the image of a country road bathed in sunshine and the colors of autumn.

We don't meet people by accident. They cross our path for a reason.

Glued to the opposite page were pictures of family friends Beck barely recognized, such as a lady from the neighborhood who used to come over for coffee and one of the teachers from school. Mama had had a whole life full of friends Beck hadn't even realized as a child.

On the next page was the image of a road sign and the words: *An unexpected detour can change your life forever.* Plus a picture of her father, looking younger than Beck was right now.

An old coil of pain curled up her chest, tightening everything in its path.

On the next page, a sunset with the silhouette of a couple holding hands, gazing into each other's eyes. *When a girl is in love, you see it in her smile. When a boy is in love, it's in his eyes.* The whole page was covered with snapshots of Mama and Daddy, dating, married, and as young parents.

Beck wiped her eyes and studied each picture, grazing her fingers over a few as if she could reach out and touch these people. Page after page, she could hear her mother's clever quotes and see how life had made these sayings real to her.

Waiting is a sign of true love. With a grainy, shiny picture from Beck's very own sonogram, too out of date to even make out the shape of a baby. She flipped another page, reading the words and ignoring the pictures. Phrase after phrase, handwritten by her mother.

Just the thought of being with you tomorrow is enough to get me through today.

If you want to know where your heart is, follow your mind when it wanders.

Love is like oxygen. You can't see it, but you need it to live.

We meet by chance. We love by choice.

More tears swam now, blurring her vision. In her head, all she could hear was the sweet, familiar, happy sound of Karen Spencer sharing wisdom, advice, and love. Wasn't that what she was doing right this minute? Using her little proverbs to guide her daughter from beyond?

Or was Beck simply an emotional mess looking for answers that were right in front of her?

She closed the book, unable to take anymore. She should give this to Gramma Finnie, and not only because that would give her an excuse to visit Waterford Farm again. She'd love—

"Oh my God, Rebecca! Rebecca!"

Beck whipped around at the sound of Aunt Sarah's high-pitched voice. She stood in the middle of the room, holding a slip of paper. "I found it! I found the recipe you've been looking for."

"What?" Still clutching the book to her chest, she scrambled over, nearly tripping on boxes. "Where was it?"

"In this folder he called 'cheat codes.'"

"I guess they're not just for video games," Beck said on an excited laugh. "What is it?"

"Baking soda!"

Beck stared at her, jaw dropped. "What?"

"That's it!" Uncle Mike boomed from the hallway, making Beck wonder how long he'd been out there, loitering and listening. He stepped into the doorway with the brightest eyes Beck had seen since the fire. "And it *was* you, Sarah. Don't you remember?"

She frowned, glanced at the paper, then up at him. "That first time I tried to make sauce? The day of the Best of Bitter Bark Festival? You got so mad because I put baking soda in by accident. Told me I needed to keep my skills in the bedroom, not the kitchen."

"I didn't hear that," Beck said on a moan.

But Mike chuckled, then let out a good, hearty laugh, the first time she'd heard that sound since before his stroke. "It was why I won, I swear. No one else ever did it."

"Actually, a guy named Chef John does," Beck said, getting them both to look at her. "I found his YouTube video and even mentioned it to Aidan, but he scoffed at baking soda in sauce."

"Who wouldn't?" Uncle Mike barked. "But then it won because it adds a certain something, like a taste you don't even know you're missing."

"Umami," Beck whispered.

"And I've been sneakin' it in ever since," Uncle Mike continued. "Won me twenty-four medallions that those nice firefighters managed to save."

"Could be twenty-five." Sarah waved the paper at him. "The contest starts in about an hour."

"Seriously?" Beck choked. "It's today? I totally forgot."

"And Ricardo Mancini called last week to offer you his kitchen if you wanted to enter," Sarah said to Mike. "I told him that was kind, but…"

"And win for what? Slice of Heaven is gone," Mike said. "Burned to the ground."

Beck glanced down at the book in her arms, conjuring up one of the pages. "Strength doesn't come from your tears," she whispered. "It comes from getting up and trying again."

Uncle Mike held her gaze for a long, long time. "If I win that contest, Beckie, you know what I'll want to do. You *know*."

"You'll want to rebuild Slice of Heaven." It wasn't a question. She knew that look in his eyes. It used to be there every morning when he mixed his dough.

He looked at Sarah. "She's right."

Sarah nodded and reached for him. "Then let's try again, sweetheart. Florida will always be there."

A smile broke over Beck's face as she squeezed her mother's scrapbook. It was like she was right there, rooting for them, sending her sage advice, loving them from her place in heaven.

"Let's go to Ricardo's!" Beck said. "Bring that recipe, Aunt Sarah."

Uncle Mike waved his hand. "Pffft. I remember it."

Sarah and Beck shared a look, and Beck snagged the paper and stuck it in her scrapbook, carrying it with her. "In case he forgets."

Chapter Twenty-Five

Ricardo's kitchen was completely unfamiliar. The proofing box was in the wrong place. The counter was slippery. The room was jammed with unfamiliar people. And, of course, the oven...well, the oven was modern and could easily hit 700. That was one big change right there.

But all in all, the experience was no different than climbing into the cockpit of someone else's bird and having to adjust muscle memory to get the job done. Bottom line, it was flying. And the bottom line *today*, in this strange kitchen, with Ruff at his feet and the owner at the next counter rolling dough with masterful moves, Aidan was just making pizza.

By now, he could do it in his sleep.

He tested the doughball and leaned back, wiping his hands on the Slice of Heaven apron he'd found in his laundry basket at home. Probably the last remaining one on earth, and Aidan had eyed it for a long time when he'd found it, thinking that it might be the perfect thing to "return" to Beck so he could see her again.

But at Wednesday night dinner, the conversation had turned to this weekend's Best of Bitter Bark Festival, and every single member of his family had pressed him to compete. Ricardo Mancini had come by Waterford Farm the day before, as so many neighbors and townsfolk had, to check on Aidan and offered the use of his kitchen to anyone from Slice who wanted to compete. He said he made the same offer to Mike, but it was turned down.

It hadn't taken much to get Aidan to agree to compete, but only as a representative of Slice of Heaven, so if he won, he could give the medallion to Mike to take with him to Florida, along with the other twenty-four that Dec and his crew had managed to save.

And his entire family had come to support him, of course, from Gramma Finnie down to newborn Fiona and every Kilcannon in between. They'd already claimed seats at the judging area on the square, ready to root for him.

If only…

Don't go there, Kil.

He worked the dough harder, stealing a glance to his left to check out Ricardo Mancini, a big personality with a shock of white hair and black brows, who spoke with a hint of New York in every word. He rolled with flair and tossed the pie in the air, making his restaurant employees break out in a cheer and Ruff bark.

"This is my year," he exclaimed, giving a friendly grin to Aidan. "With all due respect, young Kilcannon, no one whose last name doesn't end in a vowel has a shot."

Aidan laughed easily at the friendly trash talk. "But Night Stalkers don't quit, Ricky-boy. Not until we win."

The other man held up his perfectly round circle. "Look at this windowpane."

"It's too thin!"

At the exclamation, every single person in the kitchen turned toward the door from the dining room, a soft gasp rolling through the group.

"Michael Leone, you handsome *paisano*!" Ricardo dropped his pie to greet his guest, and Aidan damn near did the same. Mike was here?

And behind him, Sarah. And...and...Oh *yes*.

When Beck stepped into the room, it was like a grenade exploded in Aidan's heart. Nothing had changed for him. If anything, his feelings had deepened and grown, strong enough to strangle him when he woke in a cold sweat in the middle of every night.

Instantly, their gazes met, and her brown eyes widened in surprise and flashed with...oh, that had to be joy. He knew that look. He recognized the smile, the angle of her head, the flush in her cheeks. He'd put that expression on her pretty face so many times in the past.

"But your rep is already here!" Ricardo said, patting Mike on the back and turning him to see Aidan.

"Wasn't sure you'd make it, big guy," Aidan said, already reaching to untie his apron.

Before Mike answered, a bark below pulled his attention. Ruff stood right in front of him, at attention like a soldier under inspection, tongue out, lips back, teeth displayed in a rare smile.

"Ruff!" The older man bent over, his left arm still not at a hundred percent, but he managed to get both hands on the dog's head to love him. After a second, Mike looked up at Aidan, his eyes damp with emotion. "You keep that apron on, Son. I want you to win."

"Not a chance." He pulled the strap over his head and walked closer to Mike to slip it over Mike's head with a flourish. "I bow to the master."

"Uh, I don't know," Ricardo said, a not-too-serious frown pulling his dark brows into a V. "This could be a game changer."

"You bet it is," Mike replied, then leaned closer to Aidan. "We got the secret."

"Get out."

Mike grinned. "Why? I just got here."

"And you're here to win." The two of them shared a quick embrace, with Mike adding a cheek-to-cheek brush on each side. "What is it?" Aidan whispered when their heads were close.

"I was right. It was Sarah."

Aidan drew back, scowling, then glanced across the kitchen to where Sarah and Beck stood with their arms around each other.

Ricardo moved in closer and added his own warm hug. "It's such an honor to have you here in my kitchen, Michael. You're a blessing to this whole town."

A cheer went up with applause and hoots, making Mike blink in shock. Had he not realized that this community was aching with him over the loss of his restaurant? That he was an institution, even for these employees of the only real competition around?

"Then let's make pizza," Mike said, looking around. "Where's my Sarah? She's my secret ingredient."

More applause for Sarah as she sidled her way between the counters and planted a kiss on her husband's lips. "Let's get twenty-five, honey."

Aidan relinquished his spot and slid over to where Beck stood, snapping pictures with her cell phone.

"Whoa," he whispered, resisting the urge to kiss her. "This is a surprise."

She lowered the phone and smiled up at him, the topaz flecks in her dark eyes sparking. "She literally found the secret recipe in a pile of Call of Duty cheat codes."

Aidan choked. "Why didn't I think of that? So, what is it? Mike is still claiming it's Sarah."

"Because Sarah discovered it by accident twenty-five years ago, but had no idea." She leaned close to his ear, her breath tickling as she whispered, "I miss you."

He almost fell over, but stayed perfectly still, almost afraid to break the magic of the moment by saying a word. Instead, he let the confession fall all over him like rain on a thirsty man.

As she eased back to her heels, they looked at each other. The raucous kitchen faded into nothing but his thumping heart. The smells of tomatoes and basil evaporated, leaving the floral scent of Beck's hair. And the world around him blurred as only one thing and one person stayed in focus.

"You do."

"So much." She didn't look away, not for one second. But her lips quivered a bit as she took an unsteady breath. "I can't believe you're here."

He couldn't believe...anything. "I couldn't let him lose, Beck."

"Plus, Night Stalkers..." She let the rest go unfinished.

"Never," he said. "Unless they don't have a choice."

Her eyes flickered as his words hit home. "What if you had a choice?"

He lowered his face a millimeter closer. "Then I'd never quit you, Beck Spencer."

Just as he leaned in for a kiss, Ruff barked and pulled their attention. He circled Mike, literally blocking him from moving away from the counter. Mike tried to take a few steps to get some ingredients, but Ruff was like an eighty-pound wall, refusing to allow him to inch away from the counter.

"Ruff's protecting him," Aidan said, sliding his arm around Beck to pull her closer.

"He probably remembers the trauma up in the apartment," Beck said, some pain in her voice. "Poor thing can't let go of the past."

Aidan looked down at her, lifting a brow. "The past can be a crippling thing."

"He thinks because something awful happened once, it could happen again."

He started to smile. "Nobody ever accused that dog of being a genius."

She smiled, too. "But we are human, and we know better."

"Do you, Beck?"

Inching up on her toes again, she put the softest kiss on his lips. "I do."

The admission, simple, whispered, and powerful, rocked Aidan he put his hands on her cheeks.

"Someday, somehow, somewhere, you're going to say those two words again to me. In front of a church full of family and friends."

Her eyes filled. "Aidan, I—"

"Nope, nope. Don't argue. I'm not going to quit."

"But, Aidan, I—"

"I'm not going to stalk you or hound you or pressure you to do or say anything, Beck, but I will not give up on this. On us."

"Aidan, I—"

"Just accept it, Beck. This is it. For me and you and—"

She tapped her hand over his lips, silencing him. "I'm trying to tell you that I love you."

The rest of his argument lodged in his throat as everything ground to a halt. "You love me."

"Yes, I do. And I will say those two words somewhere, somehow, sometime again. For now, I'll say these three: I love you. I don't know where that's taking us, but I love you."

All around them, a cheer erupted, deafening and happy. For a moment, Aidan thought it was for him— the winner of everything he'd ever wanted—but it was for the two pizzas as they came out of the oven.

"Now, my friend." Ricardo put his hand on Mike's back. "Let's go see what the judges say."

As the whole lot of them poured into the dining room to march over to Bushrod Square, Beck and Aidan stayed behind to steal one more kiss in the pizza kitchen.

Beck clung to Aidan's hand all the way to Bushrod Square, stopping at various booths and displays to drink in the event that showcased just about every talent in town. In addition to the food section, where they were heading, competitions were taking place all over the square and spilling onto the surrounding streets.

They were vying for best in art from local painters and sculptors; best in dance, featuring several of the girls from the local high school; best in acting, with the Bitter Bark players reading monologues; and best in music, with a large contingent of locals singing and playing instruments. Dotted in between the big "shows" were the best in craft beer and cocktails, storefront décor, baked goods, and flower arranging.

"But what about the dogs?" Beck asked as they cruised by a juggler and a street mime competing for best of performance art.

"Oh, that's at the end," Aidan told her. "Darcy is hell-bent on Kookie winning, but she has so many dogs she's groomed for the competition, she'll win no matter who comes in best in show."

"We should enter Ruff," she said.

"Best in sad face?"

"Oh." A whimper escaped her throat. "He's not happy, Aidan?"

He slowed his step and studied her for a moment, looking at her like he simply couldn't possibly look anywhere else. Which was fine with Beck. She didn't want him to.

"I thought he was channeling my inner misery since you've been gone," Aidan said. "But you know, after seeing him in the kitchen? I think he misses Mike."

"That's who should have him," she said. "Mike's his job."

"And Charlie would know it if he saw them together," Aidan agreed. "But, I honestly don't think I could bear to have him go to Florida. Day gigs for service are one thing, but that dog is not leaving us forever."

"Well, the fact is, Mike doesn't even want to go to Florida."

"I thought it was a done deal."

"When we found the secret ingredient, he said he'd stay and rebuild if he won today."

"Are you ser—"

"Look, Aidan. There's the Food Network people." She pointed to a group gathered around the small stage set up for food judging.

"He'll really stay if he wins?" he asked, clearly more impressed with that than the VIP guests.

"Guess there's only one way to find out," she said. "Win."

As they reached the grandstand, the huge contingent of Kilcannons descended with hugs, kisses, and a buzz of excitement. Beck cooed over the newborn Fiona all tucked under a shady umbrella, and hugged Gramma Finnie, remembering the scrapbook.

"I have something I want to show you," Beck whispered to the old woman.

Gramma leaned back and searched her face. "That smile, lass? Is that what you want to show me? Because it's mighty pretty."

A line from the scrapbook flashed in her mind.

When a girl is in love, you see it in her smile. When a boy is in love, it's in his eyes. "That, and something else."

"You look happy," Daniel Kilcannon said as he gave her a warm, fatherly embrace.

"I am," she told him, beaming up at him, unable to think of anything but…*Aidan's going to be that silver and handsome in thirty years.*

And she wanted to be around to see that.

The family essentially took over the viewing stands, almost all of them with dogs in tow. Only Chloe and Shane were missing, currently running around directing the day's many contests and working with the surprising amount of media covering what had been, in Beck's memory, a tiny event many years ago.

She settled in next to Aidan, drinking in the color and pageantry of her little town and…

"My little town," she murmured.

"What was that?" Aidan asked.

"It's home," she said softly. "I think this place is finally home."

He smiled at her, his eyes as blue as the afternoon sky behind him. In that second, she remembered looking up at him for the first time right here in Bushrod Square. The first time the full impact of Aidan Kilcannon hit her…and never stopped.

"Pizza!" The announcer broke in over a crackly speaker, making them both laugh.

As the crowd hushed, Beck's gaze found Uncle Mike standing to the side. Sarah was a few feet away, holding Ruff by the leash, which was a sight Beck had never actually thought she'd see.

Next to Uncle Mike and Ricardo Mancini were a woman she didn't recognize and a young man who used to frequent Slice of Heaven a lot when she first started.

"That guy launched a new catering business in town," Aidan said under his breath. "The other woman is a local who loves to make pizza. But the kid could be a dark horse."

"How do you know?"

"I ordered his stuff one night when I was particularly miserable and missed you. The pizza was damn good."

"But did it have baking soda?"

He drew back, jaw loose. "*That's* the secret ingredient?"

"Remember the chef—"

"—you found on YouTube. Damn. I should listen to you."

She snuggled closer as each contestant was brought up, and the judging panel tasted their pizzas. Uncle Mike was last, and when they called his name, the entire square went nuts. The applause went on and on and on. Long enough for Beck's heart to fill with gratitude at how much they cared about the tragedy that had struck one of their own.

Not far away, one of the fire trucks parked for the kids to climb and explore sounded a long blast of a horn, making most of the dogs bark in response. While that little bit of madness was going on, the Food Network producer walked closer to Sarah and Mike, and reached out a hand in greeting.

Beck and Aidan shared a look, both silent. Everyone was quiet, though, as if they didn't want to disturb the quiet discussion among the judges.

Then Uncle Mike waved at Beck, gesturing for her to come down.

"Come with me," she said to Aidan, sliding off the little bleacher, still holding his hand as they walked to join her aunt and uncle.

"Beckie, this is Tom Marshall with the Food Network," Mike said as they reached the small group. "My niece, Rebecca, and the man who saved my life, Aidan Kilcannon."

The producer lifted two dark brows at Aidan. "Oh, I've heard a lot about you," he said. "Nice work, soldier."

Aidan nodded, but gestured to Mike. "This man is the star today."

"And maybe for a lot longer," the man said, looking questioningly at Mike and Sarah.

"Beckie," Mike said, "Mr. Marshall thinks they could produce a documentary about the rebuilding of Slice of Heaven. They'd have a camera crew for the whole thing."

"That's amazing!" She looked from her aunt to her uncle, not surprised at how her chest tightened with happiness. She wanted them to stay here so much.

"I understand there was an apartment upstairs," the producer said. "I'm thinking we could rebuild that, too, and maybe coordinate with a sister show on another network, one that specializes in building and design. That way, we could hit some real viewer hot buttons with food and home décor."

"Would you like that apartment rebuilt, Rebecca?" Aunt Sarah asked, unable to hide the longing in her voice.

Beck let out a breath and tightened her grip on Aidan's hand. "Actually..." She glanced at him and winked. "I'd really rather turn that space into a photography studio. Do you think the design people would be interested in that?"

"Absolutely," the man said. "Another local business would be terrific."

Sarah made a soft hooting sound and reached to hug her, and so did Mike, making the producer laugh at the moment he'd brought about.

"Then we can have Slice of Heaven downstairs," Beck said. "And Angel Face upstairs."

"Angel Face?" Aidan asked. "Not Baby Face?"

She gave a shrug. "Think I'll branch out. Babies *and* dogs."

"We have a winner!" The announcement drew them all apart again, turning toward the stage where one of the judges stood with a microphone. "By unanimous decision, our judging panel awards the Best of Bitter Bark—"

"Better Bark!" someone in the crowd called out.

"*Better* Bark," the judge conceded. "The best pizza in town is made by Slice of Heaven! Congratulations, Michael Leone!"

Beck barely heard the insane response that got, because Aidan pulled her right into his arms for a kiss that felt like New Year's Eve met Christmas morning and threw in a little of her birthday. Celebration. Joy. Success. And so much love.

Beck couldn't even remember what it was like to fear losing someone, not with these arms and this man and all the hope in her heart.

The party didn't stop until everyone had hugged everyone and Uncle Mike tearfully accepted his medallion and announced he and Sarah would be rebuilding Slice of Heaven. More cheering, clapping, and hugging.

A few minutes after that, Gramma Finnie sidled up to Beck. "What did you have for me, lass? Liam and Andi are driving me home now. Old women and newborns are done in today."

The scrapbook! "It's in my car parked across the square. Can you wait while Aidan and I run to get it?"

She nodded. "As long as you don't stop and kiss each other's face off for an hour."

"No promises, Gramma," Aidan said, pulling Beck away.

They were halfway across the grass when Aidan stopped. "We left Ruff back there."

"With Sarah and Mike. He's fine."

"He's where he belongs," Aidan agreed.

For a long moment, they both looked at each other, silent, but saying so much.

"Mike is like Charlie to him," Beck whispered. "Mike is his purpose."

Aidan nodded. "We should give him to Sarah and Mike. Charlie would approve. I feel it in my bones."

"I think you're right, but we have to have a dog."

"A boxer?" he suggested. "I'm sure I could find us one."

She shook her head. "I have a better idea. Any of those Fabulous Fifteen left?"

"Most of them are adopted or spoken for, but not that little Yorkie, Bonnie Blue. She's still a scared little mess."

Beck smiled. "I know what to do with scared little messes. I was one once. Can we take her?"

Aidan kissed her on the forehead. "You had me at 'we.' I think that's a great idea, although Charlie would laugh his ass off if he found out I had a four pound dog named Bonnie. And what are we on our way to get again?"

She unlocked her car and pulled open the back door. "It's a scrapbook my mother made," she said. "It has sayings that Gramma will like."

He took the book from her and frowned. "I've seen this before. Where was it?"

"In Charlie's night table, of all places."

"Oh yeah!" He let out a bark of a laugh. "He hid condoms in here in high school."

"In my mother's *scrapbook*?" She choked the question. "What the heck was wrong with him?"

"Nothing. He was safe and smart. And didn't want Aunt Sarah to find them. He said if he stuck them under the mattress, he might not be able to get to them in an urgent need."

She rolled her eyes and flipped open the book. "Well, let's make sure they're gone before I give this to Gramma Finnie."

The back cover had a flap, and Aidan reached right in, clearly knowing exactly where the condom stash had been kept.

"Nope. He probably used them all."

She made a face.

"But he left this." He slid out a piece of paper folded into a square, turning it over. "Charles John Spencer. Bucket list."

They both blinked at it, inching back.

"Charlie left a bucket list?"

Aidan sighed. "My guess is he didn't get to everything on it." He unfolded one corner. "You want to read it?"

Did she? Today was perfect in every way. Glorious and right and good. Would Charlie's list of things he'd wanted to accomplish in a life cut short wipe all that away?

"Yeah," she said softly. "He should be here with us today."

"He's always here," Aidan said, fully opening it. "Let's see what the lug nut wanted to do in his life."

Beck closed her eyes and pictured her brother, with his crooked smile and dancing eyes. His big hands and occasional bouts of bathroom humor. His steady love for his family, his country, and his friends. She said a silent prayer of gratitude for everything her brother had been and sent it to heaven, hoping he heard her.

"Fly a Black Hawk," Aidan said.

"Well, he certainly did that."

"See the Eiffel Tower."

"He went to France on leave once," she recalled. "I have a postcard."

"Have sex with Dana DeWitt." Aidan snorted. "He did *not* do that."

"Ya never know, Kil," she teased. "The condoms are missing."

But Aidan didn't laugh. His gaze was on the page, not moving. "And...and..." Aidan's voice trailed off. "There's one more thing, Beck."

She searched his face, her throat tightening at the stunned expression on his face. "Tell me."

Aidan tried to talk, but couldn't. His eyes filled,

and he closed them, his dark lashes damp. "All I can say is, now I know why he wrote one thing to you and another to me, two days apart."

He turned the paper and showed it to her. She scanned the page of familiar handwriting, landing on the last thing on the list.

Dance at Beck and Aidan's wedding.

Speechless, she stared at the words, unable to even breathe.

For a long time, neither one of them spoke, but then Aidan folded the paper, put it in his palm, and placed her hand on top.

"Rebecca Spencer, will you honor the wishes of my best friend? Marry me, and we'll have a dance for Charlie."

She squeezed his hand and lifted her face to his. "I wouldn't have it any other way."

And there in the sunshine of the square, with Charlie's deepest wishes pressed between their hands, Beck and Aidan sealed their promise and their love with a kiss.

Don't miss the next book in The Dogfather series:

Double Dog Dare

Daniel Kilcannon has one more child...but Darcy Kilcannon has no interest in her father's matchmaking shenanigans. What she wants is her own small business where she can come and go as she pleases, surrendering to her wanderlust whenever the travel bug bites. But in order to achieve that dream, she'll have to prove to her father that she's mature enough to handle responsibility and rooted enough to live on her own. A condo in town? Sounds great to Darcy, as long as she can bring Kookie, her beloved Shih Tzu.

Joshua Ranier is out of town when the realtor leases one of the town houses he owns and has recently refurbished, but he's assured that his new tenant is from a fine local family, is starting her own business, and has most certainly not broken his cardinal "no pets" rule. One glance at the gorgeous blonde sneaking a fuzzy white dog tucked in a designer bag in and out of his brownstone and he knows that someone hasn't told him the truth. Darcy Kilcannon will have to go. And her little dog, too.

Except, Darcy defies every convention and expectation Josh has. And the big, sexy, tool-toting landlord makes Darcy suddenly want to...stay put. From the moment they meet, Darcy and Josh clash and spark and think about things neither one of them should be thinking about. And it isn't when the rent's due.

But when someone from his past shows up to wreck his present and saddle him with the last thing in the world he wants—his own dog—Joshua needs something only Darcy can offer. It'll take one wild and crazy dare, two incredibly cute puppers, and, of course, a little help from the Dogfather, for this one to have a happy ending.

Find out the day *Double Dog Dare* releases! Sign up for my newsletter—you'll get previews, prizes, and a personal note the day the next book is released!

www.roxannestclaire.com/newsletter-2/

I answer all messages and emails personally, so don't hesitate to write to roxanne@roxannestclaire.com!

Fall In Love With
The Dogfather Series...

Watch for the whole Dogfather series coming in 2018!
Sign up for the newsletter for the next release date!

www.roxannestclaire.com/newsletter/

The Barefoot Bay Series

Have you kicked off your shoes in Barefoot Bay? Roxanne St. Claire writes the popular Barefoot Bay series, several connected mini-series all set on one gorgeous island off the Gulf coast of Florida. Every book stands alone, but why stop at one trip to paradise?

THE BAREFOOT BAY BILLIONAIRES
(Fantasy men who fall for unlikely women)
Secrets on the Sand
Scandal on the Sand
Seduction on the Sand

THE BAREFOOT BAY BRIDES
(Destination wedding planners who find love)
Barefoot in White
Barefoot in Lace
Barefoot in Pearls

BAREFOOT BAY UNDERCOVER
(Sizzling romantic suspense)
Barefoot Bound (prequel)
Barefoot With a Bodyguard
Barefoot With a Stranger
Barefoot With a Bad Boy
Barefoot Dreams

BAREFOOT BAY TIMELESS
(Second chance romance with silver fox heroes)
Barefoot at Sunset
Barefoot at Moonrise
Barefoot at Midnight

About The Author

Published since 2003, Roxanne St. Claire is a *New York Times* and *USA Today* bestselling author of more than fifty romance and suspense novels. She has written several popular series, including The Dogfather, Barefoot Bay, the Guardian Angelinos, and the Bullet Catchers.

In addition to being a ten-time nominee and one-time winner of the prestigious RITA™ Award for the best in romance writing, Roxanne's novels have won the National Readers' Choice Award for best romantic suspense three times, as well as the Maggie, the Daphne du Maurier Award, the HOLT Medallion, Booksellers Best, Book Buyers Best, the Award of Excellence, and many others.

She lives in Florida with her husband, and still attempts to run the lives of her young adult children. She loves dogs, books, chocolate, and wine, especially all at the same time.

www.roxannestclaire.com
www.twitter.com/roxannestclaire
www.facebook.com/roxannestclaire
www.roxannestclaire.com/newsletter/

71230420R00205

Made in the USA
Middletown, DE
21 April 2018